Readers love the
Stud Games series by CINDY DEES

Poker Face

"The characters are well crafted and totally lovable, even Jack Lacey is the kind of character I love to hate. Thoroughly enjoyable story."
—Open Skye Book Reviews

"This book is unique. I say that because even though there is a somewhat serious aspect about the book, there is also a huge amount of humor as well. I loved it!"
—Rainbow Book Reviews

Dead Man's Hand

"It's entertaining and fun to read, has a good dose of mystery and intrigue with interesting characters, both good and bad."
—Paranormal Romance Guild

By Cindy Dees

BLACK DRAGONS INC.
Out of Control
Over the Top

STUD GAMES
Poker Face
Dead Man's Hand
Showdown

Published by Dreamspinner Press
www.dreamspinnerpress.com

CINDY DEES

OVER
THE TOP

REAMSPINNER
PRESS

Published by
DREAMSPINNER PRESS

5032 Capital Circle SW, Suite 2, PMB# 279,
Tallahassee, FL 32305-7886 USA
www.dreamspinnerpress.com

This is a work of fiction. Names, characters, places, and incidents either
are the product of author imagination or are used fictitiously, and any
resemblance to actual persons, living or dead, business establishments,
events, or locales is entirely coincidental.

Over the Top
© 2021 Cindy Dees

Cover Art
© 2021 L.C. Chase
http://www.lcchase.com
Cover content is for illustrative purposes only and any person depicted
on the cover is a model.

Mass Market Paperback ISBN: 978-1-64108-234-1
Trade Paperback ISBN: 978-1-64405-867-1
Digital ISBN: 978-1-64405-866-4
Library of Congress Control Number: 2020946056
Mass Market Paperback published April 2021
v. 1.0

Printed in the United States of America
∞
This paper meets the requirements of
ANSI/NISO Z39.48-1992 (Permanence of Paper).

Chapter One

CHASTEN REED took an appreciative sip of his beer—cold and foamy. It had been a rough week, and he looked forward to a quiet, relaxing weekend. It had taken all of his patience to keep order in a classroom full of five-year-olds anticipating Halloween next week. He loved his kids' energy, but sometimes he just wanted to slow down for a minute and be an adult.

He'd left a good mystery novel on the coffee table, and he planned to finish off a few more beers, then fall asleep on his couch reading it.

It was on nights like this, when Misty Falls, New Hampshire, was quiet, its citizens tucked into their cozy homes, that he felt most alone.

It was also when he most seriously considered getting a dog. Maybe a Corgi. He would name it Sir Fluffington—

Pop. Pop, pop, pop.

It sounded like some local kids had gotten ahold of some firecrackers leftover from the summer. He shook his head and reached for the book. Not his circus, not his monkeys. Some nosy neighbor would call the police and the kids would run away, laughing their heads off.

Ba-da-da-da-da-da-da-da.

Jeez. That almost sounded like a machine gun. The kids must have lit off a whole string of firecrackers.

Bang! Bang!

Okay. That sounded close and much bigger than a simple firecracker. Shooting off fireworks this close to the historic wooden houses on this street was a fire hazard. He got up and headed for the door to tell the kids to cut it out in his sternest teacher voice.

Something thudded against his front door.

Oh, for the love of Mike. Kids were pranking the neighborhood *already*?

Tires squealed as he reached for the handle and threw open the door. He started to step out and literally tripped over the woman sprawled across his front porch.

"Leah? Is that you?"

His next-door neighbor lay half on her side, awkwardly curled around her middle. Something dark was smeared in a wide streak down his front door—and the unmistakable iron smell of blood slammed into him.

He jolted in shock and squatted down, reaching quickly for the middle-aged woman who rented the one house that was the only remaining eyesore of this newly gentrified neighborhood.

"Leah, honey, are you hurt?"

He pulled on her shoulder and she rolled limply onto her back, her eyes glassy and staring up at the porch ceiling, unblinking. She looked freaking dead.

"Leah!" He felt under her chin for a pulse. *Nothing. Holy crap.* He pushed his hand hard along the junction of her neck and jaw. *Still nothing. Jesus, Mary, and Joseph.* He fell to his knees beside her, frantically reviewing his CPR training from high school lifeguarding class a million years ago.

He yanked open her bulky coat, reaching for her sternum, and realized there was blood everywhere. Her shirt was soaked; her coat was soaked. In fact, he was kneeling in a spreading puddle of blood. Frantically, he tore open her shirt buttons and counted eight ragged holes in her torso. She'd been *shot*? The holes were oozing sluggishly but couldn't account for all the blood he saw.

He started chest compressions, counting in his head in panic. He bent down, pinched her nose closed, tilted her jaw back to breathe into her mouth, and that was when he saw the ragged tear all along the far side of her neck. Dark red meat and white tendons stuck out along with the fibrous tube of her esophagus as he tilted her head back, and blood seeped sluggishly from the devastating wound.

A bullet must have torn through her throat and split open her carotid artery along with ripping up everything else in its path. Nobody could survive this. Frankly, he was shocked she'd stayed conscious long enough to make it onto his front porch. He fumbled in his pants pocket for his cell phone to dial 911, but his fingers were slippery with blood and he dropped the phone. He leaned across Leah's body to grab it, and that was when he heard the noise. A terrified whimper coming from the wadded blanket lying on the porch beside Leah. She must have been carrying it when she staggered onto his porch and collapsed.

Quickly, he unwrapped the bundle and stared at a toddler, covered in blood, looking so terrified she couldn't even cry properly. He plucked the child, dressed in pink, perhaps eighteen months old, out of the blanket and used a corner of it to wipe the blood off her face, urgently searching for injuries. As best as he could tell, the baby was unhurt.

He heard another squeal of tires and looked up. A black SUV was careening around the corner.

Why he panicked, he didn't know, but he did. Call it instinct.

Scooping up the baby and his cell phone, he sprinted for the end of his porch, hurdled the low hedge, and took off running around the corner of his house into the dark.

He raced across his backyard at top speed. Brakes squealed in front of his house. Swearing in a continuous mental stream, he unlatched the gate, slipped out of his yard, and relatched the gate quietly behind him.

A barrage of gunfire exploded from the street, making him crouch instinctively. The sound of glass shattering announced that his front windows had been destroyed. Terror gave wings to his feet as he flew down the alley. He swerved between two houses without fenced yards and raced down the next street.

He ran for perhaps a dozen blocks, until he was so out of breath it felt like a knife was buried in his side and the panic finally abated enough for his brain to actually function.

What the hell had just happened?

His information was limited. His neighbor had died on his front porch, apparently protecting and possibly delivering to him the toddler now in his arms. The child hadn't made a single sound since that one terrified whimper.

Where to go?

He didn't dare go back to his house. He could knock on a random door and ask for help, but he was drenched in Leah's blood, and the child was still more or less coated in it too. They looked like they'd just left the set of a horror movie.

The police. He should go to the station, report Leah's death and hand over this child, whose parents must be frantic. He looked around, getting his bearings. It wasn't far to the police station from here. Perhaps six blocks.

He walked cautiously, on the lookout for any black SUVs or armed gunmen on foot. It was surreal. This was Misty Falls, for God's sake. Possibly the most boring small town in America.

He struck out across the town square, which was occupied by a small park, and his heartbeat tripled as he scurried across the open spaces between trees, eager to get to the safety of the station.

The police headquarters were housed in the town's municipal building. It was a single-story brick building built in the 1970s—ugly, squat, and utilitarian. It came into view, but more importantly, a black SUV was parked in front of it.

He froze, then backed away slowly. Fading into the nearest shadow, he continued easing backward, his heart choking him, literally in his throat.

Who was in that vehicle, and *what* did they want?

Abruptly a cop burst out of the front door of the city building onto the sidewalk. He had his pistol drawn and was pointing it backward into the station itself. A man dressed all in black, his face covered in a black ski mask, came out behind him, brandishing some sort of assault-rifle-type weapon. There was a burst of light from its muzzle with a sharp *rat-a-tat* of noise, and the cop toppled over on his back and lay still.

The gunman calmly walked over to the passenger side of the SUV and climbed in. The vehicle pulled away from the curb.

Chas tried desperately to read the license plate, but the SUV was too far away. All he saw was a blur of black. The vehicle turned a corner, and silence fell in the town square.

Lights were coming on in apartments over the stores, and he suspected people were dialing 911 without realizing there was a good chance that everyone who might answer their call was dead. Why else would that gunman have been so casual about leaving the department unless he knew there would be no pursuit from within?

Holy what the heck, Batman?

Now what was he supposed to do?

Someone came out of a building a few doors down from the cop and raced over to check the downed officer. Whatever the guy saw caused him to reel back, turn, and vomit. The man did pull out a phone, however, and appeared to be talking to whomever answered it.

Chas assumed the bystander was calling in help, perhaps police from the next town over.

Logic told him to return to his house and wait for law enforcement to arrive. To make a witness statement and hand over this kid, who was starting to feel more than a little heavy in his tired arms.

But something in his gut stopped him. His home was no longer safe. His porch was the scene of a murder, and he had no way of knowing if the bad guys would be lurking nearby, waiting for cops—or him—to show up.

Had they seen him leap off his porch? Had they entered his house in search of him? If so, they'd found his cold beer. They would know he'd fled on foot and was somewhere nearby.

He looked around frantically. He had to hide. Get to cover. Call someone, anyone, for help. But who? It wasn't like he had a contact list full of commandos—

Whoa. Rewind. He did know one commando.

And he even had Gunner's phone number. He'd had it for years but never had the guts to call it. His mother had gotten it from Gunner's mom and passed it to him. He couldn't count how many times he'd looked at that name in his contact list. Pulled up the number, hovered his finger over the Dial button, and then chickened out.

There had to be somebody else. Anybody. But it wasn't like he could call up any of his one-night stands and open with, "Hey, it's Chas from spring break last year. You know, Miami. So, my house just got shot up and a woman died on my porch, and I've got this bloodied kid with me, and I don't know where to go. Mind if I hop on over and shack up at your place? Don't mind the armed killers who may be hunting me and this kid. Oh, and they just took out an entire police force, but that's no big deal, is it?"

Cripes.

With his forearm under her diapered behind, he propped the child against his shoulder, where she huddled shivering, her face buried against his neck. Poor kid was scared out of her mind.

He fished out his phone with one hand and, shielding its light against his chest as much as possible, opened his contact list.

Vance, Gunner.

He pressed the Call button.

GUNNER WOKE up slowly, groggy. Disoriented. What was that beeping noise? The vague thought crossed his mind that somebody should make it stop.

He cracked one eye open. Weird. It wouldn't open all the way. He tried the other eye. Better, but he was in a darkened room. In a bed. How in the hell did he get here?

As he regained more awareness of his surroundings, pain began to flood his consciousness. Layer upon layer of it. Sharp surface pain of lacerations. It felt like a few of his cuts had been stitched. The deeper throb of bruises. Damn. He felt that all over his body. Top to bottom, front to back… he felt like one giant bruise. And beneath that, the intense ache of cracked bones. Felt like several ribs had been busted, if the pain whenever he inhaled was any indication. What the hell had happened to him?

Accident of some kind? He didn't remember one. Car? Motorcycle?

He sat up—or at least he tried to—but was swamped by a whole new layer of pain so bad, he fell back to the mattress, groaning at the pounding waves of agony rolling through his skull.

A door opened into the room, throwing a wedge of light on the floor. A big, thick shadow entered, and he braced himself for more pain. Was he a prisoner? Was this some kind of mind-bending interrogation? Had he been drugged? Alarm that he couldn't remember ripped through him.

A gray-haired man stepped up to his bed and turned on the light beside it. Gunner squinted and registered that his bed was elevated well above the floor, kind of like a hospital bed. No, wait. His body was inclined gently upward from the hips, and the sheets were white. He wore some sort of thin cotton gown thing.

Jesus H. Christ. He was in a hospital.

"How'd I get here?" he rasped.

He squinted through his good eye and made out a black uniform. A shitload of colorful medals splashed all over the burly chest. A whole lot of gold braid on the lower sleeves. The bright gold of a Budweiser pin—

The symbol, an eagle holding a three-pronged trident and a rifle, slammed into his memory gap, shaking a big chunk of it loose all at once. His name was Gunner Vance, Navy Master Chief, SEAL Team Ten. And the man standing beside him was Rear Admiral Jonathan McCarthy, commander of all the SEAL teams on the East Coast of the United States.

Well, go fuck a duck.

What had he done to rate the big kahuna coming out to see him like this? No doubt it was either stupidly heroic, or just stupid.

"How're you feeling, son?" the admiral asked.

"Like I got into a fight with a locomotive and the train won."

"I'm told you'll make a full recovery."

"If you don't mind my asking, sir, a full recovery from what?"

"Well, you sustained quite a few superficial injuries this morning. Although from the look of you, I imagine they don't feel so superficial."

No lie.

"What... happened?"

"You don't remember?" the admiral asked with a sharp edge in his voice.

Well, duh. If I remembered, why would I ask?

"Winds changed direction and went out of limits while you were on a training jump. The jumpmaster threw you men out at low altitude, and you were blown way off course into a wooded area. Came down through some trees. Could've been real bad."

No shit, Sherlock. He could've died. Two things that did not mix at all were trees and parachutes. Horror unfolded in his gut, a slow burn that ate through his innards with the indecent agony of acid eating through steel. It bubbled and hissed, chewing through sinew and muscle and soft organs until all that was left was a goo of pain.

He closed his eyes, suddenly too exhausted to hold them open. "How did it happen?"

The admiral said candidly, "Weather shop screwed up. They didn't pass the updated winds to the flight crew."

"The pilots should've known they were encountering strong winds and told the jumpmaster."

"Same difference." Admiral McCarthy shrugged. "Communications broke down."

"Anyone else get hurt?" he asked quickly.

"No. Just you. Rest of the jumpers made it over the trees to a field."

He shifted slightly and piercing pain shot down his spine. Oh no. Not his back. The two parts of the human body prone to letting down special operators like him were the back and the knees.

He missed the next few platitudes the admiral uttered, something about hoping he got well soon. But then the old man said something that got his full attention. And fast.

"…afraid you're done in the SEALs, Chief Vance."

"I beg your pardon?"

"This is your third hard landing. Doc tells me your back isn't looking real good, and apparently you were complaining about it when the medics brought you in. After this incident, it's unlikely your body's going to let you return to an operational team."

"I feel fine," he lied.

"Doc injected some sort of painkillers around your spine. They tell me those will last a few weeks. But it's not a permanent fix. According to the doc, you've got a couple disks that are completely shot."

"Since when?"

"Since the Navy got a good MRI of your spine this morning."

"Sonofabitch."

"Did you know your back was on its last legs, son?" The admiral stared down at him awkwardly.

Gunner said bitterly, "We all have aches and pains. So what if my back gives me a little discomfort now and then? We all run on missions dinged up."

The admiral shifted weight uncomfortably. "The doc said he didn't know how you were walking."

He snorted. "I'm a SEAL. Pain has no meaning for me."

"Come now, Chief Vance. That's a bit of an over-statement. All of you guys have your limits. And it appears you've reached yours. The doc was clear. Your back is done for. Your career as a SEAL is over."

He stared at McCarthy until the man finally looked away.

"I'll rehab it. Strengthen it—"

"Chief Vance. You don't understand. I wasn't offering you a choice. I was giving you an order. You're finished as a SEAL."

Goddamn, I'm dense.

"I've put in an order for you to get a desk job where you can finish out your twenty years and retire. I can keep you in the SEAL community, but not as an active team member."

The paperwork had already been filed while he was knocked out. They knew he'd fight it tooth and nail, so the fuckers had gone behind his back.

He rolled onto his side at great cost, stoically bearing the pain of moving his body. But it was worth it to turn his back on the admiral, to silently let McCarthy know he didn't appreciate being treated like some meathead grunt. He was a senior NCO, for fuck's sake.

He listened bleakly to McCarthy's footsteps retreating from his room.

Jesus. Now what?

He'd joined the Navy straight out of high school and gone into the SEALs as soon as he was eligible. He had never done anything else, *been* anything else, in his life. And they wanted him to spend the next eight years driving a damned desk? Pushing paper? He wasn't some damned admin weenie. He despised being cooped up inside. But he was also pushing thirty years old, a lethal special forces operator with an aging back. He had nowhere else to go. Nothing to do. No assignments to save the world. No wars to stop—or start.

He had nothing. He was… nothing.

He lay back and stared at the ceiling in shock. He passed through dismay to rage and from rage to tired, cynical acceptance. He was just passing through cynicism into the cold dread of having to face the real world—a world he'd never really lived in and had no idea how to live in—when his phone rang.

He was inclined to ignore it, but old habits died hard. It could be something important. He reached out painfully to the bedside table and picked it up, looking without interest at the caller ID…

Chasten Reed.

His childhood best friend and worst enemy.

What. The. Actual. Fuck?

Chapter Two

CHAS CROUCHED beside a fetid-smelling dumpster, chanting under his breath, "Pick up, pick up, pick up."

A familiar voice, deeper than it had been the last time he heard it and with an edge he didn't recall, growled in his ear without even a greeting, "To what do I owe this surprise?"

Not a pleasant surprise, Chas noted. Just a surprise.

He whispered urgently, "I'm in trouble and couldn't think of anybody else to call. There's been a shooting in Misty Falls. All the police are dead. A woman died on my front porch. She was carrying a baby. I've got the kid with me now. I don't know where to go or what to do. The shooters seem to be… hunting… someone. They're killing everyone who gets in their way."

"How many are there?" Gunner's voice was clipped, abruptly terse. The SEAL had taken over his old friend.

"I don't know. I saw an SUV. Or maybe there was more than one SUV. I never did catch any license plates."

"How big are their weapons?"

"They look like, umm, rifles. They fire a lot of rounds fast. Like a machine gun."

"Assault weapons. Heavily armed, then. And you say they took out the police? How do you know that?"

"I was heading for the police department to turn over the kid when a cop ran out on the sidewalk. A bad guy followed him out and mowed him down. No other cops came out, and the shooter left super casually, as if he knew nobody else would be giving chase."

Gunner swore. "Where are you now?"

"Hiding in an alley behind a dumpster."

"Can you get indoors?"

"I don't know. Everyone's inside hiding. The town's locked up tight. I knocked on a few doors of people I know, but nobody's answering. Everyone's panicked."

"Break a window if you have to, preferably at the back of a building. Let yourself inside and find a hiding place. A small room you can barricade yourself into. Hunker down."

"Then what?"

"Don't come out until you're absolutely certain the threat has passed and law enforcement is on the other side of that door."

"How will I know? What do I do with this baby? Is she the reason these guys went on a rampage?"

"Just get inside, okay? I'm on my way. I'll call when I get close."

"Are you close?"

"No, but I'll call in a favor. I can be up there in a few hours. Just sit tight until then, okay?"

"Okay. And Gunner?"

"Yeah?"

"Hurry."

"Got it."

The line went dead in Chas's ear.

He looked around the alley. It was mostly brick walls and security doors. But down near the end, he spied a window. He crept toward it, hugging the wall. He reached the window, which was conveniently right beside a rusted metal door. Using his elbow, he hit the glass hard.

Ow.

Sharp pain shot up and down his arm. He probably should have looked for a rock to smash the window with. But soldiers and cops on TV always used their elbow. Of course, they were busting out prop glass, and he was an idiot for not thinking of that before attempting it.

He did pick up a rock, though, and used it to knock the remaining shards of glass out of the frame. He bent down to set the kid on the ground so he could reach inside and grope around for the lock. But she wailed the moment he set her down.

Crap! He scooped her back up, joggling her and whispering frantically to her to hush. He looked up and down the alley in panic, expecting men with assault weapons to come around the corner and make swiss cheese of him any second.

Fortunately, the little girl quieted almost immediately. Unfortunately, it wasn't so much that she was a good baby as a traumatized one. But he would take it if it meant she was quiet and didn't draw the shooters to this alley.

It was awkward as hell to reach through the window while holding the kid, and he had to use his left hand to find the lock, but he did eventually feel a deadbolt. He turned it ninety degrees and tried the door. Still locked. Damn. Must be another lock. This time he groped lower and found the doorknob. It had one of those little turn locks in the center of it, and he gave that a twist. This time, when he tried the door, it opened.

Thank God.

He slipped inside and quickly locked the door behind him. Using his cell phone flashlight, he took a quick look around. He was in the storeroom of a pub or restaurant. He found an empty cardboard box, put it up against the broken window, and held it in place with a tall coat stand he dragged over to the window. If it looked like the window wasn't recently broken and had been patched over, maybe the bad guys wouldn't feel the need to come in and slaughter whoever was hiding inside. What the heck did they want, anyway? And what did this kid have to do with it? For as sure as he was standing here, Leah had brought the baby to his front door for a reason.

He grabbed several coats and a sweatshirt from the coat stand and went hunting for a hiding spot. A pair of disgusting bathrooms were a possibility, but there was nothing inside to use to barricade the doors. He kept searching and found a tiny, cluttered office with an oversized desk taking up most of the space. And the door opened inward. Better.

He locked himself and the baby inside and braced his feet against the far wall to shove the massive desk up against the door with his hip. He pulled the desk chair out of the way and made a nest out of the coats under the desk. He crawled under it, curling up awkwardly in the little cave with the child.

Finally, he could stop and take a real look at her.

Using his cell phone light again, he examined her, looking more closely for wounds. She had big dark eyes, straight black hair, and almond skin. Petite. She was Asian, Japanese if he had to guess, and cute as a button. He stuck with his first estimate of around eighteen months of age.

She was starting to tremble—maybe cold, maybe shock setting in. He wrapped her in the sweatshirt and cradled her in his arms so her ear was pressed against his heart. He didn't know much about toddlers, but in his experience with the occasional freaked-out five-year-old, the sound of a heartbeat was calming.

His own shock started to set in, and he pulled one of the coats around both of them, then huddled together in the dark under the desk. All they needed was a blanket over the desk to have a perfect fort. If only.

He was too wired to sleep, too scared by every little noise to do anything but sit there, clutching the little girl close and periodically reassuring her that they were both going to be fine. He hoped.

GUNNER SWUNG his bare feet to the floor, so relieved to have a mission to do, a crisis to handle, that he was nearly sick with it. He eased his weight onto his feet and straightened carefully.

What the hell were they all going on about? His back felt fine. In fact, he didn't feel it at all. Must be the meds they'd allegedly injected him with. Hell, all they had to do was keep him on these painkillers and he'd be good to go for another few years.

A quick search of the wardrobe in the corner of the room revealed a large plastic bag holding his personal possessions. And more importantly, his rucksack stuffed full of combat gear was stowed inside. Praise the Lord and pass the potatoes. He tried to dress quickly, but truth be told, it was a slow, creaky affair. He pulled on camo pants and his olive-green undershirt and carefully zipped up his jump boots.

All the while, images and snippets of memory kept flashing through his head. Riding banana-seat bicycles with Chas out to the reservoir to swim in the icy cold pond. Sitting in the back of seventh-grade English class blowing spit wads at the blackboard. Getting sent to the office together for that stunt. Crying in Chas's arms when his dad left him and his mom.

Gunner shook off the flashbacks and used his cell phone to call an old buddy, Rafael Adler, who'd been medically retired from the Air Force after a helicopter crash a few years back. Nowadays Rafe flew chartered jets, mostly. He'd been flying since he was a kid, starting out with crop dusting. He even did some stunt work in Hollywood before landing in the military. Dude had never met a flying machine he couldn't handle like a pro.

"Hey, Rafe. It's Gunner Vance."

"Gun, man. How ya doin'?"

"I've been better, but that's another story. I need a favor, dude. I gotta get to New Hampshire ASAP."

"How ASAP? I get to stick around a few hours and fuck this hot guy I'm with ASAP, or ditch the date and get my ass to the airport ASAP?"

"Ditch the date. This one is life-or-death. I need to go now."

Rafe muttered off the line for a second, telling someone to hit the road, and then said briskly, "Where am I filing a flight plan to?" It sounded like he was jogging as he talked. Good man. The guy had worked with the SEALs long enough to understand that now meant *now*.

"I need to get to a little town upstate called Misty Falls. North of Manchester."

"'Kay. I'll find it. How long till wheels up?"

"I can be there in a half hour."

"I'll be ready. White Learjet with a red stripe down its side. Tail number Yankee X-ray 84 Zulu."

"Got it." He added, "Any chance you could bring me a couple of boxes of 7.62 mm ammo?"

"Regular or Teflon? And do you want hollow points or hydra-shock rounds?"

"Bring me whatever you've got on hand, and I'll be mighty grateful." Since it had been a training jump, he had his sidearm in his gear, but he hadn't been carrying live rounds.

"See you soon, Gun."

"Soon."

Sneaking out of the hospital turned out to be as easy as looking like he was supposed to be walking down the hall and knew where he was going. He stepped outside just as the ride-share car he'd called pulled up.

"Norfolk International Airport?" the driver called through the open window.

"That's me." He was tempted to offer the guy an extra twenty bucks to get him there fast, but the man looked to be pushing sixty years old and was not likely trained in combat driving.

The car pulled away from the hospital sedately, and he leaned his head back and closed his eyes. The memories of Chas continued to flow. Sneaking *Playboy* magazines into his bedroom. He looked at them for the naked women, Chas looked at them for the fashion and the articles. Who in the world opened a *Playboy* for the damned articles? He snorted over that, even now.

He recalled Chas surrounded by a half-dozen football players taunting him for being a fag and working themselves up into beating the life out of him. He'd stepped in on that one, and as captain of the football team, he'd threatened to kick their collective asses and turn them in to the coach if they didn't scram. Chas had cried in his arms, that time.

They'd been to hell and back together as kids. He'd had to survive his parents' rotten marriage, and Chas had had to survive being gay in a small conservative town.

He felt like a steaming pile of crap by the time he reached the airport, checked in at a fixed base operator's hangar, and walked out to the plane.

Rafe was indeed waiting for him, along with another pilot he introduced as Noah. The new guy didn't offer any information about himself, so Gunner didn't ask. There was an understood etiquette among operators about such things, and Noah had the hard look of one around his eyes and in the set of his shoulders.

"You look like death warmed over, man," Rafe declared as Gunner hauled himself up the steps into the plane.

"I feel worse," he grunted as he eased down carefully into a seat.

"Sleep, then. We'll be there in about an hour and a half. That fast enough for you?"

"No, but it's gonna have to be."

"Balls to the wall, I can make it in an hour and fifteen. But that's the best I can do."

"Thanks," he sighed.

Chasten Reed had reached out to him, huh? That was a name he'd never thought to hear again in this life. Not after the way they'd parted. Chas had figured out Gunner was gay, or at least bi, before he had, for Chrissake. And he'd never forgiven Chas for it.

The jet's engines whined to life. They made a short taxi out and then lifted off into the night. He had no idea what kind of shitshow he was walking into, but it couldn't be any worse than the one he was leaving behind.

CHAS LEARNED quickly that time passed differently when a person was scared half to death. Each minute dragged on forever. He kept expecting to hear sirens, but they never came. Instead, almost exactly two hours to the minute after his call to Gunner, his cell phone vibrated, startling the living heck out of him.

The little girl, who'd finally dozed off, lurched awake, flinging her arms wide in terror and whacking him on the face. She started to cry, and then, as if she abruptly remembered to be frightened, went silent. For which he was inordinately grateful.

The caller ID on his phone said it was Gunner.

"Hey," he said, low.

"You still alive?" Gunner asked.

"Obviously. You're talking to me."

"I just landed at the airport. Where are you?"

"In the back of a restaurant, or maybe a bar. North-east corner of Fifth Street and Maple Avenue."

"Got it. I'll come into the building, so don't shoot me when I do."

"You're hilarious. I wouldn't know the front end of a gun from the back end."

"That's the bore from the butt."

"Huh?"

"Never mind," Gunner bit out. It sounded like he was running, the way he was breathing hard. "I've got to acquire wheels, and then I'll have to move in cautiously, clear the area before I make my approach to your position. I'll text you when I'm about to breach the building so you'll know it's me. Hang on, dude. I'm almost there."

The wash of relief that flooded his gut was overwhelming. Not much longer now. He continued rocking the toddler, murmuring nonsense to her, but the rigidity never left her little body. Still, he took comfort from her presence, and goodness knew having someone else to focus on helped him not obsess about how freaked-out he was.

It was perhaps twenty minutes later when his phone vibrated with an incoming text. *Cardboard over a busted window?*

He texted back, *That's the place.*

Coming in.

In an abundance of caution, Chas stayed under the desk, waiting in an agony of anticipation to hear Gunner's voice on the other side of the door. He, by God, wasn't unlocking the thing until he knew for sure it was safe out there.

A quiet knock made him jump violently. Dang, he was on edge.

"Chas, it's me. You can open up now."

"Just a sec. Gotta move the desk. It's against the door."

"I can help with that."

Chas crawled out from under the desk and watched in shock as the door lock clicked and the door began to slide open. A large dark shadow filled the doorway, and the beam of a flashlight abruptly illuminated the space. Familiar dark hair. Same dark eyes. The tan was deeper now. And that face—

He raced forward, baby and all, and shocked himself by throwing himself against Gunner. The man was a living, breathing wall of muscle, and every inch of him felt like safety. Strong arms came up around him, forming a cage of protection that he huddled within. He realized his whole body was shuddering.

Gunner mumbled, "I've got you. You're safe now. Or at least safer."

"What's going on outside?"

"Town's locked down. Cops are crawling all over the police department and your house. What the hell did you get mixed up in?"

"Nothing. I was sitting in my living room having a beer when I heard noises outside. And then my neighbor died on my porch and—" He broke off, the horror of his memories too graphic for words.

"Ready to blow this Popsicle stand?" Gunner asked gently.

"Is it safe to go outside?"

"Probably, but we're going to assume otherwise for now and be ultra cautious."

Chas stepped back out of Gunner's hug, startled at how bereft he felt. Good golly Miss Molly, he was a mess.

"How did you unlock that office door?" he demanded as he shifted the baby in his arms and followed Gunner out into the main storeroom.

Gunner shrugged. "It was a simple interior lock. Used the tip of my knife to turn the lock mechanism from the outside."

Belatedly, he realized Gunner was holding a bi-gass knife in his right hand. The blade was squarish and black and looked positively lethal. He watched as Gunner slipped the blade into an ankle sheath and pulled his pant leg down over it. He was shocked at how comforting the mere presence of another human being was. Particularly a big, capable, armed one.

"Any black SUVs with blacked-out windows cruising around?" Chas asked.

"Nope. Is that what the hostiles were driving?"

"Yep."

"My guess is they skipped town a while ago. Probably when the police started rolling in from surrounding towns."

"Are there lots of police?"

"Oh yeah. I must've seen thirty squad cars. They've come in from all over this part of the state." Gunner reached for the same door Chas had come in through before asking, "Who's the kid?"

"No idea. But I think she may be involved somehow."

"A baby? How?"

"I'm not sure. But my neighbor carried her to my front porch for a reason."

"Good point. What do you think about taking the kid to the cops who are milling around?"

Chas's gut tightened with anxiety at the idea. "What if they don't believe me? What if they don't think she's in danger, but she is? What if the bad guys come back for her—?"

"Slow down, there. We don't have to hand her over right away. I happen to agree with you. The presence of this kid in the middle of a mass shooting is a little too weird to be pure coincidence."

Thank God.

"Let's get out of here," Gunner continued. "Put a little distance between us and whatever went down here. Lemme make a few calls and see if I can find out what happened and how the kid fits in."

Chas was massively relieved that Gunner didn't want to just hand the child over without figuring out what her role in this mess might be. She'd been thoroughly traumatized tonight but seemed to have latched on to him as a safe human. He hated to turn her over to strangers again, particularly cops who might handle her like a piece of evidence.

"I never thought I'd find myself sneaking out of this one-horse town with you," Gunner muttered.

Chas snorted. "I never thought I'd see you again after the way you left the first time."

Gunner paused in the doorway, scanning up and down the alley before waving for him to follow. Chas had to hustle to keep up as they swept outside and rushed to a nondescript sedan.

Gunner slid into the driver's seat, grimacing, and Chas slipped into the passenger's seat.

"Get down," Gunner ordered.

"How down?"

"Totally out of sight."

Frowning, Chas tried slouching, but it wasn't enough. He ended up lifting the armrest and lying on his side across the center console, the baby cradled protectively against his middle—kind of how Leah had been holding her.

What had Leah been doing with this kid? To his knowledge, she had been divorced for years and had only one grown son, who was both single and a bad egg, in and out of trouble with the law and in and out of jail. Did this baby have anything to do with him?

Chas was surprised at how conservatively Gunner drove, passing through town at exactly the speed limit. But he did notice from his contorted position that Gunner's posture was tense, very much on alert the whole time. Good to know he wasn't the only one freaking out a little, here.

"Is it weird being back?" he asked from the vicinity of Gunner's right thigh, trying to distract himself from thinking about being hunched on the seat of a car, driving through a war zone with Gunner Vance.

"You have no idea."

"Tell me. I need to think about something else."

"Everywhere I look, I see memories."

"Good or bad?"

"Some of each."

Chas said reflectively, "My early childhood memories are mostly good. You and I had fun as kids. Before all the adult stuff caught up with us."

"Yeah. Good times," Gunner said quietly.

A world of pain was packed in those simple words. So Gunner hadn't escaped Misty Falls unscathed after all. Chas had assumed Gunner had left town and never looked back. Apparently he still carried around some baggage from those last difficult teen years. Chas fell silent. He'd no doubt been part of what had made them difficult.

They drove for perhaps a half hour in silence. The toddler finally relaxed against him and might even have dozed off. She, too, seemed to sense that the worst of the crisis had passed.

"You can sit up now," Gunner finally murmured.

Chas pushed himself upright, his body stiff from being all crunched over. His yoga instructor would be disappointed in him. "Where are we?"

"The old reservoir road, north of town."

"Why here?"

Gunner shrugged. "It's a deserted road. I'll be able to see anybody approaching from either direction from at least a mile away. And it has decent cell phone reception. Besides, if I were a bad guy, I'd likely be heading south after the fact, toward a major city where I can blend in anonymously."

"Or maybe they'd head for the Canadian border, which would take them right through here," Chas disagreed.

"Maybe. But if that's the case, they'd have passed through here a couple of hours ago."

"God, I hope so."

Gunner smiled briefly as he pulled out his cell phone, and Chas was struck by how wolflike that smile was on Gunner's face. The guy's cheeks had leaned down over the years and at the moment were covered in a dark three-day stubble that was sexy as hell. His skin was deeply tanned, even at this time of year when the sun was low and winter was on the horizon. He still had that killer jaw, but his once perfectly straight nose had a slight crook in it now. Must've broken it at some point.

It was his eyes that had totally changed, though. Sure, they were still as blue as a summer sky, but they were hard now. Like steel. And they had an edge that warned off a guy from messing with him.

"Hey, Spence. Gunner Vance here. You said to call if I ever needed help."

Chas didn't hear Spence's response, but Gunner continued, "I may have a bit of a situation on my hands. An old acquaintance called me tonight. Got caught in the middle of some kind of gunfight in my old hometown. Multiple armed assailants with assault weapons shot up a bunch of folks. My friend has ended up with custody of a baby who was caught in the middle of the incident, and he doesn't know what to do with it." A pause. "Local cops got killed. Yeah. All of them, apparently."

Another, longer pause.

Gunner continued, "I'm on scene. I've evaced the guy and the kid. He thinks the baby may be part of the incident." And then he surprised Chas by saying, "Yeah. Of course I've got a clean credit card. We can grab a motel and hunker down."

Chas had just assumed they would head for the nearest police department, or maybe an FBI field office. Gunner disconnected the call, and Chas demanded immediately, "Who was that? And why does he not want us to go to law enforcement to turn over the kid?"

"That's an old friend. Smart guy. Used to be my commander on my SEAL team. I trust him with my life. He and I both are... concerned... about what you've gotten tangled up in."

"Concerned how?"

Gunner shrugged as he put the car in gear and pulled back out onto the road. "Call it an intuition."

"I need you to be more specific."

In the glow of the dashboard lights, he saw Gunner frown. "In my line of work, a guy learns to listen to his gut. And mine's telling me there's more to this shooting spree, and that kid, than meets the eye. I called Spencer to see what his gut reaction was. And his gut agreed with mine."

"Now what?"

"Now we're gonna drive for a few hours, find ourselves a nice anonymous little motel, and grab a room. How's the kid doing, by the way? You two are covered in blood."

"I had noticed that," Chas replied dryly. "It's my next-door neighbor's blood. She died on my front porch. She had the baby with her."

"Is the kid hers?

"No. She was in her midfifties."

"Grandkid?"

"Not that I'm aware of. Besides, this child looks Asian to me."

"Asian?" Gunner exclaimed. "From where?"

"Best guess, I'd go with Japanese."

"Interesting."

"You used to be more talkative. What do you mean by 'interesting'?"

"Nothing. I just mean it's interesting. Spencer's gonna ask around. Find out if anyone's heard anything over the grapevine."

Chas huffed. "What grapevine?" The guy could quit being an asshole now and give him a straight answer.

"Just… the grapevine. Intel guys, operational guys, maybe some guys in the alphabet agencies."

"Alphabet agencies?"

"FBI, CIA, NSA…. Alphabet agencies."

"Ahh. What guys?"

"I don't know exactly who all Spencer's contacts are. But he'll work his little black book and see what he can find out. In the meantime, we're going to sit tight and lay low."

"This kid's parents are gonna be frantic."

"Spencer will tap his law enforcement contacts. If there's a missing child report floating around, he'll find it for us. A few hours from now is soon enough for the worried parents to get their kid back. She's safe, and I want to keep her that way until we know who she is." Then he added, "And I don't want to hand her over to anyone until I have some idea of what the hell happened in Misty Falls."

Chas snorted. "An invasion. That's what happened. That SUV drove all over town, and the gunman inside shot anyone who crossed his path."

"I need to know more. How many SUVs were there? How many shooters? Who were they and what did they want? Why kill your neighbor? What's her connection to them? Why, with her dying breaths, did she bring you that kid? Why not call for help for herself?"

Chas looked down curiously at the little girl, finally asleep in his arms. Poor tyke looked exhausted. He knew the feeling. "It's been a hell of a night, hasn't it, kid?" he murmured.

He glanced over at Gunner, and in the glow of the dashboard, he noticed the guy looked like he'd gone a few rounds with a heavyweight boxer and lost. "Why's your face all cut up? Did you get into a fight?"

"Yeah. With a tree," Gunner mumbled.

"Are you okay?"

"I'll live."

"How about the tree?" he asked dryly. "Did you kill it?"

Gunner glanced over, one corner of his mouth turning up wryly.

Chas sighed, then said, "Thanks for coming on such short notice."

"No prob."

"Are you always this talkative? You used to have more than two words to say at a time."

That only earned him a noncommittal lift of a shoulder—a shoulder that was heavily muscled without being overly bulky. Gunner looked like he worked out a lot and was insanely strong, but not as if he'd bulked up just for the sake of looking like a bodybuilder. Sure, he'd been an athlete in high school, but this level of fitness was new.

Chas worked out as well, but he doubted that bicycling, lifting a few weights, and the occasional boxing lesson compared to what a military commando did. He exercised to be healthy and blow off stress, not to prepare himself to kill enemy soldiers.

They drove in silence for a while. It was hard to believe it was only a little after midnight. Eventually, Gunner pulled in at a cheap chain motel and went inside to get a room. Chas stayed in the car, slumped down low in his seat again.

Gunner returned, drove around back, and parked the car. Chas climbed out carefully, trying not to jostle the baby… although the way she was currently sleeping, he suspected a marching band could play full blast beside them and she wouldn't wake up.

He followed Gunner to a basic hotel room with two beds and watched with a combination of dismay and amusement as Gunner peered in the closet, looked under both beds, and checked the bathtub. "Looking for the boogeyman?" Chas asked.

Gunner scowled. "OPSEC 101."

"OPSEC?" Chas echoed.

"Operational security. Never stay in any room you haven't thoroughly cleared and don't know for a fact to be empty."

"Jeez. Paranoid much?"

Gunner didn't bother to answer as he moved to the window and quickly pulled the curtains shut. He asked over his shoulder, "What are you gonna do with the kid?"

"Me?" Chas squawked. "Do I look like Mary Poppins to you? I'm no nanny."

"She was a governess, not a nanny."

"You've watched *Mary Poppins*?" Chas asked skeptically. "I challenge you to hum a few bars of any song from it."

Gunner ignored the challenge. "I heard from my mom that you're a schoolteacher. Little kids, right? Which means you'll have a better idea of what to do with a kid than I will."

He'd gotten updates from his mom on what Chas was up to? Color him shocked. Chas frowned and looked around the room. "Can we ask for a crib from the motel?"

"We could, but it would draw attention to us. Make us memorable. Better to, I don't know, put pillows around her to keep her from rolling out of bed?" Gunner suggested.

"Sounds good to me."

They had to borrow the cushions from the crappy sofa, but they made a cage of pillows around the sleeping toddler.

"How old is she?" Gunner asked quietly as they stood side by side, staring down at her.

"I'd guess a year and a half."

Gunner reached for her, and Chas restrained him, grabbing his biceps quickly. Sweet baby Jesus, Gunner's arm might as well be carved from granite, it was so hard. "Don't wake her up. She's traumatized as heck."

"Gotta check her clothes for labels. Might be a name written in them."

"Oh." He hadn't thought of that.

It turned out the baby didn't give a flying fig if someone was poking or pulling at her clothes. She slept through Gunner's whole label inspection. He took pictures of her and the clothing labels with his phone, and the flashes didn't even make her stir.

"Labels are Japanese. No name in her clothes." Gunner quickly sent the pictures over his phone, presumably to Spencer. "Should we clean her up?" he asked doubtfully.

"Grab a hand towel, and I'll make a makeshift diaper for her. There's a sewing kit here in the bathroom, and it has a couple of safety pins in it. They're small, but they'll have to do for now. As for getting the dried blood off her, let her sleep. Tomorrow morning is soon enough to give her a bath. Assuming the police won't want to collect samples of the blood on her."

Gunner snorted as he handed over the towel. "They can pull all the samples they need from you. Have you looked at yourself in a mirror recently? You look like an extra from a Friday the 13th movie."

He flipped Gunner off and headed for the bathroom, where he tossed the toddler's diaper in the trash. He gave himself a nasty start when he glanced up at the mirror. He was caked in dried blood. It was in his hair, under his fingernails, and had stiffened to kidney brown in his clothes. Even his face was liberally smudged with the stuff.

He stripped off his clothes and took a shower, scrubbing both himself and his shirt until they were more or less blood-free. The shirt was trashed, but at least he didn't look like an axe murderer now.

As the blood washed away, so did some of his earlier tension, and the reality of the situation finally started to sink in. He was alone in a motel room with his first and only true love. The same guy who'd immediately left town and never come back when he'd found out how Chas felt about him.

He dried off and reluctantly donned his jeans, which were only brown with dried blood from the knees down. Shirtless, he stepped out into the bedroom.

The baby was awake and Gunner was sitting on the floor with her. She had something in her mouth, long and metal. "What is that?"

"Ammo magazine."

"You gave a baby bullets?" he exclaimed.

"Of course not. I took the ammo out of the mag first. And it's not like I gave her the pistol too."

Chas raced over and snatched the gun part out of her mouth. "You've never been in the same room with a child under the age of five in your life, have you?" he accused.

"Not since I was under the age of five."

Chas bent down to scoop up the baby and deposit her back on the bed. Glaring at Gunner, he gave her a clean washcloth to play with. She promptly commenced sucking it, and her eyes closed.

Gunner rose smoothly to his feet, and their gazes met. And it was all there again, hanging between them. The desperation. The attraction. And the betrayal. Oh God. The betrayal.

Chapter Three

WHAT THE hell was he doing here with Chas? He knew the guy was his personal kryptonite. He shouldn't have picked up that call. No, he should have stayed far, far away from Misty Falls. Even briefly driving through town had been painful. So many damned memories flooding back. Memories he emphatically did not care to stir up.

The parking lot outside was perfectly still, but he watched it cautiously nonetheless. Chas had disappeared into the bathroom a little while ago, mumbling that he needed to wash off the blood. The bathroom door opened behind Gunner, and he glanced over his shoulder at—

No shirt. He wasn't wearing a fucking shirt. And that perfect torso was still fucking perfect. Chas ran to the lean side, but that didn't stop him from having sharply cut muscles. He obviously still lifted weights. Looked like he did something aerobic too. Maybe running. The guy could've posed for the great sculptors. He would look like a god captured forever in marble as smooth and sleek and alabaster as his skin.

A new, more mature dusting of blond chest hairs matched his headful of still unruly golden curls. And his eyes were still that light gray-green that made Gunner think of early spring and more innocent times.

Gulp.

"Lose your shirt somewhere?" he asked past his parchment-dry mouth. He swallowed convulsively.

"Washed it out. Letting it dry."

"What about the munchkin? Are you sure we shouldn't wash her off?"

"Let her be. She's had a hell of a night."

"I know the feeling," Gunner muttered.

Chas's eyes went nearly black, his pupils were dilated so hard. The guy was as aware of him as he was aware of Chas. Every hair on Gunner's body stood up, as if an electric charge raced through him in fruitless search for an outlet to ground itself.

"She asleep yet?" Chas asked quietly, moving over to the bed to check the kid.

"Out cold. She crashed the second you gave her that washcloth to suck."

Gunner eyed the one remaining bed. It was queen-sized but suddenly seemed far too small for both of them to share. "I'll sleep on the floor," he volunteered gruffly.

"Dude. You look hurt. You take the bed. I'll take the floor," Chas argued.

"Share?" Gunner offered. Chagrin roared through him the second the word slipped out of his mouth. He didn't want to share. Not with Chas. Not like this.

"Uhh, sure?"

Don't be an ass. Don't make a big deal out of this. It wasn't like they hadn't shared a bed a thousand times as kids. They used to have sleepovers at one of their houses almost every weekend. Chas sounded as freaked-out by doing it now, though, as Gunner felt.

Why this guy? Why did the one and only boy he'd ever been attracted to have to come back into his life like this, bringing all that emotional baggage with him? Gunner felt about seventeen again. That had been how old he'd been the first time Chas showed him he might be into guys.

His mom wouldn't let him go upstairs to his bedroom with a girl, but she had no problem letting him go up there alone with Chas. To study, of course. She'd had no idea what kind of education he'd gotten—

"You okay?" Chas was asking.

"Yeah. Fine."

"You checked out on me, there, for a sec."

"I was thinking."

"About what?"

"Were you always this nosy? Oh wait. I remember. Yes, you were."

Chas grinned, and for an instant, he was that cheeky teen who'd seduced Gunner and shown him a side of himself he'd had no idea existed. "Any word from your contacts about who she is?" Chas jerked his head in the child's direction.

"Not yet. They're working on it."

"So, we… what? Cool our jets here until they get back to us?"

Gunner considered the options. "Let's catch some sleep now, before anyone's chasing us. Spec Ops 101: sleep whenever you can. You never know when you'll get another chance."

"Ugh. I love me my sleep," Chas declared. "I would make the world's worst special operator."

Gunner's lips twitched. That was no lie. For more reasons than he could count.

Chas grinned. "I need my eight hours or I'm a total bastard when I wake up."

Gunner shook his head. "Longest I ever went without sleep was six days."

"Six—" Chas started to squawk. He lowered his voice quickly with a glance at the baby, who stirred slightly. "Six days?" he murmured. "How did you manage that?"

"Stim pills. Fuckers are straight amphetamines. Jack you up like nobody's business. The most you're supposed to use them is five days. But we were in a world of hurt and ran on 'em for six."

"Then what happened?" Chas asked quickly.

Oh. Right. Sometimes he forgot that outsiders saw his world as glamorous, exciting—romantic, even. "Then we made it to our egress point. A helicopter was waiting for us, and every last one of us spent the next week in a hospital sleeping it off and recovering."

"Yikes. Intense."

He shrugged. "All in a day's work." Cripes. Chas was looking at him as if he was some kind of superhero. He didn't care when women in bars looked at him like that. They were just looking for bragging rights at having slept with a SEAL. But Chas—he was different. They had a history together.

Which didn't make being alone in a motel room with the guy any easier. His sweatshirt started to feel uncomfortably hot and tight around his neck, in fact.

Dammit, if Chas could go topless, so could he. Gunner stripped off his hooded sweatshirt and T-shirt and stopped short when Chas gasped.

"My God. How are you standing upright?"

Gunner glanced down at his chest and stared. His entire torso was one giant mass of purple bruises. No wonder he'd been hurting like hell ever since he woke up. He was lucky crashing through that tree hadn't done more damage than crack a few ribs. Punctured lungs could be dangerous if not treated quickly and properly.

He couldn't believe McCarthy had already signed off on his transfer out of the SEALs. Why hadn't the guy at least given him a chance to come back from this? Bastard didn't know anything about the determination of SEALs to recover from injuries, obviously. This admiral was an interim guy until a permanent replacement could be found for Jerome Klausen. Gunner hoped that replacement was found soon. The SEALs were going to chew McCarthy up and spit him out.

"What happened to you?" Chas asked lowly, concern vibrating in his voice. He moved swiftly to Gunner's side and laid his hands lightly on the worst of Gunner's bruises.

Gunner couldn't help it. He flinched away from Chas's touch.

Chas flinched in turn, almost as if he'd been slapped.

"It's nothing personal," Gunner mumbled at Chas's back as his old friend turned away, a hurt expression plain on his face. Dammit, he was so bad at this relationship stuff. Not that they still had a relationship, of course. Or did they? Hell if he knew. He was confused as all get-out, though.

Silently, Chas turned back the covers on the far side of the bed and crawled in, turning his back to Gunner.

With a heavy sigh, Gunner sat on his side of the bed and, rather more painfully than he let on, lifted his legs onto the mattress and stretched out. God, he hurt from head to foot. A pinch of pain in his spine warned him of the agony to come when the epidural painkillers wore off in a week or two.

Chas reached out and turned off the lamp beside the bed. Darkness embraced them, and Gunner sighed in relief. He was most at ease in the night. He loved its concealment and silence.

"I had a bad parachute jump," Gunner said into the darkness.

Chas made a soft sound of distress that went straight to his heart. Gunner wasn't used to anyone caring about him like that. Not in a personal, intimate way that wasn't backslapping dude affection. "What constitutes a bad jump?"

"Too windy. I got blown into some trees."

Without warning, Chas asked, "Do the SEALs know you're gay?"

The words hung in the air, heavy and loaded, hovering over him in a smothering blanket. "I'm not even sure I'm gay."

Chas grunted. "Huh."

At great personal sacrifice, Gunner turned on his side, facing away from Chas. Two could play that game. Except in order for his knees to rest on the mattress, his back ended up pressing against Chas's warm, muscular one. For the moment, his spine wasn't complaining. In fact, Chas's body heat felt good on it, although the longer they lay like this, the more the back-to-back contact felt as if it had completed a massive electrical circuit, the way attraction zinged through him and tingled all the way to his fingertips.

He lay perfectly still, as if he was in a hide with an enemy passing by only a few feet away. He drew in his presence, his personal aura, as close to himself as he could, shutting down completely. It was a SEAL trick that had saved his life more than once.

Gunner had no idea how long he lay there before he felt Chas's body relax and lean back more fully against his, that lithe rib cage rising and falling lightly in sleep. Only then was he able to let go of the tension in his body, releasing each muscle group one by one until he could sleep, himself.

He was lying on his back, sprawled lazily, and Chas rolled over beside him, draping a leg across his thighs, reaching down to cup Gunner's junk. Chas ran his fingers around his ball sac, lightly squeezing the family jewels before sliding up to make a fist around the base of Gunner's rigid and ready rod. It felt so good having that fist stroke up and down, up and down, over and over until his entire being narrowed down to the pleasure pounding through him, the orgasm building toward a gigantic release—

Gunner woke up breathing hard. No surprise, he had the mother of all hard-ons. He still lay on his side, which was the only reason he wasn't making a circus-sized tent of the bedsheets with his dick as the center post.

It was a long, long time before his erection subsided enough for him to think about sleeping again. He repeated his own instructions to himself. He might not get another chance to sleep again for a while. He'd better take this opportunity now. Too bad he couldn't brute force his brain into forgetting who he was plastered up against from neck to buttcrack.

He'd had so many fantasies over the years. So many regrets. And here Chas was again, showing up in Gunner's life in the split second it took for a phone call to connect them. Had Chas always been so close and he just hadn't known it? What an idiot he was.

Sleep, dumbsquat.

Right.

It took doing every relaxation exercise in the SEAL training manual to finally drift off, but eventually he slept once more.

CHAS WOKE up as the first rays of morning sun slipped between the drapes. He rose on one elbow to check the baby. She was still out like a light. Poor kid. He relaxed back onto the bed, and as he did so, Gunner shifted beside him, turning onto his side to face Chas.

Gunner's big body curved into his, his nose burrowing against Chas's shoulder, his forearms and knees pressing against Chas's ribs and thighs. It was weird feeling Gunner relaxed in sleep. He was softer. More approachable. The hard shell was temporarily set aside, and he felt like nothing so much as a child in need of love.

Which wasn't, in fact, far wrong. Gunner's dad had been a hard man, demanding of his only son and determined to turn him into a man's man. His mother had been the sort of person Chas didn't notice when he entered a room. She just faded into the background. It wasn't that she was fearful. She was just... bland. Emotionally absent.

She'd been so unlike his own mother, who'd been a fierce warrior on his behalf. She claimed to have known he was gay since he was about four years old, and she'd ferociously defended his right to be exactly who he wanted to be for as long as he could remember. He'd been out and proud in high school. Gunner, not so much. Heck, it didn't sound like the guy was out yet. Not even to himself.

They would both turn thirty next summer. Chas couldn't imagine having lived his twenties in the closet. He'd had a ton of fun in college and enjoyed being young and carefree to the fullest. But Gunner had apparently spent his twenties learning how to kill people. It was hard to square the funny, smart, generous kid he'd grown up with becoming a coldhearted, serious, grim SEAL. And now here he was, curled up against Chas's side like a needy kid. It was enough to give a guy mental whiplash.

The baby stirred, flinging her limbs wide and letting out a wail. The sound cut off abruptly, though. She was still scared, obviously.

Chas rolled away from Gunner's warmth and moved over to the little girl, scooped her up into his arms, and murmured, "It's okay, baby girl. Cry all you want."

He carried her into the bathroom and ran a warm bath. While the tub filled, he stripped her down and tossed her makeshift towel-diaper in the trash. They would have to see about getting her real diapers and some food pretty soon, but right now he wanted to get all that blood off her.

She relaxed in the bath, lying back and letting him support her head. She even closed her eyes and let her limbs float in the water as he gently washed her off and shampooed her hair. Poor tyke needed the relaxation something fierce.

After he'd rinsed the soap off, she sat up, waist-deep in the water. He coaxed her to play, and she hesitantly slapped the water a few times with her little hands.

He smiled and nodded encouragingly, and she slapped harder. A splash of water drenched his chest, and he laughed in delight. Her rosebud mouth curved into a tentative smile. Thank God. She wasn't so traumatized that she could feel no joy at all.

They played the splashing game for several minutes, until the little girl really got into it, sending waves of water up and out of the tub onto him.

A movement in the doorway startled him, and he looked up to see Gunner leaning a shoulder against the doorjamb, his arms crossed against his chest.

"You're really good with her."

Chas shrugged. "It's all about getting in touch with your own inner child. You have to relate to kids at their level. See the world through their eyes."

"If you say so."

"I do. Pass me a towel, will you?"

He drained the tub and wrapped her in the big white towel Gunner handed him. He was gratified when she trustingly laid her head on his shoulder.

He used a hand towel to dry her hair, and made a makeshift diaper out of another hand towel. He moved into the bedroom. "Here. Take her."

Gunner took a step back in alarm.

"She won't bite you. Well, she might, but she's just a baby. It won't hurt much."

"I don't do babies," Gunner bit out.

"You do now. I need to dry off and put my shirt on, and I can't do that while I'm holding her." He thrust the baby into Gunner's arms, not caring whether the big bad commando liked it or not.

Dried and dressed, he emerged from the bathroom to see Gunner staring down at the little girl, who looked up at him solemnly, as if she was deciding whether to scream her head off or accept this stranger.

"We'll need to get her food and diapers pretty soon."

Gunner lurched. "She could pee on me?"

"There are worse things in life, dude. It washes off. I'm going to rinse out her clothes and use the blow dryer on them, so you're going to have to hold the small alien being a bit longer. We'll probably need to get her new clothes too, but in the meantime, she needs something to wear. Hence the impromptu laundry. Unless you're willing to stay here with her alone and let me run out to shop for her real fast."

"Uhh, no. You stay with her. I'll shop."

"Do you know what size clothes she wears? Or what size diapers? And while we're at it, what do eighteen-month-olds eat?"

Gunner scowled. "Fine. Wash her clothes and then we'll go out together. I don't want to let either of you out of my sight."

Chas looked up quickly. "Do you think we're in danger here? We're nowhere close to Misty Falls."

Gunner shrugged. "The baby was last seen in the arms of a woman who died on your porch. If this kid is, in fact, the reason the shooters went on their rampage, they'll know by now that you're the guy who owns that porch. They'll have to assume you took the kid and ran. You said they came back and shot up your house, right?"

"Well, yeah."

"Then they're after you. No, they won't know where to start looking, but there are ways to find people. They can hack credit card systems and closed-circuit TV cameras. Use facial recognition programs... hell, even pay informants."

"I get the idea."

"Thus, I stick to you two like glue until we figure out what's going on."

Chas gulped. "Who are they? Who would shoot up a town over a little kid?"

"Depends on who the kid is, I suppose. Her diaper wasn't full of diamonds or anything, was it?"

"No. Just pee and a little poop."

"TMI, man. TMI."

"Oh, you think you're dodging changing diapers, do you, big guy? You can let go of that idea right now. If we're babysitting this kid for any length of time, you get to pull your fair share of daddy duty."

For the first time since Gunner had walked into that office last night, Chas saw fear—stark, cold terror, actually—pass across Gunner's face. The chiseled jaw tensed, and the laugh wrinkles around Gunner's eyes tightened in stress.

Chas took pity and held out his arms. "I'll take the baby so you can put on your shirt. You know, we need a name for her. We can't just keep calling her 'the kid.'"

Gunner's face emerged from his shirt, and the blank look on his face made Chas grin and tease, "Feeling a little out of your depth when it comes to baby names?"

"Fuck off, Reed."

Chas grinned.

"You teach kindergarten, right? You know all the kid names. You pick one."

Chas considered. "Her shirt has a big red flower on it, kind of like a poppy. How about we call her Poppy?"

"I like it."

"You actually have an opinion about it? Huh. Maybe your soul isn't totally cold and dead after all."

"I repeat: fuck off."

"Don't swear in front of a child. They learn words like lightning at this age."

"She doesn't talk, does she?" Gunner blurted in alarm.

"If we're right about her age, she's starting to."

"I've barely heard a peep out of her since I picked you two up."

Chas looked down at the little girl, who was currently tugging at the collar of his shirt. "She's been scared silly ever since I plucked her out of Leah's arms. I think that's probably why she's been so quiet."

"Great. So once she relaxes, I'm going to have to evade armed killers with a screaming kid in tow? Jesus. It's an operator's nightmare."

"Stop. Swearing," Chas said firmly.

"I don't know if I can. Every third word the guys I work with use is obscene."

"Well, you're going to have to clean up your act as long as you're around Poppy."

"You sound like a mama bear."

Chas's eyes narrowed. "Just because you have the parental instincts of a single-celled organism doesn't mean I'm the same as you. I teach kids every day. Over the course of a school year, they all become *my* kids. And until we find Poppy's parents, she's *my* kid."

Gunner threw up his hands in surrender. "You'll get no argument from me. You deal with the kid, I'll deal with the tangoes."

"Tangoes?"

"Tango for the letter *T*. *T* for terrorists."

"You think the shooters are terrorists?" Chas squawked.

"I have no idea who they are. I think it's more likely they're child traffickers or something criminal along those lines."

Chas looked down at Poppy in shock. "As in, she was stolen from her family and is being sold to someone here in America? That's barbaric!"

"It's just a guess. I've never heard of an op where a kid was the primary package."

"She's not a package, Gunner. She's a human being. With feelings and needs. And right now she needs breakfast. And a diaper."

"All right, already. Let's go shopping."

They found a superstore nearby and went inside. Chas put Poppy into the child seat of a grocery cart and gestured for Gunner to push it. Gunner scowled and took command of the cart. Poppy commenced pulling at his fingers, and Gunner fished a plastic comb out of his pocket and handed it to her. Chas watched in amusement as it immediately headed for Poppy's mouth and Gunner had to make a quick grab to save it from slobberdom.

Poppy, however, took umbrage at the maneuver and let out a high-pitched squeal. Gunner jumped about a foot in the air, and Chas laughed aloud.

"She sounds like a velociraptor," Gunner muttered in distress. "Make it stop. Everyone in the store will look and take notice of us."

"Honey, nobody will stare at a toddler screaming. It's what they do."

"Still. Make her shut up, will you?"

"If only magic spells were real, eh? You could swish and flick a silence spell at her," Chas commented, amused out of all proportion at Gunner's freak-out.

They turned a corner into the baby section, and Chas grabbed a stuffed toy off a shelf and passed it to Poppy. She hugged the plush blue elephant close and quieted.

Gunner let out an audible sigh of relief.

"Don't get too comfortable, buddy. That'll keep her quiet for about sixty seconds, and then she'll be wanting something new to entertain her."

"Sixty seconds?" The horror in Gunner's voice was palpable.

Chas laughed aloud. "Oh man. Breaking you into parenthood is gonna be fun."

"You can fuck all the way off," Gunner muttered.

"Language," Chas said mildly, his attention on the shelves beside them. "Diapers. Let's see. Do we go for the twelve-to-eighteen-months size or the eighteen-to-twenty-four months size?"

"Just get them both," Gunner grumbled, clearly disgruntled at Chas's amusement.

"I think the smaller size. She's actually fairly petite. Bottles, pacifier—I don't know if she uses one, but it could help keep her quiet in a pinch—baby wipes, lotion, bib, sippy cup, bowl, spoon, baby bag."

"Why do we need one of those bags?" Gunner demanded.

"Have you seen all the gear we're buying?" Chas argued. When Gunner continued to look skeptical of the pink polka-dotted bag in the grocery cart, he added, "Think of all the guns you can hide inside it."

Gunner looked mollified at that.

Chas pulled out his cell phone and did a quick internet search.

"What are you looking up?" Gunner asked suspiciously.

"What foods kids this age eat." He read from a list. "Finger foods. Avoid added sugar and salt. No artificial colors or preservatives. Oh, interesting. She should still drink milk or toddler formula. See if you can find that, Gunner."

"What the hell does that look like?"

"Amateur. It'll be a container of dried powder. Bigger than a soup can and smaller than a coffee can."

"Here's infant formula," Gunner announced.

"Great. Now look for a picture of a kid about Poppy's age on one of those containers."

"I'm not a complete moron."

Chas grinned. "Had me fooled there for a minute." As Gunner opened his mouth, he added, "And you don't have to tell me to fuck off again. I already got that memo."

A mother with a little boy about Poppy's age was passing by and threw him a dirty look. "Sorry," he mumbled guiltily.

Gunner grinned. "Hah. Busted."

Chas glared at Gunner. "I'm picking out the girl-iest clothes for her I can find so you'll have to carry around a kid decked out in pink lace and bows."

"Hey. I have nothing against girls."

"Yeah, except sleeping with them," Chas added under his breath.

"I've slept with plenty of women, thank you very much," Gunner declared.

The mom with the kid was passing by again and threw Gunner the dirty look this time. Chas slapped a hand over his mouth to hold back the laughter as Gunner glared at him.

"How many outfits, do you think?" Chas asked Gunner.

"Not many. I'm getting rid of her at the first opportunity."

"Six, maybe?" Chas picked out a couple of dress-es, some rompers, matching stretch pants and shirts, a one-piece winter snowsuit, and an adorable pink paja-ma onesie with a hood, bunny ears, and a fluff-ball tail on the butt.

Gunner eyed the armload of clothes. "That looks like serious overkill."

"She may go through several outfits a day. Little kids make messes all the time."

"Oh God."

"I don't know about you, but I left home with the clothes on my back. I could use a coat and some clothes of my own. Maybe a change of underwear? Oh, and a phone charger. I'm just lucky I had my wallet in my pocket."

Gunner rolled his eyes. "I'd kill for a field kit right about now."

"What's a field kit?"

"It's a prepacked bag with everything I'd need to survive in the field for several months."

"Does it include weapons?"

"You do know what my job is, right?" Gunner asked dryly.

"Yes, dear. I'm aware of what you do," he answered in his best television-mother voice.

"Fu—"

"Don't do it. That mom with the death-ray stare is at the other end of this aisle."

"Fuck her too," Gunner breathed.

Chas chuckled under his breath.

Their cart was shockingly full by the time they were ready to check out.

"Oops. Forgot one important thing," Chas added.

"What's that?"

"Car seat."

"Come again?"

"Poppy needs a car seat."

Gunner rolled his eyes so hard, Chas wondered how they didn't pop out of his head. They duly returned to the baby section, grabbed a car seat, and returned to the checkout line.

"This kid is costing a fortune," Gunner complained when he saw the rung-up total. He pulled several hundred-dollar bills out of his wallet.

"Let me charge it to my credit card, then—"

"No," Gunner said sharply. The clerk looked up, startled.

When they left the store, Chas held out the long receipt. "Here. Charge the US government for it if you're so freaked about me not charging it."

"This isn't an official operation."

"Fine. Send me a bill. I'll pay you back."

"I can afford it," Gunner snapped. "It's not like I ever take any time off to spend my salary."

"Really? You never take vacations?"

"Where would I go?"

"Home? To visit friends? Someplace pretty and relaxing, perchance?"

"I don't speak to my parents, I work with my only friends, and I don't do 'relaxing.'"

"Dude. You have to get a life."

They reached the car, and Gunner tore open the cardboard box with the car seat in it.

Chas said drolly, "Because I know you pride yourself on being a lone wolf, I'm gonna let you figure that out and install it while I load everything else in the trunk and put a diaper on Poppy."

He laid the toddler down in the front seat and dressed her from the skin out in a proper diaper, new outfit, and a cute pair of tiny running shoes. By the time he put her arms into the windbreaker he'd bought for warmish fall days like today, Gunner was swearing freely in the back seat.

"How's parenthood going back there?" Chas called.

"Don't. Even."

"Need some help?"

"No. I need decent instructions in actual English."

"I'll just go put the cart in the cart corral. C'mon, Poppy. Let's let Daddy Number Two have a little tantrum in private while he defeats the big, bad car seat."

"*If* I figure this out. And I'm totally Daddy Number One," Gunner called after him.

Chas let his laughter float back over his shoulder toward Gunner. By the time he and Poppy returned to the car, however, Gunner stood triumphantly beside it and gestured with a flourish for Chas to put Poppy into the seat, which was duly installed and secured.

"Congratulations. I guess you can be Daddy Number One… for now." Chas passed Poppy a plastic toy that was inset with colorful rubber pieces that popped back and forth with a smacking sound. She went to town on it in the back seat as they pulled out of the parking lot.

Chas noticed Gunner spending a lot of time watching his rearview mirror, and he asked in alarm, "We're not being followed, are we?"

"Not that I can see. But I'm playing this cautious, not letting my guard down because we're on American soil and appear to be in the clear. I'd like to put some more miles between us and Misty Falls, to be honest."

"Why did you freak out back there when I tried to use my credit card?"

"Credit cards are trackable. If our bad guys have connections to even a semi decent hacker, we can be tracked through your credit cards."

"What about yours? You used one last night to pay for the motel room."

"I have sanitized cards in fake names."

"Fake names? Seriously?"

"Sometimes SEALs have to live off the local economy, but we can't afford to leave trails."

"Nice."

Gunner pointed the car south but turned onto a winding two-lane road instead of the major highway only a few miles away.

"Umm, I hate to be a buzzkill, but I have to teach school on Monday. I can't exactly go on a road trip with you for grins and giggles."

"What if the shooters are hanging around Misty Falls, waiting for you to show back up with the kid?"

Chas stared at Gunner in dismay. "What am I supposed to do?"

"Go on a road trip with me for grins and giggles until we figure out who the shooters are and what they want. And then we eliminate them."

"Eliminate, as in kill them?" he squeaked.

Gunner shrugged. "Whatever works."

"What about my job?"

"Call in sick. Tell them you're suffering post-traumatic stress after your house got shot up and your neighbor died on your porch. You might want to ask your boss to call the police and let them know you'll be back in town in a few days and will make an official statement to them then."

"The police?" Chas blurted, alarmed.

"They surely found your neighbor on your porch, and they know you're missing. They may have the cavalry out looking for you already."

"Great. Just what we need."

"What we need is some time to figure out what the hell happened and who the kid is."

"That's no lie," he muttered. He called the phone number teachers reported sick to and left a message that he would be out for a few days, recovering from the events of Friday night. Then he used bottled water to make formula for Poppy. She drank it hungrily from one of her sippy cups as they rolled down the road. Next, he put dry Cheerios, strawberries he sliced with a pocketknife Gunner passed him in silence, and banana pieces into a plastic bowl and passed those to her.

"She acts like she hasn't eaten in a week," Gunner commented.

"I know the feeling," Chas replied. He dug out granola bars and bananas and passed one of each to Gunner.

"What? I have to eat like a baby too?"

Chas shrugged. "Unless you have a cooked steak in the grocery bags that I didn't notice, you get no-cook snack food too, until you want to stop at a restaurant or somewhere we can cook real food."

Gunner said nothing but went back to staring at the rearview mirror.

"Why aren't we getting on Highway 91? We'd make better time."

"Because I'm going to turn west at some point, and we're a whole lot harder to track if we stay off major highways."

"Track how?"

"There are traffic cameras at intervals along major highways. And where there are cameras, there are hackable feeds."

"Paranoid much, are we?"

"Not in the least. I've used those feeds in my work. And if the SEALs can use them, so can hostiles."

Chas quieted, more alarmed by the idea of being surveilled on American soil than he wanted to let on.

About midmorning, Gunner's phone rang, and he put it to his ear. He listened intently for a long time and then said merely, "Got it."

"Well?" Chas demanded when the call ended.

"Well what?" Gunner asked blandly.

"You're just teasing me now. Getting even for the car seat, are you?"

"Might be," Gunner said cryptically.

"C'mon. This isn't funny. What's up with Poppy, and what happened in Misty Falls? Who were those guys?"

Chapter Four

SPENCER NEWMAN stepped into the guard shack at Norfolk Naval Air Station. It felt weird as hell to be signing in as a civilian visitor. His companion, Drago Thorpe, murmured as they headed back to the car, "You okay?"

"No, actually. I don't like being back here one bit."

"I'm sorry, man. Just remember, I've got your back."

Spencer flashed an intimate smile at his best friend and brand-new husband. "Let's just get this over with."

"Then up to DC?"

"Yeah. I don't think we're going to get anything out of your old contacts unless we speak with them in person."

A shadow passed over Dray's handsome face. He, too, had recently lost his job at the CIA. They'd killed possibly the most dangerous terrorist on earth a few months back, but it hadn't been a sanctioned mission, and Uncle Sam had sacked them both. It was a shitty deal, but those were the rules. At least neither of them had ended up in jail over the incident.

Spencer drove to a nondescript building that housed the largest intelligence unit on base and parked in a visitor's space. It had been his decision to sacrifice his career. No use being bitter over it. And hey, he'd gained Dray out of the deal.

They went inside, and the clerk at the front desk started in recognition. "Lieutenant Newman. It's been a while."

"It's Mr. Newman now. Is Penelope Walker in the office today?"

"Yes, sir. Uh, yes."

"Can you ring her up? Let her know I'm here to see her?"

It took only a few minutes for the civilian intelligence analyst, a smoking-hot redhead in her early thirties, to come down to the lobby. She handed Spencer and Dray visitor's passes, which they clipped to their collars, and then led them to an office barely large enough to fit her desk and two chairs.

When Spencer and Dray sat down, she asked, "What can I do for you, gentlemen?"

"Did you happen to hear about a shooting in New Hampshire last night? And an Asian toddler who may be involved?"

"Oh. I thought you were here to check on Gunner Vance. He worked for you, didn't he?"

"Yeah. Number two in one of my platoons. What are *you* talking about?"

"He was put in the hospital the day before yesterday. Low altitude parachute jump went bad. He went into some trees and got banged up pretty bad. The Navy's investigating it, but it looks like a communication breakdown. Winds went out of limits and nobody relayed that information to the jumpmaster."

"How bad is he hurt?" Spencer asked, concerned.

Penelope winced. "The way I hear it, he messed up his back pretty seriously. The paperwork is already filed to retire him out of the SEALs."

"That's freaking fast. Who signed the papers?" Spencer exclaimed.

"Admiral McCarthy. He has temporarily replaced Admiral Klausen."

"McCarthy's not an operator. What's he doing deciding for a SEAL when his career is over?" Spencer ground out.

Penelope shrugged. "Above my pay grade to answer that one."

Spencer leaned forward and pinned her with a hard stare. "Gunner's a fine operator. Even with a busted-up back, he's the kind of guy I'd want to work with. Any chance you can pull some strings and land him a training job, or maybe a supervisory job in an ops center?"

She nodded, her expression grim. "I can put in a good word for him with a few people."

Spencer leaned back hard. "Thanks. I owe you one."

A short silence fell in the small office. When Spencer had regained enough cool not to put his fist through a wall, he asked her, "New Hampshire? Shooting spree? Young Asian child in the middle of it?"

"How did you hear about that?" she countered. "The shooting hasn't hit the news yet. The blackout on journalists doesn't lift for a few more hours."

"Why's there a news blackout?" Spencer asked, surprised.

"Whatever happened up there is quite a mess. FBI's involved on it. Homeland Security shut down the news coverage and made everyone in town sign NDAs."

"What the hell?" he blurted.

"I got a rather terse call from an assistant secretary of the Navy this morning telling me to keep my perky little nose out of it," she added bitterly.

Spencer stared, shocked. What the hell had Gunner wandered into the middle of? "So you can't tell me anything?"

"I didn't say that." She smiled archly.

"What have you got?"

"Close the door, will you?" she said to Drago.

He reached out and pushed the panel closed without leaving his seat.

"Four cops were killed by automatic weapons fire. Five civilians dead. Four of them in a house, one—a woman—dead outside the house next door. Presumably she fled the scene of the house shooting and died from wounds sustained."

"And the shooters?" Spencer asked tersely.

"They drove at least two blacked-out SUVs, possibly three. Unknown number of occupants. Armed with assault weapons and body armor. Surveillance cameras inside the police station show the police firing multiple shots at the assailants at close range using weapons as big as .45 without seeming to injure any of the bad guys. So… we're likely looking at high-end body armor. Military grade."

"If there's film of them, do we have any IDs on the shooters?"

"They all wore ski masks and gloves. Proficient with the weaponry. Knew how to control field of fire."

"They're military?" Spencer blurted.

"Not necessarily. But they've had military-style training."

"Anything else?"

"Their license plates were covered with tape, so it was a premeditated attack."

"Have you got anything on the occupants of the house who died?"

"Nope. FBI's got that information locked down tight. Sorry."

"What about the kid?"

"I haven't seen any reports about a missing child. That's the sort of thing that would get broadcast wide across multiple law enforcement agencies."

Spencer and Drago exchanged frowns at that.

Dray piped up, "Any missing persons reports floating around the system for Asian female children?"

"Lemme check." She typed for a few seconds and read information scrolling across her monitor for several minutes.

"There are hundreds of missing Asian girls worldwide, but none with any link to Misty Falls, New Hampshire," Penelope answered. Then she added, "I'll put a request in to the State Department to contact all the Asian embassies and ask them specifically about a missing toddler. I'll let you know if I get any hits."

"Have you got anything else for us?" Spencer asked.

"No. But I'll keep poking around. Nobody in the government can keep their mouth shut for long. Information will start to leak out soon enough."

Spencer and Drago both snorted at that.

Then Spencer stood up. "Thanks for your help."

"It's good to see you again, Spencer. Any chance I can convince you to come work for me here? You'd make a hell of an intel specialist for the teams."

"Not only am I retired, but I'm done with the military. They tossed me out on my all-American ear."

"What will you do now?" she asked.

"Dray and I are looking into starting a security company. Small outfit to begin with."

"Cool. If I hear of anyone who needs your kind of help, I'll send them your way."

"Thanks, Pen. I guess I owe you another one."

She laughed. "I'll keep that in mind. It's always good to know an ex-SEAL who I can call in a pinch."

"Anytime. You're good people. And if you ever need a job, give us a call, eh?"

She nodded thoughtfully as he passed her a business card with his personal cell phone number on it.

They left the base, and Drago looked over at Spencer from the passenger seat. "What has your guy gotten mixed up in?"

"No freaking clue. But my gut says there's more to it than meets the eye."

"Yeah, my gut's in total agreement with yours."

Spencer glanced over at Drago grimly. "Now we try your contacts."

"To Langley it is, then."

Chapter Five

GUNNER SPOKE while keeping his eyes on the winding road. "My contact—my old boss, actually—can't get any information out of anybody. And that is weird as hell. It tells me you're tangled up in something bigger than a simple domestic violence incident."

"You call a bunch of dead people an 'incident'?" Chas replied. "It was more like a massacre."

"A massacre is a whole village wiped out." Gunner knew. He'd seen a few of those, and they sickened a man all the way to his soul. "Nine people died last night in Misty Falls. Four cops, the lady on your porch, and four more inside her house."

"Four in her house? Leah lived alone. She was quite the hermit, in fact. Her son never came to visit her. It was almost as if—" Chas broke off.

Gunner prompted, "Finish that thought. Intuitions are right more often than they're wrong."

"As if she was living in hiding. She rarely came outside, and it was only for quick trips to the grocery store or to run an errand, and then she ducked back indoors. And she always kept her curtains closed."

"Interesting. Who could she be hiding from?"

Chas shrugged. "My guess would be her son. She sounded afraid of him the one time she ever mentioned him to me."

Gunner passed his phone to Chas. "Text Spencer Newman what you just told me. And the name of your neighbor's son, if you know it."

Chas sent the text and then got distracted entertaining Poppy for a while. They managed to drive for about two hours before she had a total meltdown. Who knew a child that tiny could make so much noise in an enclosed space, and at that particular earsplitting pitch?

"We're gonna have to pull over," Chas announced. "Poppy needs out of her car seat, and she may be finally releasing some of the stress from last night. This could go on for a while."

"Say it isn't so," Gunner muttered under his breath, deeply regretting having not bought a bunch of earplugs while they were at a store.

He slowed the car and turned off onto a dirt road that didn't appear to lead to anywhere. It did feel good to get out and stretch. His body was sore and stiff from the accident.

The air was crisp and cool, the trees around them arrayed in their full fall glory. Yellows, oranges, reds, maroons, and even purples cloaked the margins of the rolling field they'd parked beside.

Poppy took off running the second Chas set her down, and Gunner grinned as Chas had to dart after her. The pair got busy picking up leaves, and the little coos she made when she found a particularly big and bright leaf were kind of adorable.

When they finally returned to the car a half hour later, Chas and Poppy's cheeks were rosy, and they both had big grins on their faces. Gunner was staggered by the wave of warmth that rolled through his gut at the sight of them laughing and talking. Well, Chas talked. Poppy responded in her own private language of baby gibberish. But it was good to see her interacting with Chas and not totally shut down in terror like she'd been last night.

"Did you tire her out?" Gunner asked Chas over her head.

"You're hilarious. All I did was run off the worst of her frustration. She'll go like the Energizer Bunny for several hours before she crashes."

"We can't sit here for several hours."

Chas waxed thoughtful for a minute. "If you'll give me your phone, I ought to be able to download some TV shows she'll watch. It might buy you an hour or so of quiet from her."

Gunner stared at her like the alien creature she was to him. "Better than nothing, I suppose," he mumbled.

"Next stop, you get to change her diaper and entertain her."

"Oh, hell no."

"No swearing, dude."

Gunner huffed. "I can't swear at all now?"

"Not in earshot of Poppy."

"She's not my kid. I don't care if she learns how to swear like a sailor."

Chas shot him a silent, waiting look that challenged him to think about what he'd just done and how guilty he should be feeling.

"You do that accusing-teacher-glare thing pretty well."

"Thank you," Chas replied, magnanimous in victory.

"Let's hit the road. I want to put more distance between us and Misty Falls."

Chas took a lace out of a tiny pink tennis shoe and tied Gunner's cell phone to the back of his head rest, hanging it in front of Poppy but safely out of her reach. Entertainment for the tiny velociraptor procured, they got back on the road. Before long they crossed into the eastern edge of New York state.

The kid seemed happy, and Chas turned around to face front. "So, what have you been up to the past few years, Gunner?"

"A little of this, a little of that."

"Is that SEAL speak for 'don't ask me questions about my missions'?"

"Pretty much."

"Anything you *can* tell me about?"

"Nope."

"Talking with you is like bouncing a ball off a wall," Chas muttered. "It just comes back and smacks me in the face."

"Sorry, bro. Tell me about you." The easiest way to avoid talking about himself was to get other people talking about themselves.

"Not much to tell. I went to UMass. Partied hard. Got a teaching degree. Moved back home to teach kindergarten."

"Why back to Misty Falls?"

"My mom worked in the superintendent's office. She got me a job interview, and having an in with the school district helped."

"But you stayed. I thought you wanted out of there."

Chas frowned and stared straight ahead. Hit a nerve, had he? Gunner waited out Chas's silence.

Finally Chas replied, "I did a little traveling after college. Turned out the big city and bright lights weren't all they were cracked up to be. Perfect Gaylandia doesn't exist. There are assholes everywhere and tolerant folks everywhere."

"Maybe. But there are more tolerant people in some places than others."

"Whoa. That sounded bitter," Chas commented. "Care to elaborate?"

"Nope."

"It had to be hard juggling being gay and a SEAL."

"Thanks for that observation, Einstein," Gunner replied dryly. "I would never have figured that out on my own."

"Jerk."

"Double jerk," he responded automatically with the insult they'd used all the time as kids.

Chas smiled fondly.

God, it felt good to be back with someone who'd known him forever. Someone with whom he didn't have to pretend to be or not be anything. He could just relax and be himself for a change.

They drove on and off for the next several hours, taking breaks to let Poppy out of the car seat, change her diaper, feed her or themselves, and to refresh her entertainment options. He had to give Chas credit. The guy was creative and good at guessing what would occupy her.

But by about four in the afternoon, Poppy and his aches and pains were simultaneously about done with cars. He would love to cross over into Canada, but without any ID for Poppy, he wasn't willing to risk it. Instead, he found a small town in the middle of the Adirondack Mountains and snagged a room at a national hotel chain. The clerk at the counter went on at length about how lucky they were to get a room, but there'd been a cancellation. With the fall colors peaking, everything was booked, apparently.

The only room they could get had a single king bed, so Gunner reluctantly asked for a crib. They ate at the buffet-style restaurant next door, but Gunner was glad to get back to the room. Far too many people had taken note of the two men and a baby eating together for his comfort.

Once back in the room, though, Chas announced, "You're up, Daddy Number One."

"Me? Up?" he echoed in alarm.

"It's your turn to give her a bath and get her ready for bed."

"I have no idea what to do—"

"And you won't until you try it. Just dive in and give it a go. Encourage her to play and move around in the tub. It'll tire her out. Help her go to sleep. You're in the Navy, right? You can do water."

Scowling darkly, he took Poppy under her armpits and carried her into the bathroom at arm's length in front of him. She seemed to think it was a game and kicked her feet joyfully. Which, as it turned out, made putting her down and taking off her shoes an ordeal in its own right.

"What temperature should the water be?" he called out.

"Warm but not hot," Chas called back. "Comfortable for you will be comfortable for her. She's a human being, after all."

Gunner heard the TV go on in the other room. The bastard was enjoying abandoning him with Poppy.

Fine. He could do this. How hard could it be to give a little kid a bath?

After chasing her around the bathroom a couple of times before getting her out of her clothes, he finally scooped her up and plopped her the tub. She settled in and played with a couple of floaty toys he now understood Chas buying. Gunner sat on the toilet and watched her play. Okay. This wasn't so bad—

Whoosh.

The little squirt had swung her arm across the surface and sent a sheet of water arcing all over him. She giggled tentatively, as if unsure of his reaction. Remembering Chas laughing last night at the antic, he forced a smile onto his face.

Whoosh. A bigger wave smacked him. Resigned to getting soaked, he reached into the water and threw a little water back at her. That earned him a squeal of laughter. He did it again. Her joy was contagious, and before long he was sitting beside the tub, his arm hanging over the edge, making balloons of washcloths, submerging them, and blowing all the air out of them in cascades of tickly bubbles under Poppy's feet. She howled with laughter.

Chas eventually called in, "You'd better let her wind down a little or you'll never get her down to sleep. My kindergarteners never go down for nap time right after recess. Try shampooing her hair. That knocked her out last night."

Shampoo. Right. He grabbed the bottle of baby wash and dumped out a big handful of it. Suds went *everywhere*. Which, of course, Poppy thought was fantastic. It took him several minutes of emptying the tub and running more water to corral the suds, but eventually, he got the mess under control, the kid rinsed off, and the tub emptied.

He picked her up—who knew a human being could be so slippery?—and got her wrapped in a towel without dropping her on her head. He mimicked Chas's drying her hair last night and stepped out into the bedroom.

Chas held out a white rectangle without saying a word. *Diaper*.

Oh God.

He took it without comment, laid Poppy on the floor, and unfolded the bath towel. She flipped over and took off crawling like a shot, and he had to dive after her. He happened to glance up and caught the unholy amusement on Chas's face.

"Not a word," he bit out.

Chas made a zipping motion across his lips and threw away an imaginary key.

Scowling, Gunner unfolded the diaper, chased down Poppy again, and eventually got the thing taped around her lower torso. Whether it was on backward or not, he had no idea.

A hand appeared in front of his face with the bunny onesie dangling from it. He snatched the thing out of Chas's hand and wrestled it onto Poppy, who, to her credit, was relatively cooperative with his awkward efforts. She was so tiny and soft. And she felt so breakable. He snapped the last snap and scooped her up in his arms as an odd burst of protectiveness filled his gut. He just wanted to wrap her up and keep her safe from harm.

He glanced up and was shocked at the warmth glowing in Chas's eyes.

"Parenthood looks good on you, Gunner."

Gunner snorted inelegantly.

Chas handed him a bottle already made up with warm water and formula. Frowning in concentration, Gunner carefully tipped her onto her back in his right arm and poked the bottle at her mouth with his left hand. Poppy reached up and guided it into her mouth, bless her.

Her dark eyes drifted closed as she sucked on the bottle. She was so warm and relaxed in his arms, it started to rub off on him. He sat down gently in an armchair and propped up the bottle as she started to fall asleep. Sucking lazily, she mostly finished the bottle before she passed out.

Gunner rescued the bottle from falling and looked up at Chas. He mouthed, "What do I do now?"

Chas answered quietly, "I'd hold her for a few minutes to let her get good and asleep. Then, very gently, I'd lay her down in the crib."

Gunner nodded and settled in with Poppy. Even in sleep, she moved a little bit. So alive, she was, and so vulnerable and trusting. He'd never felt anything remotely as peaceful as it was to hold her. And he had to admit, it was kind of magical.

He ended up sitting with her in his arms for close to an hour before he was willing to risk putting her down in her crib. At least that was his excuse, and he was sticking to it. Holding her for that long had nothing to do with the sense of calm that came over him as he stared down at her tiny, perfect face and watched her sleep.

When he finally turned away from the crib, Chas was holding out something else without comment— this time a glass with ice and what looked like whiskey from the refrigerator's stock.

Gunner sipped at it as he sat down on the bed beside Chas and put up his feet. "Yep. I'm definitely Daddy Number One," he said with relish.

Chas grinned. "I'll hold you to that when she's screaming her head off in a massive tantrum and refusing to stop."

"Poppy? Never. She's a sweet princess."

Chas's grin widened. "I work with kids all day, remember? Even the most angelic child has demonic moments."

"Kind of like adults?" he asked cynically.

"Yeah."

Chas had on a news channel, and Gunner asked him, "Any mention of Misty Falls?"

"Not a word."

"Spencer said Homeland Security had shut down the press."

"Can they do that?"

"Oh yeah."

"Are we going to keep moving indefinitely?" Chas asked quietly.

"I hope not. Ideally, Spencer will figure out what happened in New Hampshire and that Poppy has nothing to do with it. Then we can turn her over to the authorities and they can work at finding her family."

Except even as he said the words, he got a strange, painful pang in his gut.

Without comment, Chas turned off the lights and crawled into the king-sized bed, and Gunner followed suit. Sleep eluded him as he tried to figure out the source of that pang.

After about an hour of staring up at the ceiling in the dark, Gunner was startled when Chas rolled over and flung an arm and a leg across his body. He froze.

All the years' worth of fantasies tore through his head. He'd imagined sex—all kinds of it in every conceivable way—made up pillow talk conversations that they might have had in his head, even envisioned simply snuggling with Chas. Like this. Exactly like this.

To be here now, with Chas draped all over him, warm and lithe and relaxed, was more than the universe could possibly have paid him back for stealing his career out from under him.

Gunner's right arm happened to be over his head when Chas rolled against his side; he'd been stretching out an old shoulder injury. Now he eased his arm down, sliding it carefully under the pillow Chas was lying upon. It was a tense few seconds, but at last, Chas's head was resting on his shoulder beneath the thin pillow. It would be so easy to flex his forearm and embrace Chas, drawing him closer and holding him there all night long—an event ranked much higher on his life's bucket list than he'd admitted to himself until this exact moment.

Chas shifted a little in his sleep, and his palm slid down Gunner's belly, perilously close to his private parts. Whoa. He would never forget the first time they'd been having a sleepover and Chas had, in his sleep, fondled Gunner's cock. It had woken him instantly. He'd lain there in the dark, his face flaming with shame, loving every second of Chas's fingers wrapped around his eager erection.

He'd attributed it to the general horniness of being a teenager, but that wasn't all it had been, and he knew it. He'd responded to Chas's touch, to Chas's young body pressed against his, the smell of him, the feel of him—

Umm, it was exactly the same way he was reacting now. In fact, he was rapidly acquiring a painfully insistent boner. Chas's fingertips rested close enough to his pubic hair to twine into the curls, to wrap around the base of his throbbing dick, to measure the length of him by feel—

Chas shifted in his sleep, and instinctively, Gunner wrapped his arm around Chas's shoulders. *Don't go. Don't stop.* The words burned into his brain with searing directness. He wanted this man. Wanted to be touched by this man. Wanted to make love to this man.

He wasn't in the habit of admitting to himself that he was gay. It felt weird now, but thankfully the weirdness had nothing whatsoever to do with Chas. Chas felt great. More than great.

No matter how awkward and clumsy he'd ever been, Chas had always made it all feel exactly right. Back in high school, neither he nor Chas had known what they were doing. Oh, Chas had known what he wanted, but he'd been too shy to spell it out clearly for Gunner. As for Gunner, he'd never given the idea of sex with a boy much thought prior to that first sexually charged encounter with his best friend. The one thing he hadn't counted on was being so turned on by the sight of Chas's tight, pale ass just waiting for him to plunder it that he'd nearly exploded before ever actually getting to the sex act.

It was a memory he rarely allowed himself to access. For the most part, he kept it locked away tightly in the furthest, darkest corner of his mind. But lying here tonight with Chas's fingertips moving ever so slightly on his belly, easing toward his hungry cock millimeter by millimeter, he went there in his mind.

The thing he never ever admitted to himself was that it hadn't been just about the sex, although the tight heat of Chas's body accepting him into it had been so graphic a turn-on that he could barely control himself while Chas panted and adapted to the invasion.

No, it had been an emotional thing for him. He loved Chas. As his best friend, as the brother he'd never had... and as the one person on earth he wanted to share the intimacy of sex with more than anyone else. And that had been a staggering revelation at the ripe old age of seventeen. He wasn't ready to love anyone, let alone his male best friend.

He'd been a giant jerk about it. Said the wrong things, acted the exact wrong way. Chas had laid himself and his heart on the line for him, and Gunner had emotionally kicked the guy in the teeth. Told him it was a terrible mistake. That he felt taken advantage of. That it would never happen again. And worst of all, that he wasn't attracted to Chas in that way.

Every word had been a lie.

And that was the thing he hid the most from, that he rarely confessed to himself. Only in moments like this, late at night, alone with his thoughts and regrets, did he dare confront his hypocrisy.

Tonight, the guilt overwhelmed him, flooding through his consciousness, lodging underneath his breastbone with a burning sensation ten times worse than indigestion.

He'd treated Chas like crap. Sweet, loving, generous, *honest* Chas.

Which made him a gigantic asshole.

He sighed and turned his head, burying his nose in Chas's blond hair. They lay like that for a while, him inhaling the wholesome shampoo scent of Chas's hair, and Chas's palm, warm and light, on his lower belly, just above his groin.

It was intimate and personal, and Gunner took a while to absorb that. Truth be told, he'd never lain with any human being afterward like this. He always felt dirty afterward. Sullied.

All that time, the only person he'd wanted was Chas. How had he not seen it earlier?

Chapter Six

WHAT. AN. Idiot.

How had he missed it all these years? He wanted Chas as his lover.

The notion exploded across his brain with all the fiery brightness of a fireworks display. And in its black, echoing wake, the questions poured in. Was it a bad idea? Should he risk their friendship in that way? What if it didn't work out? But what if it did? It was one thing to know that he was attracted to guys sexually, but was he ready for a full-blown gay relationship?

He thought back over the years, and certain aspects of his life clicked into place. He'd never been interested in the porn magazines the guys snuck into their gear and jerked off to in the field. He'd privately wondered if something was wrong with him.

For a few years, he'd wondered if his high school encounter with Chas had ruined him somehow. Changed him. Made him incapable of getting satisfaction with women. As he'd gotten a little older—and a lot less ignorant about sex—he'd figured out that was ridiculous, of course.

But he'd never made the leap of logic to identify himself as a man who wanted a long-term relationship with another man.

Which, in retrospect, was not only stupid but a massive act of denial. He'd known somewhere, buried deep in his gut, that he was all-the-way gay. He'd just been desperate to avoid the complications it would bring to his life. He loved being a SEAL. Loved fitting in. Being part of a band of brothers. He hadn't wanted to risk all of that. But he'd denied himself even thinking about the kind of relationship that might bring him long-term happiness. Not to mention an actual happy ever after.

Nope. He'd chosen to pretend for years that he wasn't gay at all rather than admit that he wanted the whole gay enchilada.

And then Chas had called him, scared out of his mind and in deep trouble.

Everything else had fallen away. The SEALs. His career. All that had mattered was getting here. To Chas. To the only person he'd ever loved. The person he'd always loved.

The only thing that mattered was that he loved this human being.

He desperately hoped that his decade of epic idiocy running from that truth hadn't destroyed all of Chas's feelings for him.

He sighed deeply, and the lift of his chest made Chas shift against his side. His hand slipped lower, and Gunner gasped.

Chas's fingers landed against his semirigid dick, which lost the "semi" quality in the time it took his heart to beat twice. And then his cock was rock-hard and he could count his pulse in its nearly painful pounding.

His engorged flesh jumped under Chas's touch, and he bit back an urge to groan aloud. He squeezed his eyes shut and concentrated on controlling his body. *Must not blow my load. Must have self-control.*

Chas's magic fingers slipped beneath the waistband of his underwear and slid around the base of his cock, caressing and lightly pulling at it so as to tug gently at his balls—his ready-to-burst balls that ached like mad between his legs. They drew up against his body like eagerly ticking time bombs, awaiting the signal to explode.

Gunner realized his lower back was arching slightly, his hips lifting hungrily into Chas's hand. His whole existence narrowed down to a single spot—his crotch and Chas's fist around his cock.

Lazily, as if Chas wasn't actually awake, his hand slid up and down the shaft once. Again. Gunner literally started to quiver in anticipation. An urge to wake Chas up and beg for more hovered on the tip of his tongue.

At what point Chas woke up, and at what point he shoved down and kicked off his underwear, Gunner wasn't sure. But gradually Chas's fist tightened, moved more purposefully, gripping his dick with more authority and stroking it with a hint of demand in it. As if he was claiming Gunner's cock for himself and expected it to perform for him.

Gunner's whole world became that fist on his erection in the dark. Waves of pleasure broke over and through his body, washing away everything else that had come before. This—*this*—was the thing he'd been craving all these years. The sex he'd had with women paled by comparison.

Chas's hand pumped over the head of his cock, gathering the precum collecting there and smearing it around the engorged hood. Oh Lord, that felt good. A faint groan escaped the back of his throat as his entire body clenched around the slippery, tight sheath of Chas's hand pumping up and down with more intent now.

With shock, Gunner realized his hips were matching the time of Chas's fist. He was a puppet on strings, totally controlled by Chas's hand. He wanted this too much, had wanted it for too long to deny it, to deny Chas, to deny himself. He gave himself over to it with a long, low groan and let his need take over.

Chas pushed up on his elbow and then knelt beside him, never letting go of his cock. He pulled on it hard enough to make Gunner arch up off the mattress, and then slammed his fist down on it hard enough to pull the head almost painfully tight. Gunner's nerves screamed their pleasure as they also screamed for release. Chas gripped the base of his steel-hard erection tightly, and then—

Oh God, he circled the tip of Gunner's erection with his tongue. His wet, slick, quick tongue that flicked across the sensitive tip hard enough to send a micro-orgasm shivering through him. But those fingers ringing the base of his cock so tightly prevented a full volcanic eruption. His ball sac contracted in anticipation, demanding in no uncertain terms to come, and come *now*.

"Give yourself to me," Chas whispered around his cock. "Surrender."

Not a word in his vocabulary. His body tensed.

Chas slurped at his shaft, running his tongue in a lascivious line along the underside of his cock from base to tip. He then gave a long, hard suck on the tip, easing up to circle the tender flesh lightly. "Surrender."

"No."

"Huh."

Gunner heard the challenge accepted in that single grunted syllable. He should have known better. He should have known that while he was busy playing straight dude, semi-monk, Chas might have gone out and gotten himself an education in sex.

Chas's lips closed around the head of his cock, and Gunner had just long enough to register what was about to happen before Chas's mouth slid down his erection, taking more and more of it into that wet, hot, dark cavern that was the best blow job he'd ever had.

Deeper and deeper Chas pressed. Gunner felt the muscles at the back of Chas's throat moving against the tip of his penis, and it was a huge turn-on. Who knew? And then Chas was moving to straddle Gunner's thighs, getting the angle just right, and slowly, he pushed even farther down on Gunner's erection.

A swallow. So. Damned. Tight. The guy was actually deep-throating him.

Disbelief exploded behind his eyes as the tightness and intimacy of it blew his mind. He heard a gurgling noise and realized that it was coming from his own throat. His body was trembling now, shaking with the effort of not slamming his dick all the way down Chas's throat. He felt more helpless than he could believe, but more shockingly, he loved it. He loved having this man play him like a violin, demanding responses from him that he couldn't stop himself from giving if he tried.

Kneeling over him now, Chas slid his free hand lower. He cupped his balls, lifted them and rolled them around in their sac. They felt like stones, they were so tightly drawn at this point. And then one of Chas's fingers slid even lower, pressed against the clenched sphincter of his ass.

No one had ever penetrated him there, and he froze. But then Chas's mouth slid up and down his shaft, his tongue doing swirling things all around his engorged flesh, erasing all thought and leaving him a mass of jangling nerves in desperate search of release.

The finger probed again while Chas's tongue wove its magic. This time his muscles didn't have control and he didn't have the focus to stop the intimate invasion.

The number of nerves that reacted, sending bolts of electricity shooting through him, was stunning. How come nobody ever told him he could feel this plundered? And then that tongue whisking up and down, around and under, sucking and pulling, erased even that thought.

White lights began to erupt like tiny fireworks behind his closed eyelids, and his breathing came in quick pants that he was completely incapable of controlling. His body felt like a massive bow pulled tight by its master, waiting with quivering anticipation for when Chas would let loose the arrow and allow an epic orgasm to crash through him.

A single word repeated in his mind. Now. Now. Now….

He realized he was chanting it aloud under his breath, at first a command and then a plea. When he was practically sobbing it, Chas let go of the base of his cock, slammed his mouth all the way down the shaft, and rammed a finger into his ass, curling it forward to stroke his prostate gland from the inside.

Gunner threw his forearm across his mouth, shouting against his own flesh as a massive orgasm detonated without warning, ripping through him, reverberating on and on as his entire body clenched, pumping and pumping and pumping into Chas's mouth.

He fell back to the mattress, completely wiped out, totally out of breath, without words. He didn't have the strength to lift a finger or even a toe as his body continued to shudder with aftershocks. Wave after wave of pleasure vibrated through his being.

Eventually, a single thought formed in his mind. He'd been missing out on *this* his whole life?

He lay there a long time, too shocked to form words. Unlike last time, he couldn't bring himself to deny that he'd loved it. He couldn't lie to Chas that it wasn't the best orgasm he'd ever had. And he couldn't lie to himself and say that he didn't want more of that.

He wanted to do that again—Chas to do that to him again—worse than he wanted to live to see another day. He wanted to do that over and over for the rest of his life.

And he wanted more. He wanted to make love to Chas, to return the favor and make his best friend and lover shout with pleasure. He wanted to be inside Chas's body the next time he came. He wanted to make Chas pant the way he had the last time, the only time, they'd had sex. He wanted to see his dick taken into Chas's beautiful, slim body, wanted to fuck until neither one of them could stand upright.

"You okay?" Chas asked cautiously.

"Yes. No. Yes."

"Which is it?" Chas asked.

"I'm...." Gunner searched for words. "Utterly wrecked." Then, lest he fuck it up again like he had last time, he added hastily, "In the best possible way."

"You sure?"

"Mind blown."

"You're not mad at me?"

"I'm mad at me," Gunner replied.

That made Chas press up onto an elbow to stare down at him in the dark. "Why?"

"I could've been doing that for the past decade."

Chas laughed under his breath, a gust of humor that slid across Gunner's chest like a blessing. "Thank God. When I woke up and realized I was giving you a hand job, I thought you might kill me."

Gunner rolled over on his side and gathered Chas against his chest. "You *did* kill me."

They lay together, their legs entwined and Chas cuddled with his ear to Gunner's chest, for a long time. The late hour was deep and still and matched the peace settling into Gunner's soul. Finally. He'd made up for getting it so terribly wrong the last time. Twelve years' worth of guilt was lifting away from his heart as he lay there with his lover.

He heard a noise outside and turned his head toward the window. It sounded like a car door latching gently. Too gently, as if someone had closed it with the intent to muffle the sound.

The skin across the back of his neck prickled.

He rolled out of bed and gained his feet all in one smooth, athletic move. Naked, he moved swiftly over to the window. Standing to one side of it, he peered around the curtains without moving them.

Three men dressed in dark clothing stood behind a black SUV. As he looked on, they pulled ski masks down over their faces.

"Get up, Chas. Right now. Get dressed and grab what you can. We need to be out of here in thirty seconds."

"What?" Chas mumbled.

"*Move.*"

Gunner threw on clothes, stomped into his boots, and was ready to go before Chas, so he scooped up all the baby gear and crammed it into the baby bag. He opened the hallway door and peered out cautiously while Chas scooped up Poppy behind him and wrapped her in a blanket.

Signaling with his hand for Chas to follow, he raced out into the hall and took off running on his toes, as silently as possible. Chas was relatively quiet for an amateur but breathing heavily in what sounded like near panic.

They reached the stairwell door, and he threw his shoulder against it as the elevator dinged in the middle of the long hallway. Gunner held the door for Chas to slip through ahead of him, and then Gunner leaned against the back side of the door to force it closed more quickly.

There was no way of telling if the hostiles spotted it closing or not.

"Run," he breathed.

Fortunately, they were only on the second floor, and it was a fast sprint down the stairs. They emerged into a hallway that matched the one overhead, and Gunner took the lead, running full-out to the middle of the building and turning left to the exit closest to their car.

He slowed at the exit and eased the door open. Then they slipped outside, hugging the wall of the building. They were leaving footprints in the mulch under the bushes, but there was no help for it. Hopefully their pursuers weren't trained trackers.

They reached the car, and he eased the passenger door open for Chas, who slid in with Poppy. The toddler was starting to wake up.

"Keep her quiet," Gunner muttered as he closed the door. Chas stuffed a pacifier in her mouth as he let down the door handle slowly enough to make minimal noise. Then, with a sprint around to the driver's side and a repeat of closing the door silently, he threw the car into Neutral and released the parking brake.

He'd chosen this parking spot for its proximity to the exit and its slight downhill slope. Slowly, the car rolled forward. He turned the wheel and let it roll for perhaps thirty more seconds. It had nearly reached the end of the building before it started to lose momentum. At that point he started the engine and pulled away from the building.

He accelerated away into the night, praying that the hostiles did not pursue them in their faster, more powerful SUV. To that end, he didn't take the same road they'd come into town on and changed directions to head south and then back to the east. Most civilians fled in a single direction, straight away from pursuit, and he hoped the circuitous route would throw off the bad guys for a while at least. Long enough to figure out how in the hell they'd found him, Chas, and Poppy.

"Chas, did you use a credit card in the past day without me seeing you do it?"

"No."

"Make any phone calls?"

"None. Why are you asking?"

"They've got to be tracking us somehow. There's no way they randomly showed up in a dinky town, hours away from Misty Falls, and went directly to our hotel. They even knew the floor we were on."

Chas's eyes went wide. "How could they do that?"

"Poppy," he answered grimly. "They've got some sort of tracker on her. Or in her."

"*In* her?"

"Sure. I've got one implanted under my shoulder blade. If I ever go missing, Uncle Sam can find me anywhere on earth."

"Are you kidding me?" Chas blurted.

"Nope. Hurt like a bitch when they put it in too."

Chas frowned. "I don't remember seeing any scars on Poppy when I gave her a bath."

"Tracker's probably in her clothes. Do we still have the shirt and pants she was wearing the night you found her?"

"Yes."

"Check them over. It'll be a small metallic device about the size and shape of a grain of rice. It may be glued to the fabric, or it may be tucked inside a seam."

Before he checked the clothes, Chas turned around in the front seat, got on his knees, and carefully lifted Poppy into her car seat. "I'm worried about her. She's gone silent again."

"She definitely picks up on fear in the adults around her," Gunner agreed. "It's come in handy a couple of times now."

"But it can't be good for her emotional health," Chas commented. "Here, sweetie. Suck on your pacifier while I make you a bottle."

Gunner snorted. Just like his mother, Chas was. When in doubt, feed people's hurts and pains away.

Once Poppy was sucking sleepily on a bottle, Chas dug in the baby bag and came up with a plastic grocery sack. He flopped back down in the front seat.

"I wrapped her clothes up in case they were needed for evidence or something. I never dreamed they'd be used to follow us." He paused, then added apologetically, "I'm sorry. I didn't know."

"You're a civilian. It's not your job to live in my world. I'm the one who should've thought to check for a tracking burr earlier." Damn, he'd been off his game ever since he woke up in that hospital room.

Chas opened the bag and began checking over the baby's clothes. He found the burr in the hem of Poppy's pants. "Oh my God. There it is. Should I throw it out the window?"

"No!" Gunner exclaimed. He headed for the nearest highway, which took about a half hour to reach, and then he headed north until he found a truck stop at an exit. Chas started to pump gas for the car while Gunner jogged to the diesel fuel pumps where a few trucks were filling up. He found one with Canadian plates and surreptitiously opened the passenger door of the cab, dropped the burr on the front seat, and backed out of the truck.

He checked on Poppy, who was fast asleep in her car seat, carefully locked the car doors, and headed inside quickly to find Chas.

"Looking for the pretty blond guy?" the clerk asked.

"Yeah."

"In the bathroom. But you'll have to get in line. Couple other truckers followed him in there for a quickie."

Jesus H. Christ. Gunner charged down the aisle on full battle alert. He slipped into the bathroom low and fast, his blood ice cold in his veins.

Chas stood with his back against a wall beside the sinks. He stood in a boxer's stance, his fists up defensively, and he looked as if he was getting ready to kill these guys.

"Can I help?" Gunner asked lightly.

"With what?" Chas asked back coolly.

"Beating the shit out of these assholes."

The two burly truckers crowding Chas spun around, scowling. They looked Gunner up and down, obviously weighing whether they could take him.

"Don't try it, boys. I'm an active-duty Navy SEAL, and my hands are considered lethal weapons. Consider yourself officially notified that I will fuck you up bad—or kill you—if you attack me."

One of the truckers snorted in disbelief, but the other looked a little less sure of himself.

Disbeliever demanded, "What team you on?"

"That, my friend, is none of your business. Which one do you want to take to school, Chasten?"

"I'll take the one on the left."

"Any bets on how long it'll take to drop them both?"

"Are we going for unconscious or in need of an ambulance?" Chasten asked casually.

"Your call."

Chas nodded. "Ambulance." He moved smoothly around the undecided truckers to stand shoulder to shoulder with Gunner, then murmured, "Show them your knife."

Chas had seen the Ka-Bar field knife he kept strapped in an ankle sheath, had he? In one blindingly fast motion, Gunner reached for it and held it out in a fighter's stance, low and deadly. "Now with this little beauty, I can give you the closest shave of your life… as well as carve my initials on your faces." He gave the knife a couple of graceful swings in front of him that made it crystal clear he knew how to handle the blade.

Both of the truckers backed away.

Gunner sheathed the knife as smoothly as he'd drawn it and smiled politely at the two men as Chas opened the door and slipped out into the hall. "Have a nice evening, gentlemen. You drive safe out there."

He followed Chas to the car and Poppy, and once on the road again, they headed south on the highway. Gunner's hands shook on the steering wheel, and more than once rage nearly made him turn the car around to go back and kill those bastards.

Chas was pale and tense beside him. No surprise. Those truckers had thought they were going to gang rape the guy. Thank God he'd gotten there before things had become rough. Chas had always had fast hands in their martial arts classes down at the YMCA. Really fast. Which was a hell of an asset in a hand-to-hand fight.

"You okay?" he finally asked when chatterbox Chas continued to be silent and withdrawn beside him. He was kind of like Poppy, come to think of it. "Talk to me. Please. You're scaring me."

Chapter Seven

"I'M SCARING you?" Chas exclaimed. He stared across the interior of the vehicle at Gunner, whose jaw looked carved from the same granite as the old mountains they passed by outside. "You're a SEAL. Hell, you pulled out a knife back there as casual as can be. What the heck do you have to be afraid of?"

Gunner snorted. "I'm scared shitless that something bad will happen to you and I won't be there to protect you. Has anything like that happened to you before?"

Chas looked away, staring out his window into the night. "Yeah. Now and then. I make no secret of being gay. I've had to defend myself a time or two. I took up boxing when you left Misty Falls, you know. I can handle myself in a fight."

"Have you been…?" Gunner hesitated and then said in a rush, "Have you ever been assaulted?"

"As in raped? No. But I've had to beat up the odd asshole now and again."

"Who?" Gunner demanded. The cold steel in his voice was deeply gratifying. He sounded ready to kill whoever'd laid a hand on him.

"It's old history. And I'm better at spotting and avoiding jerks than I once was. I'm tired tonight, though, so I wasn't paying attention."

A low sound emanated from Gunner's throat, and it took Chas a second to identify it. The man had growled. Actually growled. The beginning of a smile curved his lips. It was nice to have someone be so protective of him. It had been a long time since—

His train of thought derailed. The last time anyone had been this protective of him had been back in high school, when Gunner had scared off anyone who even thought about bullying him.

"What?" Gunner asked quickly.

"You've always been my knight in shining armor, haven't you? You're the only person who has always come to my defense, roaring like a lion and chasing off anyone who tries to mess with me."

A snort. "I'm a lot of things, but a knight in shining armor is not one of them."

"I dunno. Those truckers backed off plenty fast when you showed up."

"Don't remind me of them. I'm already fighting with myself about going back and teaching them both a lesson."

"They're not worth it. The world will always have its share of ignorant jerks. I learned a long time ago to just live my life and let others live theirs. You can't change people who don't want to be changed."

Gunner's voice lowered into the tone of a confession. "I'm still pretty new to this. It may take me a while to arrive at your sense of calm over what other people think of you."

"You mean because I'm gay?" Chas was star-tled. "What do you mean, you're new to this? New to what?"

"New to embracing being gay."

A laugh escaped him before he could bite it off. "Well, of course you're gay. I've known that since high school."

"How in the hell could you know when I didn't?"

"Dude. Every girl in the school threw themselves at you, and you didn't even notice, let alone have any interest."

"Yeah, but that doesn't mean I was gay. It could have just meant I wasn't interested in sex."

"Ahh, but you forget. I knew you *were* interested in sex."

Gunner's knuckles turned white on the steering wheel.

A memory flashed through Chas's mind of Gun-ner's head thrown back, his young, athletic body arch-ing forward, his cock thrusting into Chas's mouth. The first time he'd given Gunner a blow job, it had almost been an accident. They'd been spending the night to-gether at Chas's house—Gunner's parents were fight-ing again. Chas had a double bed they usually shared, and that night had been no different. He'd woken up from a hot dream about crawling all over Gunner, only to realize he actually was.

He'd started to roll away, but Gunner had reached out wordlessly and stopped him. And by the time he'd gotten his mouth around Gunner's cock, Gunner had been groaning in pleasure. He hadn't stopped Chas from sucking him to a massive orgasm.

The second time, he was supposed to pick Gunner up from football practice and drive him home, but he'd gotten off work late, and Gunner had been alone in the boys' locker room by the time he arrived.

Yeah, it was cliché. Blow jobs in the locker room. But damn, it had been hot. The danger of discovery had added an edge to that encounter that had both of them so turned on, it had only taken a few minutes to bring Gunner to a shouting orgasm he'd muffled with the sleeve of his varsity jacket stuffed in his mouth.

After that they'd snuck away whenever they could. They never spoke of it, never even acknowledged it. But surely teen Gunner had known teen Chas was hopelessly in love with him.

Chas sighed. He'd have done so many things differently if he had it to do over again. He'd have confronted Gunner about what was going on between them, forced him to acknowledge the mutual attraction. He wouldn't have let Gunner float along pretending it was just sex—sex he could have had just as easily with any of the girls in school.

He'd watched Gunner like a hawk back then, and the guy never—*never*—got a hard-on when one of the cheerleaders made a point of rubbing up against him or some girl threw herself at him at a party. But all Chas had to do was arch an eyebrow or let one corner of his mouth turn up from across the classroom, and Gunner was shifting uncomfortably in his seat.

He wasn't sure why the universe had given them this second chance, but he was not planning to waste it. To that end, he said, "You may get away with pretending you're not gay to everyone else, but this is me you're talking to. I *know* you, Gunner. Better than anyone else on this planet."

"You don't know everything about me," Gunner retorted.

"Oh yeah? Tell me something I don't know about you."

"I've killed people. Lots of them. In lots of ways. I blew some up—watched chunks of their bodies go flying. I've slit throats and heard a man's death rattle as the guy died in my arms."

"Well, of course you have. You're a SEAL, for crying out loud, not a Girl Scout."

Gunner frowned.

Apparently, that grand declaration of being a killer was supposed to scare him off or something. "Why do you think I called you when I got into trouble?" Chas asked reasonably. "I needed someone who could handle serious danger and get me and Poppy out of there safely."

"So you only wanted me for my violent skills," Gunner responded. He stated it as a fact, not a question.

"In part."

That made Gunner look over at him. "What's the other part?"

"I wanted to see you again. We left a whole lot unresolved between us the last time we saw each other."

That did it. Gunner clammed up tighter than an oyster hiding a pearl, refusing to even look at Chas across the front seat.

Dammit, had he pushed too hard again? Was Gunner still having a hard time with his sexual identity? He was tempted to force the man to admit he was in love, but maybe this wasn't the moment. Chas stayed silent, unwilling to chance pushing Gunner into his cave of denial for another ten years.

It took a long time, but Gunner's fists eventually relaxed around the steering wheel.

"Where are we going?" Chas asked casually.

"We're heading toward Pennsylvania. It's as good a place as any to park while we figure out what the hell's going on with Poppy."

"Don't swear," he murmured automatically.

Gunner glanced in the rearview mirror, presumably to check on Poppy, and murmured, "Fuck off."

Chas grinned at him, and praise the Lord, Gunner grinned back.

Chapter Eight

GUNNER LOOKED around the small cabin with approval. The log walls would hold up well in a firefight. Its placement, high on the side of a mountain, gave him great sight lines to the road approaching it. The lock on the front door was sturdy. It was probably meant for keeping out bears, but it would work on humans too. And best of all, it had two bedrooms, which meant Poppy would have her own room and he and Chas would have their own space.

To do what, he wasn't sure, but he thought he might just want to find out. Last night's encounter before the hostiles had shown up had been… enlightening.

He still had it as bad for Chas as he ever had, apparently.

"What's wrong?" Chas asked from the little kitchenette in the corner.

"I beg your pardon?"

"You were frowning as if you were bothered by something about this place."

"Oh. No. It's fine."

"You wanna go take a nap? You drove most of the night. I'll watch Poppy for a while."

"I'm okay."

"Weren't you the one who told me to sleep whenever I could because I wouldn't know when I'd get to sleep again?"

Gunner rolled his eyes. The guy had a point. "Fine. I'll go take a nap."

He stretched out on the big bed and sighed at the comfort. He'd slept on the cold, hard ground more often than in a bed over the past decade, and he'd learned to appreciate having a soft mattress beneath him, with no stones poking him.

He woke with a lurch sometime later to the sound of a car engine coming to a stop outside. He rolled out of bed and pulled the pistol out from under his pillow, all in one fast move. He raced on silent feet to the living room. There was no sign of Chas. He had to be in the other bedroom with Poppy. Good. Safely out of the line of fire.

The knob on the front door moved, and he crouched in the bedroom doorway, using the log wall for cover as he took aim. He exhaled slowly as the door cracked open and his finger began a smooth pull through on the trigger. He would have a millisecond to see the tango's face and memorize it before he obliterated it with a couple of rounds of hot lead.

The intruder slipped inside as the firing pin began to engage.

Shit.

He yanked the pistol up at the last possible second, shocked that it didn't actually fire. He released the trigger carefully and made sure the weapon was safe before he lowered it. He couldn't say the same for his heart. It pounded like a jackhammer in his chest as he straightened in disgust and moved into the living room.

"I almost shot you," he bit out.

Chas set down several bags of groceries on the counter and turned, staring at the weapon gripped in his fist. "I thought you might want something to eat when you woke up. The only restaurant around here is the one up at the main lodge, and I figured you wouldn't want to be seen there, particularly not with me and Poppy."

Gunner sighed and shrugged into his shoulder holster. When he'd buckled the leather harness in place, he stuck the gun in it.

Chas started unpacking groceries and asked, "Don't you worry about shooting your own ass with your gun tucked in your pants like that?"

"It has a safety. I wouldn't stick a gun in my pants if it didn't. Some of the Sig Sauer models don't come with safeties, for example. You always use a holster with one of them. Otherwise you do risk shooting off some important body part."

"How would I know if the safety was on or off if I looked at your gun?"

Gunner moved over to the kitchen counter and drew the weapon. "Some weapons have a grip safety or a decocker, but mine has a simple thumb safety. See this little lever here? If it's pointed down, like this, the weapon is safe. If I flip it up, like this, pointing down the barrel, it's off. You can remember it by thinking of it pointing in the direction a bullet would travel if the trigger were pulled. It would stay down in the clip if the safety is pointing down, but would travel down the barrel and fire if the safety is pointing forward."

"I'm still stuck on what a decocker might be," Chas murmured.

Gunner snorted in humor.

"Is Poppy still asleep?" Chas asked.

"Jesus. I haven't checked on her. I woke up when your car drove up and headed straight out here."

"To kill me."

"Well, to kill the intruder I thought you were."

"Why not try to apprehend one of the bad guys? Make him talk? Find out what they want with Poppy and me?"

Gunner shrugged. "We could. But it's not as easy or pretty as it is on TV to get a prisoner to spill their guts. You have to be prepared to do some bad things to break a really determined prisoner, or you have to be super patient and prepared to take your time earning their trust. Either way, it's messy and time-consuming."

"That's disappointing," Chas replied.

Gunner moved swiftly to the second bedroom, which had come with a crib, and checked on Poppy, who was sprawled on her stomach with her face mashed against the mattress. She clutched the stuffed elephant and drooled a little in her sleep.

"She's passed out like a cheap drunk," he announced, returning to Chas's side.

"She's not a cheap drunk," Chas declared. "Well, she probably would be at this age, but don't ever give her alcohol, okay?"

"Never," Gunner agreed. "Watchya got in the bags?" His stomach was growling something fierce.

"Nothing fancy. This place doesn't have much by way of cooking equipment. When we get back to my place in Misty Falls, I'll cook you a dinner that'll make you weep with joy. But for now, you're getting hamburgers."

"I'll take 'em."

They worked together for the next few minutes, Gunner mashing hamburger into patties and frying them while Chas thin-sliced potatoes and fried them. When he pulled the fries out of the pot, he sprinkled them expertly with some sort of spice combination.

"You some kind of gourmet chef these days?" Gunner asked in surprise.

"I don't know about being a gourmet, but I do like to cook, and I know what kind of wine to serve with what food."

"I probably shouldn't tell you about eating bugs, then, should I?"

"Why on earth would you do that?" Chas responded in horror.

"When you've got no food, you make do."

"You always have the means to hunt or fish or something, don't you?"

Gunner shrugged. "Sometimes a hide runs longer than you humped in supplies for. Or you're in a place with no game to hunt. Or you can't move or make noise because you're too close to hostiles. Food's not the problem—a guy can go a couple of weeks without eating. Water's the thing. You've only got about five days in the field without that before you die."

"And on that grim note…." Chas poured two big glasses of water and carried them over to the table.

A wail from the second bedroom announced that Poppy had woken up.

"Just in time to eat with us," Chas announced. "If you'll go get her and pop a fresh diaper on her, I'll finish up getting the meal served."

"Handy being a great cook all of a sudden," Gunner grumbled.

Chas grinned at him, and he couldn't help but smile back. An infectious joy had always clung to Chas, and it was impossible not to feel good in his presence. He was probably a great teacher.

Gunner picked Poppy out of the crib, and she snuggled against his chest, only half-awake. She was warm and soft and trusting, and something cracked inside his heart. Feelings he'd never had before flooded through him. As he laid her down on the bed to change her diaper, he tried to give them a name. Protectiveness. Affection. Even a parental urge. What was up with that? He had no desire to have a family of his own. Hell, he didn't even have a relationship of his own—

His gaze lifted to the doorway and the man moving efficiently around the kitchenette. Chas. It was always Chas. In his life for as long as he could remember, a steady friend and loyal supporter. The guy had been a constant throughout his childhood. Maybe the only constant, in fact.

He picked up Poppy, who promptly stuck her finger in his ear and squealed with laughter when he turned his head and pretended to bite at her fingers. She did it again, and he played the game with her as he carried her to the high chair Chas was putting up.

"We were lucky to get this place," Chas commented. "They're really set up for kids."

"I had no idea kids needed so much stuff."

Chas shrugged. "We could make do without most of it. Diapers, the right food, and lots of love are pretty much the only mandatory bits. The rest of this stuff is just for convenience."

Chas buckled Poppy into her seat, and Gunner pulled out a chair for Chas in turn.

Chas glanced up at him, his big green eyes bigger and greener than usual. "Thanks," he murmured.

"I appreciate how you're taking care of Poppy and me," Gunner ventured to murmur back.

"You would do the same for her if I wasn't here."

Gunner snorted. "I would have no idea what to do with a kid by myself."

"You'd figure it out."

"Doubtful. They might as well be tiny aliens to me."

"Cute tiny aliens," Chas corrected as he broke bits of hamburger and french fries onto the tray in front of Poppy along with pieces of cut-up apple.

"You're great with her."

"I love kids."

"Do you want to have some of your own eventually?"

"Not that eventually. I'm almost thirty."

Fear shivered down Gunner's spine. Chas and kids. Big commitment. Huge—

Whoa. Wait. Why did that stray thought pop into his mind? Was he subconsciously considering entering into an actual adult relationship with Chas? *That* kind of relationship? Complete with feelings and shared lives and… shared bank accounts? Mortgages? Forever?

Abruptly, the succulent hamburger in his mouth turned to sawdust. He'd never considered settling down at all, let alone with, well, a dude. Even if Chas wasn't just any dude. It would be a huge step—the kind he couldn't walk back from if he took it. The whole world would know he was gay, and there would be no undoing that—

His brain hitched yet again. Would it really be so bad to fully embrace who he was and who he loved? A band of steel tightened around his chest until he struggled to draw a full breath. Sonofabitch. He was panicking.

He laid his hamburger down and pushed back from the table.

"What's wrong? Did I overcook it?" Chas asked in alarm.

Gunner shook his head and rushed out of the cabin, grabbing his coat and shoulder holster on the way out. It was cold outside, a gray, wet afternoon with a raw wind that would knock down most of the rest of the fall foliage by tomorrow. It made for quiet movement through the trees, though. He made a full circuit around the cabin, mostly by rote as his brain spun out in every direction and that steel band refused to loosen.

All of his life had been one giant lie. He'd known he was gay since he'd been about fourteen but had refused to acknowledge it. Granted, his old man had been part of that. The bastard had never missed a chance to bash Chas for being gay once the boys had reached their teens and Chas had come out. The only reason his father had let him and Chas continue to hang out together was because it hadn't ever crossed the bastard's mind that his own son might also be gay. Gunner had known if he ever admitted to being interested in a boy that he'd have been lucky to live another day.

He'd spent his entire adult life assuming that being gay meant never having a family of his own. Never having a partner to love and live out his days with. He'd been so stupid. So stuck in denial. So afraid to allow himself to be happy. Hell. Had all the past lonely years been some elaborate means of punishing himself for being who he was?

He made another full circuit of the cabin, this one wider. He memorized terrain, scoped out possible escape routes, and considered how he would assault the cabin if he were a bad guy.

Gradually, as the shock of really owning the idea of being able to be both gay and happily in love sunk in, it dawned on him that nothing had ultimately changed. He was still a SEAL, he was still out here doing recon, he would still protect Chas and Poppy from whoever was after them. He was still… himself.

The panic eased slowly as he made a third circuit around the cabin, this one nearly all the way to the base of the hill and back. There was too much brush and cover for his comfort. Too easy for hostiles to sneak up on the cabin. But hopefully whoever'd shown up at that last hotel was on their way to Canada now, fruitlessly chasing the truck he'd planted the tracking burr in.

When he returned to the cabin, Poppy was parked on the floor in front of the television watching some kiddy show with lots of bright colors and noise. She was enthralled. Chas had cleaned up after the meal and was dozing on the sofa behind Poppy.

"Go take a nap. I'll take baby duty for a bit," Gunner murmured.

"You sure?"

"We'll need to tag team the munchkin to make this op work. I'll take a nap later and be awake the rest of the night. Get some rest while you can."

"We're a team?" Chas asked cautiously.

"Yeah. I guess we are."

Chapter Nine

CHAS WOKE up feeling refreshed and took over Poppy duty. Gunner looked frazzled after a couple hours of cartoons and peekaboo, which amused Chas to no end. "Parenthood's not as easy as it looks, is it, Mr. Commando?"

"Hardest thing I've ever done," Gunner replied deadpan. But Chas thought he heard a note of honesty in the remark.

"What's the game plan for tonight?"

Gunner replied immediately—obviously he'd been thinking about it. "I'll sleep for a few hours. When you get tired, wake me up and I'll stand guard. Hostiles tend to attack late at night when everyone's asleep or not functioning at full capacity."

"You think we're still in danger?" he asked quickly.

"I think an ounce of prevention is worth a pound of shitshow."

"I don't think that's how the saying goes."

Gunner shrugged. "I stand by it. I'd rather be cautious and not get caught with my ass hanging in the wind."

"Hmm. I rather like the idea of your ass hanging out."

Gunner's gaze snapped to his, and Chas held his breath for a moment until Gunner grinned and rolled his eyes.

Okay, then. Gunner was settling into the idea of being in a relationship with him. This was good. Very good.

Gunner retreated to the adult bedroom, and Chas turned his attention to Poppy. She was repeating the sounds from the TV, and he thought he detected an Asian accent in her pronunciation. Was she from overseas? Startled, he spent a while trying to capture audio of her baby babble with his cell phone. Maybe one of Gunner's contacts could identify where she was from by the things she was saying.

He pointed at his chest and said, "Chas," clearly and slowly.

She mimicked him, enjoying the game but saying "Chi" instead. He laughed in delight and said again, "Chas."

"Chichi," she said clearly. She squealed, and he shushed her quickly. Hopefully Gunner had worn ear-plugs to bed.

They played and watched more cartoons until she started to get tired and cranky, and then he gave her a quick bath, popped her into her jammies, and gave her a bedtime bottle. She snuggled against him trustingly, and he was pleased that she seemed to be recovering from her recent trauma.

If they could just keep her life calm for a while and establish a routine for her until they found her parents, maybe she would come out of this mostly unscathed. He knew from working with little kids that they were resilient beings if they were just given love, support, and a chance to thrive.

He laid Poppy down in her crib and stretched out on the bed in her room. He woke up to the vibration of his phone at midnight. Time to go wake up Gunner. He rolled out of bed and padded barefoot into the other bedroom. It might have a king-sized bed in it, but Gunner sprawled across most of it on his stomach, out cold.

Chas tugged back the sheet to bare Gunner's muscular back and grimaced at the patchwork of bruises. He bent down to kiss Gunner's shoulder carefully on an unbruised spot.

Gunner groaned a little, but his eyes stayed closed. Placing a knee on the bed beside him, Chas kissed his way lightly across Gunner's shoulder blade to his spine, where he headed south, down the indentation there, lined with ridges of hard muscle. Pushing aside the sheet as he went, he approached the rise of muscular buttocks, and he swirled his tongue in the faint dimple at the base of Gunner's spine just short of where that glorious ass began.

Gunner moved lazily beneath him, awake now but clearly enjoying the attention. Inspired, Chas shifted position, kneeling between Gunner's spread thighs, and commenced massaging those powerful legs, working his way down Gunner's thighs and calves, digging his thumbs into the arches of his feet until Gunner groaned faintly. Back up his legs Chas massaged, kneading and rolling the heavy muscles under his palms.

He added his mouth to the massage, sucking the backs of Gunner's knees until he squirmed a little. Ticklish, huh? Good to know. He nipped and kissed his way up the back of one thigh until he reached the junction. He hesitated for a second and then decided to go for it. Pushing Gunner's thighs wider apart, he lightly licked Gunner's balls.

Loving the gasp that elicited, he slurped his way up the underside of Gunner's cock, which was already wide-awake. The thick vein there pulsated under his tongue, and when he swirled his tongue around the tip of Gunner's cock, a drop of precum already had gathered there.

Gunner's erection pulsed against the mattress beneath Chas's mouth, and the gathered tension in Gunner's entire body enveloped him.

Prepared to torture Gunner a little, he left off the sucking and licking and kissed his way back up Gunner's spine until his entire body lay on top of Gunner's.

He murmured against the side of Gunner's neck, "Are you ready to do this properly, or are we going to pretend all you want is the occasional blow job?"

With one quick heave, he was flipped on his back with Gunner looming over him in the darkness. "Don't tease me, Chasten."

"Who's teasing?"

"You sure you want to go the whole way? There'll be no going back."

"My dude, there's already no going back. You just haven't admitted that to yourself yet." It was a risk pushing Gunner this hard. But the guy had been living in this stupid limbo for all of his adult life. It was time somebody shoved him off the fence.

Gunner stared down at him for a long time. And then slowly, slowly, inch by inch, he lowered his face to Chas's. Gunner's lips brushed across his. Another light kiss. As if he was testing this new relationship thing out.

Chas waited patiently, letting Gunner set the pace. Gunner planted an elbow on the pillow beside his head and leaned down again, this time kissing him more firmly. Chas opened his mouth, welcoming Gunner home at long last.

Gunner's tongue swept into his mouth, and Chas moaned in the back of his throat. He'd been waiting for this, imagining this, dreaming of this, forever. He let his hand creep up to the back of Gunner's powerful neck and tugged a little, inviting him even deeper into the kiss.

It was Gunner's turn to groan, the sound muffled by their lips and tongues, now sparring with each other in a sexy duel that had Chas's cock filling eagerly and his hips rocking forward.

"I don't…," Gunner mumbled against his lips.

"Don't what?" he echoed, praying he wasn't chickening out.

"Don't, umm, know exactly how to do this."

Chas could have cried in relief. "Don't worry. I've got you. I'll show you what to do."

The big bad commando's head lowered to Chas's shoulder and rested there for a moment of vulnerability that made Chas's heart swell in his chest. Gunner trusted him. It was possibly the sexiest thing the man had ever done around him.

Chas reached out and fumbled in the nightstand drawer. "I might just have taken a chance and stashed some lube in this drawer."

"Oh, you might have, huh? Confident much?" Gunner murmured.

Chas lifted his head from the pillow and kissed Gunner firmly on the mouth. "Do you have any idea how long I've been waiting for this?"

"Yeah, actually. I do."

"Smartass," Chas muttered.

Gunner grinned and lightly bit Chas's shoulder.

Chas squirted lube into his hand and smeared it generously on himself. Next time Gunner could do the honors, but tonight was about showing Gunner the basics. He squirted another handful of lube and reached between them for Gunner's throbbing erection. He smoothed his fist up and down the shaft, loving its slippery slide almost as much as he loved the way Gunner's breath hitched in his throat at the sensation.

"Let's keep this simple since you're new to it," Chas murmured, wrapping his legs around Gunner's hips. "Pretend I'm a woman and just aim a little farther back."

Gunner laughed under his breath. "Yeah, but I'm not drunk. I have to be drunk to even think about having sex with a woman."

Pumping his fist up and down Gunner's cock one more time, he replied archly, "You obviously don't have to be drunk to have sex with me."

Gunner went still, apparently absorbing the significance of that. "Well, if I'm going to have sex sober, I'm glad the first time will be with you."

"Aww, Gunner. You have no idea what this is gonna be like." Chas did. He'd been fantasizing about sex with Gunner since high school. All of his lovers over the years had been Gunner in his mind. It might have been someone else's body, but it was always his best friend's face, his heart, in Chas's imagination.

"Let's find out, shall we?" Gunner murmured.

Gunner reached between them, and Chas relinquished control of Gunner's cock to him. He shifted a little beneath Gunner to help his aim and angle, and then that blunt heat touched his ass. Pressed a tiny bit.

He groaned aloud.

Gunner stopped immediately.

Chas's eyes flew open, and he realized Gunner had an alarmed look on his face. "You didn't hurt me. That felt amazing. Do it again."

"You sure?"

Chas laughed a little. "I've never been more sure of anything in my life. If you don't fuck me right now, I'm basically never going to forgive you."

"You'll tell me if it hurts?" Gunner asked anxiously.

"Promise."

"Okay." Gunner positioned himself again, and this time he pressed a little harder. He was a well-endowed guy, and Chas's body resisted the invasion.

"Go ahead and push all the way in," he instructed breathlessly. "Just go slow and let the lube do its job." He took a deep breath and pushed back as his muscles gave way all at once and Gunner's erection slid deep, deep inside him.

"Oh. Wow. Jeez," Gunner mumbled.

"Like it?" Chas panted as his body adapted and re-laxed. It had been a while since he'd had sex.

"Uh-huh," Gunner panted back.

"Nice and easy. Slide out a little and back in, a little deeper," Chas said.

Gunner's ass flexed beneath his legs, and Chas grunted as his entire ass filled with Gunner's cock. "Oh, yeah. Like that," Chas muttered.

Gunner withdrew partway and stroked home again, more strongly. "Oh my God," he groaned in Chas's ear.

Exultation filled Chas with every slide home of Gunner's cock, and he caught the rhythm, rising to meet Gunner's increasingly eager thrusts.

"That's it, Gunner. Fuck me." He wrapped his arms around Gunner's back and tightened his legs around Gunner's ass, urging him deeper, harder, faster.

Gunner buried his face against Chas's neck, his breathing ragged, his body arching harder against Chas's. It was, in a word, magnificent.

"Am I hurting you?" Gunter panted at one point.

"God, no. I can take it. Give it all to me. Don't hold back," Chas bit out between ragged breaths of his own.

Gunner did cut loose then, slamming into Chas's welcoming body with all of his prodigious strength. Chas's dick was caught between their bellies, and his erection leaped and throbbed, loving the friction. His balls tightened until he thought they might explode, and Gunner continued ramming into him like a piston over and over until he couldn't form words, let alone breathe properly.

Gunner's hips picked up speed, his thrusts shallow and fast, and then, all at once, he slammed all the way home, filling Chas until he thought he'd been split in two by the excessive pleasure. His orgasm exploded hot and sticky between them, and Gunner thrust his hips forward hard, his entire body arching into Chas's, and gave a muffled shout of his own into the pillow.

Pulsing heat filled his body deep, deep inside as Gunner emptied himself into him. It was bar none the most intimate moment they'd ever shared. It stripped away everything else, all the years, all the hurts, all the secrets. They were together. This was right. And they could never hide from it again.

Gradually, the tension drained from Gunner's big body, and Chas reveled in how Gunner's weight pressed him deep into the mattress. He continued to hold Gunner close with both arms and legs, their bodies still joined.

Eventually, Gunner mumbled, "I'm crushing you."

"It's okay. I like being a pancake."

Gunner rolled off him but looped a lazy arm around Chas's shoulder and dragged him against his side. Chas rested, replete, with his head on Gunner's shoulder.

They lay together like that in silence for a long time, basking in the afterglow, catching their respective breaths, and processing what had just happened.

Finally, Chas ventured to ask, "Did you like it?"

"What do you think?" Gunner asked.

"I think you've been missing out your whole life and are just now realizing how much you've got to make up for."

Gunner's chest vibrated with a silent chuckle. "Just gotta rub it in, don't you?"

"I would never dream of saying I told you so."

The chuckle became audible. "Jerk."

"Double jerk," he replied affectionately. "Wait till you take me from behind. You'll be able to fuck me even deeper and harder that way."

"I like looking at your face," Gunner objected.

"I like looking at you too. But don't knock it till you've tried it."

Gunner grinned. "I'll take you up on the offer. But right now, duty calls. I need to get outside and make sure nobody has followed us."

Chas groaned in protest as Gunner rolled out from under him and headed for the bathroom. He sprawled lazily on his stomach, loving how thoroughly fucked he felt. "What will you do if you find someone out there?"

"Depends on how many and how well armed they are. Fight if I can beat 'em, run if I can't."

"I hate running," Chas replied lazily.

"Don't fall asleep without getting dressed. And leave your shoes beside the bed. If we need to bug out, I'll need you to move fast."

"Buzzkill. You're supposed to tell me how much you liked fucking me and that you hope you can do it again."

Gunner strode into the bedroom, fully dressed, bent down, and pressed his lips to Chas's ear. "I *loved* fucking you, and I *am* going to do it again."

Chapter Ten

GUNNER FELT too damned exuberant to just sit in the living room of the tiny cabin, so he decided to run a little patrol. He preferred being outside over being cooped up behind walls in general, and he loved a brisk night like tonight, with a million stars dusting the sky and his breath hanging in the air in puffs of exhaled fog.

It was a little after 2:00 a.m. when he heard a faint whirring noise. Startled, he looked up at the sky. It almost sounded like a—

He swore as the whirring became the distinctive buzz of a drone. It was the middle of the freaking night. No amateur was out here flying a drone for grins and giggles.

Gunner took off running down the hill toward the cabin, dodging among the trees, which weren't giving him shit for cover after most of the leaves had come down in yesterday's wind storm.

He thought fast as he ran grimly.

He could shoot the drone down, maybe. Bad guys might have a second one to launch. But if nothing else, it would take them a few minutes to put a second drone in the air. Range on a small military drone could run to something like fifteen kilometers, so the hostiles weren't necessarily on top of them.

But the drone explained how they'd caught up with the three of them. It also meant these assholes were no garden-variety thugs. These guys had training, skills, and smarts. And yet again, they'd caught him flat-footed.

The noise got louder as he approached the cabin. Fuckers were hovering over it, checking it out. The drone was only about fifty feet up. He paused just inside the trees and drew his pistol. He would much rather have a rifle for making this shot, but when he'd bolted from that hospital room, he hadn't had time to grab his field kit out of his equipment locker. He had only the handgun Rafael had given him as he got off the jet in Misty Falls.

He found a tree branch about shoulder high and rested his wrists on it as he lined up the shot. He would get one chance at taking the drone out before its pilot fled the area.

He guessed the windage as best he could, took aim carefully, exhaled, and took the shot. The drone lurched sideways, pieces flying every which way. Before it had even crashed to the ground, Gunner had taken off at a dead run for the cabin.

He burst inside, calling, "We have to go. Now. I'll get Poppy. Run."

Chas bolted out of the bedroom, his hair standing up every which way. "What's up?"

Gunner scooped up Poppy, blankets and all, snagged her baby bag, which he'd repacked after supper, and ran outside without bothering to answer. There'd be time for that later, assuming they made it out of here alive.

Poppy started to cry, and he shoved her across the front seat to Chas as he started the car and hit the gas. They flew down the hill without headlights, and he was abjectly grateful he'd walked this road several times in his patrols and knew it reasonably well.

They hit the main road and he accelerated hard. Chas quieted Poppy with her pacifier and strapped her into her car seat. He flopped back down into his own seat, and Gunner said, "Look outside for me, Chas. Watch the sky for any drones."

"Drones? Like kids' toy helicopters?"

"That, or maybe bigger. Could be the size of a table."

Chas leaned forward, peering into the sky. "It's dark as heck. How am I supposed to spot a drone?"

"You'll see a black silhouette against the stars."

"Maybe you might see something like that. I don't have x-ray vision, and we're going about a hundred miles per hour."

"We're only doing eighty."

"What's the speed limit on this road? Half that?"

"Something like that," he answered grimly. Gunner drove a few minutes, thinking hard. "Can you find me the nearest tunnel?"

Chas frowned. "Like where a road cuts through a mountain?"

"Yes. Doesn't Pennsylvania have a bunch of them?"

"I guess."

Chas started poking at his cell phone, and in a minute or so he said, "There's one about forty miles south of here. Sidelong Tunnel. Over a mile long. It's on the Pennsylvania Turnpike."

"That'll work. Give me directions to it."

Chas called a couple of turns, and then they hit the turnpike, racing west on the mostly deserted highway at nearly the hundred miles per hour Chas had accused him of before. Drones might be maneuverable little bastards, but they weren't all that fast. If he could outrun the drone and get under cover, he might be able to throw the hostiles off their tails. *If* he could outrun it.

They never did see a drone, but the tightness across the back of his neck told him that one was likely up there, tracking them. His intuition was rarely wrong, and he trusted this one.

"There it is. The tunnel," Chas said tightly as a brightly lit arch came into view ahead of them.

Gunner careened into the tunnel and went about a quarter mile before he slowed the car and pulled off onto the narrow shoulder. Then he turned off the ignition.

"What are you doing?" Chas squawked.

"C'mon. Grab the baby bag. I'll get Poppy." He quickly opened the hood and propped it up as if the car had broken down. Then, leaving her strapped in, he picked up Poppy, car seat and all, and lifted her out of the car. They crossed the center median quickly and stood by the side of the road.

Gunner made sure Poppy was clearly visible to any oncoming traffic, and as an eighteen-wheeler's tall headlights came into view, Gunner waved his free arm over his head. The big rig's brakes squealed as the driver came to a stop beside them.

"Got car trouble?" the driver yelled down.

"Yes, sir. We could really use a lift," Gunner said in his friendliest possible voice. "It's cold out here for the baby."

"Get in," the driver said.

Chas climbed in first, and Gunner handed up Poppy and then climbed in the high cab. "We really appreciate this," Chas was saying warmly.

"Where you headed? I'm going the opposite direction from y'all," the driver said, pulling into the lane of traffic and accelerating slowly.

"Any place we can rent a car would be great," Gunner answered.

"No problem. I'm headed for Philadelphia, myself."

"Perfect," Gunner responded. "We're from there. We'll just head home and cancel the whole vacation."

The trucker nodded, and Gunner sat back as they exited the tunnel. It was tempting as hell to lean forward and look for a drone hovering at the entrance, but odds were the thing was waiting at the west end of the tunnel for them to emerge.

They'd caught this ride fast enough that he figured the hostiles would wait another ten or fifteen minutes for their car to emerge from the tunnel before they actually drove in to flush them out. By that point, they should be long gone from the area.

About a half mile east of the tunnel, he spotted a black SUV parked on the opposite side of the turnpike. He tried to catch a plate inconspicuously, but it was too dark for him to pick it up. Smug, he sat back in his seat and listened to Chas and the trucker chatting about where the trucker was from and what he was hauling.

It was a couple of hours later when they arrived at the outskirts of Philadelphia. Gunner picked a likely looking truck stop and got out there, claiming that they would grab a cab the rest of the way to their house.

With a word of thanks to the trucker, he ordered a ride-share service on his cell phone.

"Where are we going?" Chas asked as they waited inside the warmth of the convenience store beside the gas pumps.

"Airport."

"We flying somewhere?"

"Not without risking some difficult questions over the baby. But I can get a decent rental car there."

An hour later, as Gunner loaded a sleepy baby and a nearly as sleepy Chas into a turbocharged muscle car, Chas commented dryly, "So by decent, you meant a fast car."

"Hell yeah. I need to be able to outrun those fuckers if they manage to find us again."

"Language," Chas mumbled, his eyes already drifting closed.

Gunner was tired too. But he had a lot more experience with running on empty than Chas did. He got in the car and headed south. Time to call in reinforcements.

He drove about two hours, until the sky started to lighten in the east, and then he pulled into a random hotel—random but relatively nice. For some reason, people on the run tended to stay in dives. He supposed the assumption was a sleazy motel manager would be less inclined to talk to the police. But in their case, an upscale hotel manager would be less likely to talk to a bunch of criminals without badges asking questions about the guests.

He carried in Poppy, asleep in her car seat, and led a sleepy Chas to the room.

Chas mumbled, "Can I take off my shoes?"

"Yes. We should be safe here. Sleep. I've got a few phone calls to make."

Chas tumbled into the bed, and Gunner looked longingly at it. He would love nothing more than to crawl in with Chas, snuggle up to him, and crash for about twelve hours. Instead, he went into the bathroom and closed the door.

He called Spencer Newman. The guy wouldn't mind a phone call in the wee hours of the morning—he'd been an operator long enough to know that trouble didn't always come during daylight hours.

To his credit, Spencer sounded alert when he answered his phone. "Hey, Gun. What's up?"

"I've got a problem. I haven't been able to shake whoever followed us out of Misty Falls. I've got the kid and the guy who rescued the kid with me. We're in a hotel about an hour outside of Washington, DC."

"Just a sec. I'm gonna put you on speakerphone so Dray can hear too."

Drago Thorpe and Spencer were partners, both personally and professionally, these days. Dray was ex-CIA and apparently a hell of a black ops man.

"Hey, Gun." Drago sounded noticeably sleepier than Spencer.

"Sorry to wake you up."

Spencer said briskly, "What can you tell us about your tails?"

"They're good. They had a tracking burr in Poppy's clothes, and—"

"Poppy? Is that the kid's name?"

"Nah. It's just what we call her. The night Chas found her, she was wearing a shirt with a big red flower on it."

"Cute. Continue," Spencer said.

"I put the burr in a truck headed for Canada, but the hostiles didn't bite. My best guess is they tracked us with a drone into Pennsylvania. I shot down one drone, but they must have put up a second one. We switched vehicles in a tunnel, and I think we've lost them for the moment. But I could use some backup. I haven't gotten much sleep in the past several days, and I'll need some extra firepower if these assholes close in on us."

"An hour out of DC, you say?" Spencer asked.

"Yeah."

"Catch a nap in place if you need it. Meet us at noon at… I'm going to text you an address in Potomac. Drago and I will meet you there. We'll put together a plan to catch these bastards, or at least to figure out who the hell they are and what they want."

"Any chance you could bring an extra field kit?" Gunner asked. "I'm feeling naked as hell with just a handgun and none of my usual gear."

Spencer laughed. "I'll see what we can scrounge up for you."

"See you then. And thanks, Spence."

"We take care of our own."

"Ooh-rah."

Chapter Eleven

SPENCER STRAIGHTENED his tie as they stepped into the lobby of CIA headquarters in Langley, Virginia. He was here mostly to lend moral support to Drago. It was his first visit back here since they'd both been let go.

Still, they'd moved on to bigger and better things. They'd finished doing the paperwork to incorporate, although they were still debating what to name their new security company. It would be nested behind several other innocuous tax entities, of course.

Spencer wanted to call the company something that sounded fierce, but he had yet to land on the perfect name.

He clipped the visitor's badge Drago passed him to his lapel, and they strolled over to the wall of stars while they waited for their escort to come get them.

A rather rumpled, scholarly-looking man greeted Drago with a warm handshake. Drago said, "Good to see you again, Charles."

"Good to see you both again," Charles murmured. His lean features lit with a smile that animated his whole face.

They followed the CIA analyst to a tiny office off to one side of a cluster of people at desks. The group made up a special strategic analysis unit that Charles headed, according to the plaque in the sliding holder on his office door.

They piled inside, and Charles closed the door behind them. Spencer's ears popped a little and he reassessed the door sharply. Soundproof.

"What can I do for you gentlemen?" Charles asked, donning a pair of horn-rimmed glasses that made him look exactly like an absentminded professor.

"Have you heard about the shooting up in New Hampshire a few days ago?" Drago asked.

Charles frowned. "I'm an international specialist."

"Right. So, there was a shooting in upstate New Hampshire. A few local cops were killed. Several locals were shot as well. But what nobody except us seems to know is that an Asian child was mixed up in the whole thing and was possibly the target of the shooting."

"A child?" Charles blinked a few times. "How old?"

"Under two years of age."

"Children that young are never the targets of assassination attempts. Not unless they're the heirs to some position of power or a very large fortune. And even then, they're almost always kidnapped and not killed immediately."

Spencer responded, "It's possible kidnapping was the purpose of this attack. We do know that the adult female who had custody of her was murdered while trying to flee with the child."

"Any idea what nationality the child is? Asia's a rather large place."

"My guy thinks she may be Japanese," Spencer answered.

"Hmm." Charles typed on his computer for several seconds and then stared at his screen. Unfortunately, Spencer couldn't see it from where he sat.

As the silence dragged out, Spencer got the impression that Charles might have forgotten they were sitting in his office. Drago murmured to Spencer, "Charles's group runs simulations of global crises. He has access to real-time intel from pretty much all over the world. That's why I came to him today."

Charles jumped without warning, almost as if his chair had given him an electric shock. "What the hell are you involved in, Drago?" the analyst demanded.

"What did you find?" Dray asked quickly.

"I just got red flagged. My search parameters were apparently forwarded to the Asia desk, and they're demanding—aggressively—to know why I ran that particular search. They're sending someone down to talk to me in person now."

Spencer traded startled glances with Drago. What was Gunner tangled up in? And who in the hell was that kid?

A middle-aged man who looked to be of Japanese descent knocked impatiently on Charles's door and pushed past Charles before stopping to stare at Spencer and Drago. "Who are these people?" the man demanded.

"They're the reason I ran the search. Care to tell us what the red flag is all about?" Charles asked with admirable calm.

"Come with me, you two," the man said.

"We've never met," Drago said smoothly. "Drago Thorpe. Formerly of the Operational Security group. And you are?"

The OPSEC moniker seemed to take the man aback. As it should. The operational arm of the agency was small but very, very good at what it did. Anyone who worked there was lethal in the extreme.

"Joe Riyosuki. And you?" he asked, turning to Spencer.

"Spencer Newman. US Navy retired." He omitted the SEAL title, not only because it still rankled that he could no longer call himself that, but also because he would rather have this guy underestimate him until they knew what had him so agitated.

"I need you both to come with me," Joe said.

"Where do you want us to go?" Drago demanded suspiciously.

"Look. This isn't a request. I'm trying to be civil about it, but I'll have you both arrested if I have to. It's imperative that you come with me right now."

Spencer frowned. What in the ever-loving hell had Gunner gotten them into?

They followed Riyosuki to an elevator, and Spencer was alarmed when the man hit a button that would take them below ground level. He glanced at Drago, whose jaw was uncharacteristically tight.

They stepped out into a parking garage, and Riyosuki led them to a white SUV whose engine was idling. Spencer balked at that. "Joe, my dude, I haven't known you long enough to get into a car without knowing where in the hell you're taking me."

The guy huffed. "I have to take you to the Japanese embassy right away."

Drago's eyes widened nearly as much as Spencer's did.

"Please. This is a matter of international importance and utmost delicacy. If you insist on driving your own vehicle, you can follow me there."

Drago nodded stiffly. "I'm driving a silver pickup truck. I'll meet you outside the main gate in five minutes and we'll follow you."

Spencer followed Drago back to the elevator, and they hurried through the building to the front desk to turn in their visitor's badges. As they stepped outside, Spencer muttered, "Do you trust this guy?"

"Yeah. He's genuinely panicked. He actually broke protocol by not escorting us back to the front desk to check us out. I say we follow him and see what the Japanese are so worked up about."

The drive into northwest DC was a nightmare of morning rush-hour traffic, but they eventually arrived at the embassy, a blond brick Georgian mansion set well back from Massachusetts Ave. The guard at the front gate waved them through, and they parked in the circular drive in front of the imposing structure.

They were shown with impressive speed into a Western-style office, one with tall windows looking out on a gorgeous garden and a massive crystal chandelier dominating the center of the room. A young man served them tea, and then an older man came into the room.

Joe from the CIA made introductions all around in English, and then took off speaking with their host in rapid Japanese, and Spencer and Drago exchanged glances. Then the man from the embassy said in perfect British-accented English, "Thank you for coming so quickly."

"How can we help you, sir?" Drago asked.

"This is a matter requiring extreme discretion, gentlemen."

Drago commented dryly, "Between Mr. Newman and me, we have held most of the security clearances the United States government issues. We've worked with extreme discretion for most of our careers."

The Japanese man bowed his head briefly. "A Japanese citizen by the name of Kenji Tanaka reported his young daughter missing several weeks ago."

Great. This was going to be easy. Gunner would bring the kid to the Japanese embassy, hand her over, and she would be sent home to join her family.

"You claim to know of a young Japanese child, a girl, who might be his daughter?"

"We make no such claim," Drago said cautiously.

Spencer's gaze snapped to Drago. Dray's instincts must have fired off some sort of warning to him. Otherwise he wouldn't be so cagey with this guy.

"Who is Kenji Tanaka?" Drago asked politely. *Too politely.* What did he know that Spencer didn't?

The man from the embassy answered, "He is an architect in Tokyo. He designs and builds high-rise buildings and major architectural projects around the world."

"So he's a wealthy man?" Drago followed up.

"Yes."

"Has ransom been demanded for his daughter?" Drago asked.

"That is sensitive information, sir."

"Not really. She was kidnapped, and the kidnappers either demanded money or they didn't."

Spencer frowned. Who would kidnap a little kid and *not* demand ransom? He pondered that while the man shifted into Japanese with CIA Joe once more. Even though he didn't speak Japanese, it sounded like

Joe was being treated to a solid dose of diplomatic dou-blespeak that amounted to a nonanswer.

Joe shrugged apologetically. "He really can't an-swer that question."

"Because he doesn't know or isn't allowed to say?" Drago demanded.

Spencer was watching the man from the embassy's face closely when Drago snapped the words, and he saw all he needed to see. A shadow passed through the man's eyes. The guy knew the answer and was refusing to tell them.

The man asked, "Do you know where the child is now?"

Drago glanced at Spencer, who answered smooth-ly, "No, we don't. We merely heard that she might have been seen in the vicinity of a crime a while back, and we were asking a few questions about who she might be."

"Can you give us any further information that might help us locate her and return her to her father?" the man asked urgently.

"I'm sorry," Drago said. "We cannot share any more with you than you've been able to share with us. But we do thank you for your hospitality. If we happen to locate the child and can help return her to her father, we most certainly will."

Both of the other men looked troubled but didn't press him and Drago any further.

Spencer followed Drago from the embassy and, as they drove away, demanded, "What was that all about?"

"You've never heard of the Tanaka family who builds high-rise buildings all over Japan, have you?" Drago murmured.

"Enlighten me."

"They're only one of the oldest and most power-ful Yakuza clans in all of Asia. For decades, perhaps centuries, they've controlled the construction industry in Japan."

"You think Gunner has landed in the middle of a Yakuza feud? They're like the Japanese mob, aren't they?" Spencer exclaimed.

"Yes, and I think it's possible. Probable, even. Your boy's in serious danger if he's got one of the Tana-ka kids."

Great. Just great.

Chapter Twelve

CHAS LOOKED around in dismay as they got out of the car. They'd driven down back roads to get to this isolated place on the outskirts of the outskirts of Washington, DC, to see some apparently top-flight security types who were friends of Gunner's.

When they'd passed through a tall iron security gate, he hadn't been surprised. But then they'd followed a long driveway winding through what appeared to be nothing more than a farm, with a pasture, a few cows grazing, a big old barn, and a rambling old farmhouse that somebody was doing some work on.

"This is it?" he asked skeptically.

Gunner shrugged. "It's not the place but the people we've come to see."

"I hope they're as good as you say they are."

One corner of Gunner's mouth turned up in amusement, but that was his only response. They jogged up the front steps onto a broad covered porch that was begging for a swing to be hung at one end of it.

"This could be a pretty place when it's finished," Chas commented. "A little landscaping, maybe some antique roses, some old-fashioned flower beds. I'd plant tomatoes at that end of the porch—"

He broke off as the front door opened. A dark-haired man who looked to be of Mediterranean heritage finished the sentence for him. "Tomatoes along with some peppers, both sweet ones and hot ones. Where the sun is strong. That's the plan next spring, actually. Hi. I'm Drago Thorpe. You must be Gunner. And Chasten, right?"

Gunner stuck out his hand. "Gunner Vance. And this is Chasten Reed. And this little cutie is Poppy. At least, that's what we're calling her."

Drago looked at Poppy like she was an alien creature, and Chas grinned. "Right there. That's exactly how Gunner looked at her a few days ago too. But now he can give her a bath and feed her and dress her and yes, even change her diaper. If you'd like, we can leave her with you for a few days so you get over your terror of children, Mr. Thorpe."

"Call me Drago. Or Dray. And that's okay. I'll go ahead and hang on to my terror."

Someone laughed behind him, a rich, warm laugh. "Let our guests come inside, why don't you, Dray?"

They stepped into a big living room with gracious proportions. The furniture looked as old as the house and just as comfortable. In one corner of the large room, a very good-looking man sat at a desk in front of a computer.

"Hi. I'm Spencer. Welcome, Chas. Gunner."

"Hey, boss," Gunner said.

"I'm not your boss anymore. I'm just Spencer."

"That's going to take a little getting used to," Gunner replied.

Spencer shrugged. "You could always come to work for Drago and me. Then you could call me boss again."

"One crisis at a time," Gunner muttered. But Chas noted sharply that he didn't turn down the job offer outright.

Chas put Poppy down on the faded but thick carpet to play and pulled out several of her favorite toys to occupy her.

Carrying his laptop, Spencer came over to sit on one of the matching sofas while Chas and Gunner took the other. Drago disappeared into the kitchen and came back with four glasses of iced tea. He set the tray down on the coffee table with a flourish. "See? I can be all civilized and polite when I try!"

Spencer laughed, and Gunner grinned. Chas wasn't sure what the joke was, but he liked the easy camaraderie between these special operators. It was the most relaxed he'd seen Gunner around anyone else since he'd shown up in Misty Falls.

Spencer took a sip of his iced tea and then said, "So, you two appear to have gotten yourselves mixed up in quite a mess. Drago and I went to Langley this morning and were all but bodily dragged to the Japanese embassy for a command appearance."

"What?" Gunner squawked. "So she is Japanese after all?"

They all stared at Poppy, who froze and stared back. Chas picked up her stuffed elephant and made a silly trumpeting sound that made her laugh and grab for the toy.

"Maybe," Drago answered. "There is a high-profile girl about her age missing in Japan, but we have no confirmation that your kid is that kid."

"Who is she?" Chas asked more reluctantly than he'd expected. He actually kind of hated the idea of giving her back to her real family. He knew they would eventually have to give her up, but he'd fallen a little in love with her over these past several days. The stricken look on Gunner's face indicated that he was in the same boat.

"It's possible she's the daughter of a man named Kenji Tanaka," Drago answered.

"Who's he?" Chas and Gunner asked simultaneously.

Spencer shrugged. "I've been researching him while we waited for you guys to get here. He's an architect and heir to a construction and real estate conglomerate. His family builds high-rise apartments and major office buildings all over the world. The Tanakas are stupidly rich."

Gunner's gaze snapped to Poppy. "She's an heiress? Was she kidnapped? Is that how she ended up in Misty Falls?"

"Possibly," Spencer answered. "We'll have to DNA test her to be sure she's the Tanaka baby. As for how she ended up in New Hampshire, that's a mystery to us. Chas, what can you tell us about the woman who brought her to you?"

He frowned. "Leah Ledbetter. Single lady, lived alone. Quiet. Her son was in and out of jail, though. Maybe he got mixed up in a kidnapping plot."

"The son's name?" Spencer murmured, already typing.

"Leo."

"Got him. Released from jail about six months ago. Rap sheet consistent with low-level gang crime. There's a note in his record that he's tattooed consistent with membership in the Oshiro gang."

"Who are they?" Chas blurted.

Drago typed a bit, and then read off the screen, "Yusi Oshiro founded the Oshiro gang in 1985 in Brooklyn, New York. It spread to other major cities, including Chicago, Denver, Dallas, Los Angeles, and San Francisco. Its largest concentrations are in New York City and San Francisco. Thought to be primarily a drug smuggling enterprise. Gang membership is estimated at between three and five thousand."

"Five thousand!" Chas exclaimed. "And they're after Poppy?"

Drago responded, "Three to five thousand is small as gangs go. Some of the big ones in the US are ten times that size."

Chas frowned. "If they're drug smugglers, what do they want with Poppy?"

Silence met that question.

Eventually Spencer said, "If the Oshiro gang is doing business with the Tanaka Clan—maybe distributing drugs for them in America—the two gangs could have a beef. Or, if the Oshiros are looking to expand into Asia, they could have run afoul of the Tanakas."

Gunner commented, "If these Oshiros have decided to tangle with the Tanakas, we know one thing about them. They've got cast iron cojones."

"Why do you say that?" Chas asked.

Drago answered the question. "Clan Tanaka is one of the biggest, oldest, and most powerful Yakuza clans in Japan. Tangle with them and you *will* pay a steep price. These modern Yakuza outfits aren't like old-school Yakuza families. Nowadays they're more like Western-style mafias, motivated by profit and power. They're well trained, well armed, and violent."

"How violent?" Chas asked warily.

"As violent as any South American drug cartel."

"Holy cow," Chas mumbled.

Gunner added quickly, "Before you freak out, Chas, Japan is a significantly more lawful part of the world than certain Central and South American countries. Gang violence is tightly controlled in Japan, and because Japanese officials are generally not corrupt, the gangs don't have control of the government."

"Still," Chas retorted. "Poppy is related to these Tanaka mafia dudes?"

Drago shrugged. "Spencer's trying to find out if this Kenji guy is one of those Tanakas."

Chas glanced over at Poppy, who was sitting on a blanket playing with a set of stacking blocks. "Assuming she is one of *those* Tanakas, how did she end up in Misty Falls?"

Spencer fielded that one. "Let's assume the Oshiros have some problem with the Tanakas. What better way to hit them where it hurts? Kidnap Grandpa Tanaka's cute little granddaughter. The Oshiros snatch Poppy in Japan. If they're smuggling drugs, they obviously have shipping conduits from Asia to the United States. They smuggle her over here, hand her off to Leo Ledbetter to hide. He knows squat about caring for a baby, so he takes the kid home to his mom. And voilà, Poppy is in Misty Falls."

"Then who shot up the town and tried to grab Poppy?" Chas asked logically.

Chas looked around at all the other men, and finally Drago muttered, "I've got nothing."

Spencer added, "We're obviously missing a piece of the puzzle."

Gunner said grimly, "I don't care who all is coming after our girl. Nobody gets near her until we hand her off to her parents—Tanaka or not."

Drago fiddled with his laptop for a bit and then announced, "I'm guessing our guy Kenji is one of those Tanakas. He's in construction, they're in construction. He's rich, they're rich. His great-great-grandfather has the same name as a founder of the Tanaka Yakuza family."

Spencer asked, "Are the guys pursuing you Tanaka guys who want Kenji's kid back, or are they from some rival clan?"

Gunner frowned. "If it's Kenji's guys, it seems to me they'd be coming in a whole less hot than these guys are. When they entered the hotel the first night we were on the run, they were wearing full tactical gear and carrying Uzis and AK-47s. Would you send in armed guys with itchy trigger fingers after your kid?"

Chas answered promptly, "No way. I wouldn't want weapons anywhere near my kid. I wouldn't want to chance an accident."

"Or a stray bullet or a ricochet," Spencer added.

"So Daddy's enemies are chasing Poppy?" Chas asked.

The little girl looked up at him, and her face started to crinkle pre-tears. Did she sense his distress? Chas scooped her up off the floor into his lap and bounced her on his knee. "It's okay, squirt. Nothing's wrong." She started pulling at the buttons on his shirt, and he pretended to bite at her fingers until she was giggling happily.

"What else can you tell us about Kenji Tanaka?" Gunner asked.

Spencer typed some more, read some more, then typed some more again. "He's not married. Never has been."

"Who's her mother?" Gunner blurted, glancing at Poppy.

"Looks like he might have adopted her, or maybe he used a surrogate. The Japanese press is being cagey about how Kenji came into possession of a baby he seems to be treating as his own."

"They probably don't know," Drago responded. "They'd have printed it if they did."

"So DNA testing might not tell us if he's her papa," Chas added.

"Not if she's adopted," Spencer agreed.

"What are we supposed to do with her, then?" Gunner asked. "I'm not keen on handing her over to the first Yakuza types to catch up with us."

"I'm not keen on handing her over to *anyone* until I'm convinced she's going back to her actual family and she's going to be safe," Chas said vehemently.

Spencer glanced over at Drago. "Your instinct in the embassy was a good one."

"How's that?" Gunner asked.

Spencer explained, "Drago didn't tell the Japanese embassy staffer that we might know where Poppy was and that she might be the missing Tanaka baby. He… prevaricated… a bit."

Gunner nodded. "So he bought us some time. But to do what? Draw in the guys who've been following us and ask them which gang they work for?"

Drago snorted. "That would not go well."

Gunner snorted right back. "Not for them. I doubt they've ever run up against SEALs. I'm confident we can take them in a straight-up fight."

Catching the other men's speculative looks at Poppy, Chas stated firmly, "We're not using her as bait. No way."

Spencer shrugged. "We could use the idea of her as bait, though."

"I beg your pardon?" Chas asked sharply.

"We can stash Poppy somewhere safe. Out of the way. But if you and Gunner go on the run with a Poppy-sized mannequin in a car seat, your pursuers would be none the wiser. We could lay a trap for them."

"That sounds dangerous," Chas blurted in alarm.

The other men shrugged, supremely unconcerned.

"Hello. Civilian here. I'm a kindergarten teacher, for God's sake. I'm no commando." When nobody responded, he added a little desperately, "Just running away from those guys was more than I could handle. Knowing I'm bait in a trap—" He made a slashing motion with his hand. "Not a chance."

"It could work," Gunner said eagerly.

"No. It could not," Chas objected.

"Aww, c'mon, Chas. Have I let anything bad happen to you or Poppy? It would be a ton easier to stay ahead of these guys without Poppy to worry about. We could lead them right into a sweet ambush."

"Or end up ambushed ourselves!"

"Give it a chance. Let us come up with a plan and run it past you. Just think about it."

"Why can't you be the bait if you're so eager to die?"

"I won't die—"

"You forget, I was in Misty Falls the night they shot it up. I've seen these gangsters at work. They're vicious and efficient. I want nothing to do with them." Then, his voice sounding more desperate than he'd ever heard it, he added, "And I don't want you anywhere near them either."

"Aww," Spencer and Drago said in unison, as if he was nothing short of adorable. Gunner grinned, looking a little embarrassed.

"What?" Chas demanded, indignant.

"That's sweet of you to be so concerned for me, Chas," Gunner murmured.

"Fuck off, Gunner."

That sent Gunner's eyebrows shooting skyward as he commented blandly, "Watch your language in front of the baby, Chasten."

Chas glared at Gunner, stood up with Poppy in his arms, and marched outside to show her around the front yard. It was a warm afternoon, one of the last of the fall, and she would enjoy being outside after so much time cooped up in cars. As for him, he was going to attempt to climb down off his homicidal ledge and chill the heck out.

The other three men spent all afternoon with their heads together. They relocated to a big, scarred dining room table that must have come with the house and spread out a giant map of the United States. They seemed to think it was a good idea to draw their pursuers far away from the nation's capital before confronting them. As long as Poppy stayed in this area, Chas reluctantly agreed to lead the bad guys away from her, which was the least violent plan the group came up with. Apparently the idea was for him and Gunner to go on a road trip through rural places. Somewhere a bunch of Asian mafiosos would stand out and be hindered from operating freely.

After supper, a man named Charles Favian arrived and joined the discussion. He came armed with a ton of information about the various Yakuza clans and

American gangs. His best guess was that the Oshiros were behind Poppy's abduction.

Apparently the Oshiros controlled drug smuggling through several major shipping ports in America, and appeared to be trying to branch out into Asia. If that was the case, it could explain clashes between the Oshiro and Tanaka clans over the past year or two. The CIA analyst believed the Oshiros were attempting to challenge old Yakuza control of various Asian ports.

When Chas challenged Favian over why the Oshiros would shoot up Misty Falls if they already had possession of Poppy, he had no answers.

Chas didn't like any of this. They were all missing something big, and that big thing was the main source of danger to Poppy. They might know more about who she was, but they were still missing the key to understanding who was chasing her—and them.

Favian also swabbed the inside of Poppy's cheek and put the sample in a test tube that he sealed up and stuck in his pocket.

Chas liked him. The man wore hopelessly unfashionable corduroy pants, and his shirt looked like it had never seen the hot side of an iron. But his gray eyes were clear and shockingly intelligent.

The hour got late, and Spencer asked Chas, "What kind of sleeping arrangements do we need to make for the baby? I confess to not knowing a thing about little kids."

"She can sleep anywhere. It's containing her when she wakes up that's the problem. If you're not awake before she is, there's no telling what she could get into. She's at that age where she'll open cabinets or drawers, climb all over, and put anything she finds into her mouth."

Spencer eyed her as if she was a bomb about to go off.

"If there's a big-box store open nearby, I can run out and grab a portable playpen," Chas offered. "She could sleep safely in that."

Gunner objected quickly, "I'd rather have you not leave me, Chas. You and I both will be recognized by the hostiles."

"I thought we lost them in Pennsylvania," Chas blurted.

"Gangs will have their own full-time hackers. And where there are security cameras or closed-circuit TVs, there are searchable records of human faces," Drago explained. "Hackers are way ahead of most governments in messing with facial recognition, and we could be spotted walking into a store anywhere in America."

Chas shuddered. "We really don't have privacy anymore, do we?"

The other men shrugged. "Nature of the beast," Gunner murmured.

"I can go buy a playpen," Charles volunteered. "Nobody chasing the child knows about me."

After some discussion, they all agreed that he would be the best choice to go out in public and buy baby gear, though he looked less than excited about the prospect.

It took nearly an hour, and several texted pictures from Favian, to get the right product selected and purchased, but by nine o'clock or so, he'd returned to the farmhouse armed with a playpen and a high chair.

Poppy was in full meltdown by the time he returned, and the big bad commandos wrestled through getting the playpen unpacked and set up while Chas gave her a bath, which she screamed through. Chas laid her down in the playpen, and she crashed immediately. Thank God.

He went downstairs, and Gunner handed him a glass of white wine in silence.

"Ahh, adult time," Chas sighed in relief.

"Quite a set of lungs that kid has on her," Spencer commented wryly.

Chas responded by draining his wine and holding out the glass for a refill. Gunner grinned and obliged.

"Ready to hear the plan we've put together?" Gunner asked him when he'd put a dent in the second glass of wine.

"So the wine wasn't a reward for a good day's parenting but rather a bribe to liquor me up before you tick me off?" he asked.

Gunner shrugged. "I've been taught to use every tool at my disposal to achieve my objectives."

"Then you should have taken me to bed," Chas snapped.

Spencer laughed behind him, and Chas whipped around, his face hot. Their host was kind enough not to tease him about it, however, and merely said mildly to Gunner, "I like this man."

"Glad you approve," Gunner grumbled.

Spencer said, "Dray and I are starting a small security firm and were thinking about hiring a few people we know and trust from our former government careers." He added with a smile, "And once we get on our feet, the pay will be considerably better than Uncle Sam can offer."

Gunner glanced over at Chas thoughtfully before saying, "Tell me more."

Spencer and Gunner took off talking about the types of jobs they could do, and Drago came over to refill Chas's wineglass to the brim.

"Are all of you in on the plot to get me drunk before you spring your plan on me?" Chas asked.

"Oh yeah," Drago replied, grinning. "It's actually part of the plan."

Chas exhaled hard in disgust. "All right. Lay it on me. How dangerous is this plan of yours, and how likely am I to be maimed or killed?"

Chapter Thirteen

GUNNER POINTED the car to the west and accelerated away from the luxurious estate where Poppy was now safely installed. Charles Favian had called a woman he knew—a training officer with the CIA's Special Operations Group—to come act as her temporary nanny and bodyguard. The SOG was generally considered to be among the best of the best in the Special Forces community.

It surprised him when a middle-aged woman had shown up at Spencer and Dray's place and tartly informed Gunner that she had grown children of her own and was plenty old enough to be Poppy's grandmother.

He'd been even more surprised when Spencer and Drago had driven them all out the front gate and directly across the street to another tall iron gate. The estate they'd wound back into had been so elegant, it was frightening.

Drago explained that the neighbors, Jessica and Gershom Brentwood, had hired their fledgling security firm to beef up their estate's security, and that he and Spencer had turned the property into a virtual fortress.

They couldn't think of anywhere safer to put Poppy until the mess surrounding her was sorted out.

Gunner quizzed the security guards closely, and it turned out that Spencer and Drago had been running weekly exercises with them for several months, teaching them all kinds of advanced surveillance and security protocols.

"You're sure Poppy will be safe?" Chas asked.

Gunner snorted. "Are you kidding? She has her own personal sniper for a nanny. Not to mention, the Brentwood home has every security bell and whistle money can buy, and their staff knows how to use it all. Besides, who's gonna look for a missing kid at the estate of a stupidly rich, gray-haired hedge fund manager and his much younger trophy wife?"

"I hope you're right," Chas fretted.

"I'll miss her too," Gunner said quietly.

"Bet you never thought you'd say that in your lifetime."

Gunner glanced over at Chas. "Nope." He added reluctantly, "In the past week, I've been saying and doing a whole lot of shit I never thought I ever would."

"Sheesh. The munchkin is gone for two minutes and you're already back to swearing like a sailor."

"In case you forgot, I am, in fact, a sailor."

Chas rolled his eyes and laughed. "Did you like being in the Navy?"

"The general Navy is okay. Being a SEAL is nothing like that."

"What's it like being a SEAL?"

Gunner frowned, searching for words. It wasn't something he'd ever talked about. He just did it, and everyone he worked with just did it too. "It's… hard. Every day is hard. New challenges, new things to learn, new problems to solve. It's a constant fight to be stronger, faster, better, stay healthy, ignore pain."

"It sounds miserable."

Gunner shrugged. "I guess it would be for most people."

"What does that say about you, then? Do you have a mile-wide masochistic streak I don't know about?"

"No. Although I admit, I wondered about that during BUD/S."

"What does that stand for? 'Beating up dumbsquats'?"

Gunner grinned. "Basic Underwater Demolition/ SEAL. It's the initial training course to become a SEAL. It was… not fun."

"Then why put yourself through all of that? Were you punishing yourself or something?"

The notion startled him. "Not that I'm aware of. It was a challenge. A personal mountain to climb. And it looked like interesting work. The kind of job that would be all-consuming."

"So much that you would never have time to stop and admit to yourself that you were gay?"

"Damn, Chas. Do you have to dissect me like some dead animal?"

Chas sat back, looking smug.

"Fuck off," Gunner mumbled with no heat.

"Right back atchya, big guy."

"So why are you a kindergarten teacher? On the list of most masochistic professions, that has to rank high."

"Why do you say that?" Chas asked, sounding surprised.

"Screaming kids running all over the place. You're basically babysitting twenty heathens all day long." He shuddered just thinking of it.

"Aww, they're not that bad. You do have to establish authority with them right away, of course, and it takes a world of patience. But they're fun. They're still innocent at that age. The world is still a good place for most of them. I enjoy their optimism and enthusiasm. Five-year-olds aren't self-conscious yet. If you ask them who can sing or dance, they all raise their hands. I love nurturing that. And they're endlessly curious—" He broke off. "Sorry. Little kids get a bad rap. It's a pet peeve of mine."

"You sound pretty passionate about your work."

"I am. It's exhausting, but I love it."

Gunner nodded. "I would say the same about my job."

"How homophobic are the SEALs these days?"

"That's a hard question to answer."

"Try."

"Most guys don't give a damn who anyone else sleeps with. But SEALs do live in extremely close quarters with each other. We eat, sleep, bathe, and shit—sorry—literally shoulder to shoulder with each another sometimes. If a guy is the least bit hinky about being around a gay man, living in such close quarters could be a personal nightmare. And the guys in a platoon have to depend so completely on one another—our lives depend upon our brothers—that any disruption to that total trust is a huge problem."

"So it's not that the homophobia is bad or even prevalent. It's just that even the smallest hint of it could cause a problem," Chas said.

"Exactly."

"How are the guys in your... platoon, is it?"

"They're fine. Not that they knew I might swing the other way. But they wouldn't care—make that wouldn't have cared. Past tense."

"You're done being a SEAL? As in done, done?"

"Yup. Paperwork's already signed," he answered hoarsely.

"I'm sorry," Chas said quietly.

"What are you sorry for?" Gunner exclaimed.

"I didn't realize it was a fait accompli. That sucks."

He'd avoided thinking about it for most of the past week. Poppy and Chas had provided plenty of distraction, not to mention the carload of assholes trying to chase them down and kill them. But now, on the road, with days of travel ahead of them and nothing to do but think, he couldn't avoid the stark truth any longer. He was done as a SEAL.

"If the senior leadership had given me a chance to recuperate from my injuries, I might've been able to stay. But without that support, I couldn't have fought the doctors on my own."

"You mean SEALs don't know when to quit and have to be forcibly retired by medical experts? Color me shocked," Chas commented.

Gunner rolled his eyes.

"Are you gonna take the job Spencer's offering you?" Chas asked.

"I'm thinking about it."

"Will it be dangerous work?"

"Sometimes."

"More or less dangerous than being a SEAL?"

"Some of each. Most security jobs are less dangerous. But if they go bad, we would have less backup than a SEAL team would have."

Chas fell silent at that. Silent enough that Gunner glanced over at him and asked, "What's on your mind? You went quiet on me, and you're the most talkative person I know."

Chas made a face that made Gunner grin.

"I believe the phrase you're looking for is 'fuck off.'"

Chas smiled. "Fuck off, G."

Gunner was aware that Chas hadn't answered his question. The guy was definitely fretting about something, but he didn't want to talk about it. On the teams, they didn't usually sit around airing out their feelings. And if a guy didn't want to talk, nobody forced him to, as long as he was able to do his job effectively.

They drove for nearly an hour in silence before Chas asked, "How long until the bad guys pick up our trail and we're bait on a hook?"

"We figure they'll show up not long after we use your credit card. We've got maybe a day of relative quiet."

"Do we *have* to confront these guys?"

"We need to find out who they are and what they want with Poppy. If she's ever going to be safe, we have to at least know who hired them."

Chas sighed. "I'm secure enough in my manhood to admit that I'm a little scared."

"Being scared is rational. I'd be worried if you weren't scared. The trick is not to let fear get the best of you. Let it make you sharp. A little edgy. But don't let it overwhelm you."

"Easier said than done," he admitted.

"Spencer and Drago are an hour behind us. They'll set up surveillance on our hotel and never take their eyes off us. They're two of the best operators in the business. You're in good hands."

"I still don't like being using as bait."

Gunner snorted. "I don't like it either. Actually, I hate the idea of putting you in any danger whatsoever. The only reason I went along with this plan was because I knew you'd do pretty much anything to keep Poppy safe."

Chas reached across the center console and laid a hand on his thigh.

Gunner reached down and squeezed his hand. "I won't let anything happen to you, Chas."

But when they checked into a motel in western Kentucky, his gut was uncharacteristically tight. Usually he went into ops as cool as a cucumber. He trusted his training and preparation implicitly. But Chas was a wild card.

He'd never run an op with a civilian in the middle of it before. Not to mention a civilian he did not want to see any harm come to. His SEAL teammates knew the risks anytime they went out in the field, as did he. But Chas—he hadn't asked for any of this. He'd just been a Good Samaritan who picked up a baby and tried to keep her safe.

Gunner specifically asked for the room on the end of the old-fashioned strip motel whose rooms opened straight onto the parking lot. He backed the car into its space for a quick exit and scoped out the area behind the motel—a steep hill covered in thick brush, discarded trash, and plenty of tree cover—before entering the room. He removed the screen from the bathroom window and moved a nightstand into the bathroom for easy access to the high window. Only then did he relax a little.

"Okay. Why do we need a table next to the toilet?" Chas asked.

"To climb on so you can get out the window if we need an emergency exit."

Chas swore under his breath. "And to think, I thought we got to relax tonight."

"Ounce of prevention, remember? I just got a text that Spencer and Drago are pulling into town and will set up shop."

"How close will they be to us?"

Gunner thought about the terrain outside. "Something like a hundred yards down the road. One of them may set up on the hill above the motel with a sniper rig."

"Sniper? I thought the idea was to catch these guys alive."

"We only need one of them alive to talk," Gunner replied grimly.

Chas's eyes widened. "You plan to *kill* them?"

"We plan to neutralize them. The hostiles themselves will determine whether that means they surrender or we take them out."

Chas grimaced. "I hate violence. All violence."

Gunner shrugged. "I see it as a necessary evil, to be avoided if possible and executed with maximum efficiency if not."

"I never pictured you as a trained killer when we were growing up," Chas commented.

Gunner dropped to the floor to do some push-ups and burpees. He badly needed to work out the kinks from sitting in a car all day. His back was achy tonight, and more of those ominous pinches of pain were starting to creep through. As he pumped out reps, he asked, "What did you picture me doing with my life?"

"When I was eight, I thought you'd make a good cowboy."

"I hate riding horses. You have to have the right muscles for it; otherwise you get sore as hell and chafe in places you don't want to think about."

Chas laughed. "When we got a little older, I thought you'd be a good sports coach. You're a natural leader."

"Nah. I have no patience with people who don't put out 100 percent effort. I would've been too tough a coach to be successful."

Chas sat cross-legged on the bed and watched him work out. "What would you have done if you hadn't become a SEAL?"

"I would've tried for the submarine corps."

"I mean if you hadn't joined the military at all?"

"Oh." He rolled onto his back. "Sit on my feet while I do a few sit-ups, will you?"

Chas slid off the bed and knelt on both of his feet while grabbing Gunner's ankles. Gunner commenced doing sit-ups. "I'd have gone to college if there was money for it."

"What would you have studied?"

"History, maybe."

"And done what with a history degree?"

"Teach college. Get people to think about links between the past and present. Challenge students to learn the lessons of our forbearers."

Chas laughed. "I have trouble imagining you sitting in some book-filled office, wearing a cardigan sweater, with a pair of reading glasses perched on the end of your nose. I can see myself as that professor someday, but not you."

Gunner grinned up at him without stopping.

"How many sit-ups are your planning to do?" Chas finally asked.

"As many as it takes to tire me out."

"I can think of better ways to tire yourself out."

Gunner stopped at the top of a sit-up to stare at Chas. "Oh yeah? Like what?"

"You'll have to take a shower before I show you."

He jumped up, dumping Chas unceremoniously on his side. "Done. I'll be out of the shower in five minutes."

SPENCER LISTENED impatiently as the international call took its sweet time clicking through the satellite to Japan. The woman who answered his call in Japanese switched seamlessly into English as soon as he asked in English to speak with Mr. Tanaka.

"Mr. Tanaka is a very busy man, sir. I can connect you to one of his personal assistants who may be able to help you."

"Fine. Transfer me to the one who's handling the kidnapping of his daughter."

"Are you a journalist, sir?" the woman demanded coldly.

"No. I'm an American security contractor, and I have some information about his daughter that he'll want to hear. My name is Spencer Newman."

"One moment, sir."

No surprise, he heard the clicks of recording devices and additional listeners coming onto the line. Were they Japanese government types, or was Tanaka relying on his own private security team? Spencer would bet Tanaka had gone private. Men like him tended to want total control of what happened around them. Now to earn the guy's trust.

"Mr. Newman, you said your name was?" a man said at the other end of the line.

"Yes. Spencer Newman. You'll know you have the right person in your frantic internet search when you don't find squat about me. I'm a retired US Navy SEAL and maintain an extremely low profile."

"Uhh, thank you, Mr. Newman." The guy sounded surprised.

"I have an associate who has recently come into possession of a young child. My partner and I were taken from Langley to the Japanese Embassy yesterday and informed there that the child might be the missing Tanaka baby. Rather than continue to deal with middlemen and government flunkies, I thought it would be faster to speak directly with Mr. Tanaka."

"One moment, please."

Hah. He was right. Tanaka himself hadn't been put on the line immediately. One moment turned into more like three minutes, and Spencer could readily envision the frantic briefing Tanaka's security men were giving him about how to handle this phone call.

A British-accented voice that spoke fluent English came on the line. "Hello, Mr. Newman. This is Kenji Tanaka."

"Thank you for taking my call. I'm hoping to cut through all the layers of bureaucracy and move along this process as quickly as possible for the sake of the child involved."

"Continue," Tanaka said cautiously.

Spencer sighed. "Let's cut the crap, shall we? I'm not one of the kidnappers and I don't want a ransom. I'll give your guys my social security number if they want to run a full background check on me, and I'm only concerned about getting a little girl back safely to her family. Assuming you are her family, of course."

That caused a long silence, and undoubtedly another frantic conference.

"Who are you?" Tanaka finally demanded.

"As I told your previous guy, I'm a retired US Navy SEAL. I'm in the process of starting up a private security firm, and an associate of mine has come into possession of a little girl about eighteen months old and of Asian heritage under rather violent circumstances."

"Is she all right? Is she hurt?" Tanaka blurted.

For the first time, Spencer relaxed. There was the frantic father he'd been waiting to catch a glimpse of.

"She's fine. I'm hoping you can send me certain information that will help me verify her identity. Because of the circumstances in which my associate came into possession of her, I have reason to be cautious before I hand her over to anyone. It's nothing personal. I'm merely committed to the child's safety first and foremost."

"Fair enough," Tanaka said. "Kamiko's safety is my first priority as well."

"Ahh. Is that her name? We've been calling her Poppy."

"What information do you need from me?" Tanaka asked.

"Photographs. And please forgive me for asking delicate questions, but is she biologically your child?"

"Yes. She is. Are you thinking of asking me for a DNA sample, perchance?" Tanaka responded.

"That would be positive proof and satisfy me."

"How would you like to collect this sample so you know it's from me?"

Drago waved, and Spencer muted his phone. Drago murmured, "I know a guy at the Tokyo CIA station. I'll have him run over to Tanaka's office and swab his cheek. He can courier the sample back to the US so there's a positive chain of custody."

Spencer unmuted his phone. "We can arrange for an associate of ours to come swab your cheek. Will you be at your office through the day today?" It was morning in Tokyo now.

"I will."

"He will use my name and that of my partner, Drago Thorpe, to identify himself. And he's likely to be fairly disgusted at being sent on such an errand."

Tanaka made a brief sound of humor. "I'll make myself available to him when he arrives."

"Thank you for your cooperation, Mr. Tanaka."

"Is there anything else I can do to help you, Mr. Newman?"

Since it sounded like a fragile trust might have been established, Spencer risked asking, "Do you have any idea who kidnapped her and what they want from you?"

"Initially, we believed a local rival of my father's might have taken her. Her nanny and bodyguard were assaulted and knocked unconscious, and when they woke up, Kamiko had been taken from her stroller. But then I received a ransom demand several days ago that originated in the New York City area."

"Do you know if your family has any dealings with a group known as the Oshiro gang?" Spencer asked boldly.

Drago lurched beside him, looking startled that Spencer had shown that particular card.

"I have nothing to do with my father's... business dealings. I'm merely an architect."

"Indeed? Is it possible that a rival of your father's... in business... might target your daughter as a way of getting at your father?"

Tanaka answered soberly, "It is."

Spencer heard voices speaking in rapid Japanese behind Tanaka—no doubt his security team telling him to shut the hell up. "Did the person or persons demanding the ransom provide any proof of life and proof of custody?"

"They sent pictures of Kamiko sitting beside an American newspaper dated five days ago."

"How much did they ask for?"

"Fifty million dollars US. I told them it would take me a week or more to get that much of my assets moved into liquid cash. I expect to hear from them the day after tomorrow."

"It goes without saying, don't hand over the money until we know if the child in my associate's custody is Kamiko. If you need to stall them, demand fresh proof of possession and of the child's health first."

Tanaka made a noncommittal noise. Spencer got it. If his kid were being held hostage, he might go ahead and hand over the cash just in case the bad guys had her.

Spencer said gently, "You've been extremely helpful, sir. And thank you for trusting me. I sincerely hope Poppy turns out to be your daughter and that we can return her safely to you very soon. I do have to warn you, however, that there are people attempting to take her away from my associate. Since you trusted me, I will tell you that we do not know if the Oshiro gang or someone else is pursuing her. We hope to learn that shortly. We've set a trap to capture one of them and question him or her."

"But you will keep Kamiko safe at all costs, yes?" Tanaka blurted. "I'll pay—"

Spencer cut him off. "I don't want your money, Mr. Tanaka. And I assure you, she's not anywhere near the trap. She's absolutely safe, I promise."

"Thank you, Mr. Newman. I will be happy to fly over as many of my father's men as you might need to deal... discreetly... with these criminals."

"That's a very generous offer, Mr. Tanaka. For the moment, I can probably operate best on my own turf, using my own people. But if we should need assistance, I will definitely call you."

"Would you be willing to give me your personal cell phone number, Mr. Newman?"

"Of course."

They traded cell phone numbers, and Tanaka ended with, "Please call me, day or night, if I can be of any assistance."

"Same, Mr. Tanaka. Call me any time. And before you ask, yes, I will keep you informed of any new developments."

"You had better be who you say you are, Mr. Newman. If you are playing me, I promise you will regret it for the rest of your extremely short life."

Spencer laughed. "Never fear. I'm the real deal."

AFTER HE went through the motions of dressing the doll that Charles Favian had brought them and tucking her into the playpen, Chas hustled around the motel room, checking that the doors were locked and the blinds were closed, turning down the bed, and turning off all the lights. He turned on the TV low enough not to be distracting but loud enough to provide a little background noise. Motels like this notoriously had paper-thin walls, and he planned on Gunner making some noise in the near future.

He stripped out of his clothes and crawled into bed just before Gunner emerged from the bathroom, damp, flushed, and wearing nothing but a towel slung low on his hips. His abs rippled with muscle that terminated in a sharply defined *V* pointing down toward his groin. The man was a little intimidating to contemplate having sex with. He looked like the kind of guy who could split him open if he wanted to.

Except this was Gunner. His best friend. The boy he'd grown up with, that he'd fallen in love with, that he'd loved pretty much his entire life. He'd seen Gunner gently rescue kittens out of a rain catch basin, seen him chase off bullies when they'd picked on him. And more recently, he'd seen Gunner fall asleep with Poppy on his chest, his arms cradled protectively around her.

Gunner moved over to the bulky duffel bag he'd carried inside and pulled a large handgun from it. Chas recoiled, alarmed.

Gunner laid it on the one remaining nightstand, murmuring, "It's a precaution. Nothing more."

"You got any condoms in there?" he replied. "If we're going to be having sex regularly, we should probably invest in some."

"Yeah, actually. They're a standard part of a go-bag for SEALs."

"Of course they are," he responded dryly.

Gunner grinned. "We put them over the ends of our rifle barrels to keep sand out."

"Riiiiight. That's how they all get used."

Gunner shrugged, grinning. "It's how I used most of mine. I only had sex with a woman once when I got hassled by the guys so much I couldn't avoid it any longer."

"Did you like it?" Chas asked curiously.

"You want the truth?" Gunner murmured.

"Yes. I do."

"I closed my eyes and pretended it was you."

Chas's jaw dropped. Gunner had been fantasizing about him for all these years? Warmth started in his gut and spread outward to fill his entire body. "Well, you're in luck. The real thing is right here in the flesh. And I would purely love it if you fucked me all night long."

"Such language, Mr. Reed," Gunner tsked.

Chas held up the covers, and Gunner slipped into bed. Chas wrapped his arms around that muscular neck and pressed his body against all those acres of rock-hard muscle, and he felt as if he were exploding into a molten lava pool of desire.

"I want you, Gunner. I want to feel you inside me, filling me up until I can't take any more. Stretching me and pounding into me until I come all over myself."

"Mmm. I think that can be arranged." Gunner rolled half on top of him and stared down at him in the flickering light of the television. "Why in the hell did we wait so long to do this?"

"Somebody had to run away and join the Navy and spend ten years pretending to be straight. I never went anywhere."

"God, I'm an idiot."

Chas smiled gently up at Gunner. "Yeah. But you're my idiot." He plunged his hands into Gunner's damp, wavy hair and tugged his face down for a long, deep kiss. He felt Gunner's penis stirring against his thigh, thickening and filling. Excitement vibrated through him.

"Tonight, will you flip me over and take me from behind?"

"If you want."

"Oh, I want."

Gunner smiled tentatively, which amused him to no end. The man had no idea what he was in for.

"But first, I'd like to show you a few things," Chas murmured.

"Oh yeah? Like what?"

"Roll over on your stomach. It would help if you put some pillows under your hips."

Caution and possibly even alarm flashed in Gunner's eyes.

"Trust me, Gunner. I won't do anything you don't like. You say so and I'll stop immediately."

"Stop what?"

"Well, I'm going to start by giving you a back rub. You did a lot of sitting today, and for a guy with a back injury, that can't be comfortable. I'll bet that means you've got a few kinks to work out."

"I'm beginning to think you're the one with the kink," Gunner mumbled, his face buried in his arms.

"And you're complaining about that?" Chas demanded.

"I retract the statement."

"Better." He opened the bottle of baby oil he'd swiped out of Poppy's bag this morning and poured some into his hands. Then he smoothed his palms across Gunner's back and reveled in the groan of pleasure it elicited.

"Just relax and let me do the work," Chas murmured. He took his time, avoiding Gunner's spine, kneading out every knot he found, working his way from top to bottom and side to side until Gunner completely relaxed under his hands. Gently, he pushed Gunner's thighs apart and worked his way down both legs to Gunner's feet.

He worked his way back up to Gunner's ass and kneaded the heavy glute muscles until they, too, were completely flexible beneath his hands. He picked up the baby oil bottle and dribbled a stream into Gunner's crack and used his fingers to massage it in.

Gunner tightened up, but Chas murmured encouragement to relax him as he rubbed the oil all around Gunner's anus. Gently, he slipped the tip of a finger inside the tight ring of muscle.

"Easy, babe. I'm not going to fuck you, but I am going to show you where your prostate is and some things that will feel good to do with it."

He reached down with his left hand to clasp Gunner's hard, heavy cock from behind and stroke his oiled fist down its length as he slipped the index finger of his right hand a little deeper into Gunner's ass. In and out with his finger, up and down with his fist. He stroked Gunner's body until the man vibrated with pleasure beneath him.

He shifted his fist to Gunner's scrotum, rubbing oil into it as he probed more deeply with his finger, hooking it forward to stroke Gunner's prostate from the inside.

"Holy shit," Gunner panted.

"Like that?"

"Uhh… huh," he managed to say.

Cognizant that the man had no experience at all with this stuff, Chas was gentle in slipping a second finger into Gunner's ass. The invaded muscles clenched hard around his fingers at first, but he went back to stroking Gunner's cock until the muscles relaxed. Twisting his fingers around inside Gunner's body, he continued to stroke Gunner from the inside in time with his pumping fist on the outside.

Gunner grabbed a pillow and buried his face in it, groaning and swearing in a steady stream now. Triumph surged through Chas. He loved giving Gunner so much pleasure, loved seeing Gunner share his body with him like this, loved the trust Gunner gave him. When the man seemed coiled on the verge of an epic orgasm, Chas leaned over him and murmured in his ear, "What do you want, Gunner? Do you have a fantasy you'd like to make come true?"

"Sometimes—" Gunner's voice hitched, and he continued, "Sometimes I dream about you naked. Begging me to fuck you. And I, umm—" Another sharp inhalation of breath. "—I, umm, bend you over. Press your face into the mattress and, umm, take you."

"Ahh, sweet Gunner. Why didn't you tell me ages ago?"

Chas rolled off Gunner and stood up beside the bed. Gunner rolled onto his back, and his erection stood straight up, throbbing eagerly. In one fast, aggressive move, Gunner came to his feet beside him. Chas held out the bottle of baby oil, and Gunner took it.

"Bend over," Gunner told him a little hesitantly.

Smiling, Chas bent over and placed his elbows on the mattress. Gunner stepped back and stared at him for a long time. Frankly, it was a turn-on to be on display like this for his lover. He knew Gunner was devouring the sight of his lean, fit body and his ass sticking up in the air, begging to be fucked.

"Spread your legs," Gunner ordered a little more confidently.

He complied.

"Umm." Gunner hesitated, and Chas waited out what he wanted next. "Spread your cheeks for me."

Smiling, Chas rested his forehead on the mattress and reached back to spread his asscheeks. His entire body quivered with excitement at being this open and vulnerable to Gunner.

He never heard Gunner step close to him, and he jumped as a trickle of baby oil splashed on his asshole. Then big, blunt fingers rubbed it around, dipping down lower to oil his taint and rub around his testicles. His own erection jumped hungrily, banging against the edge of the mattress.

"Turned on, are you?" Gunner murmured, gripping Chas's dick and treating it to a lovely layer of oil too. He had to give Gunner credit. The man was a fast learner and had paid close attention to Chas's earlier lesson. But then, so had he. He propped himself on his elbows once more and looked over his shoulder at the magnificent man standing naked and aroused behind him.

"Fuck me, Gunner. Please. Bend me over and split me wide open. Fuck me until I can't stand."

Gunner groaned under his breath.

A large hand grasped the back of Chas's neck and pushed his face down to the mattress strongly enough that he couldn't have fought back if he'd wanted to, but gently enough not to hurt him in the least.

He heard the rip of a condom packet, and then another stream of oil hit his ass. "Are you ready for this?" Gunner ground out. The guy was obviously fighting for self-control, which made Chas's dick jump with anticipation. He was *so* getting fucked.

"I'm all yours," he panted.

Gunner's cock touched his asshole. It was big and blunt and hard as steel. It pushed against his entrance, and he took a deep breath while telling his body to relax. Be open. Accept the invasion. It was right on the verge of painful, but the plentiful lubrication did its job. The tip of Gunner's cock lodged inside the sphincter of his ass.

"You okay?" Gunner grunted.

"Yeah. Great," he panted.

Gunner pushed in a little farther. "You good?"

"Hell yeah," he groaned.

Gunner gripped his hips in both hands and pulled back as his cock pushed steadily forward. In one smooth, incredible stroke, Gunner seated himself balls-deep in Chas's ass. And it was so fantastic, Chas wanted to weep for joy.

His muscles accommodated the invasion quickly, adjusting to Gunner's size and heft, clenching and unclenching around the very large cock now firmly lodged in his body.

Gunner withdrew partway and sheathed himself to the hilt again, a little more firmly this time.

"Yes. Yes," he chanted.

Gunner retreated and filled him again. With each stroke, Chas's entire body quivered a little more, his own erection filled a little tighter, and delirium took over a little more of his mind.

"Fuck me, Gunner. For the love of God, fuck me."

Gunner slammed home hard, and Chas groaned aloud. Gunner's hands tightened on his hips, pulling rhythmically as he rammed into Chas's body over and over. Chas hadn't fully appreciated just how strong Gunner was until all that strength was unleashed on him in the most delicious way. He felt completely safe in Gunner's hands, but he also had never been fucked with this strength and stamina before. Thank God he stayed fit and strong himself.

On and on it went. He had a massive orgasm somewhere in the middle of it, and his body recovered and his dick filled and hardened a second time, so sensitized by the first orgasm he literally shouted with pleasure as Gunner slammed into him with abandon.

At some point he realized his legs had collapsed and that Gunner was pressing him down into the mattress, using him and taking him so completely that he lost the ability to form words. Pleasure tore through him so violently that he wasn't sure where his body ended and Gunner's began. He knew only that their joining was so ecstatically incredible, he couldn't feel anything else. Just that iron cock claiming his body and taking it with such authority, with such possessive ownership, that he was sure he would never be the same again. Gunner owned his body now and forever, and no one else would ever claim it, claim him, like this again.

An eternity later, when he was so overtaken with pleasure that he couldn't stand one more iota of it, Gunner stiffened behind him. His whole body arched into Chas's, and Chas felt the hot gush of Gunner coming deep, deep inside him. With a shout of his own, he came a second time, a hot spurt of pleasure that was more than his overwrought nerves could register. He passed out momentarily, pleasured into a little death unlike anything he'd ever experienced.

He came back to his body, realizing he was mashed flat on the mattress with Gunner lying on top of him. Never in his entire life had he felt this loved, this protected, this cared for. It was, in a word, perfect.

Eventually Gunner rolled to one side, keeping a protective, possessive arm and leg thrown over Chas's body.

As for Chas, he couldn't have moved if his life depended on it. He'd asked to be fucked until he couldn't stand, and oh baby, had Gunner delivered.

It took a long time for Chas's breathing to return to normal. He felt wrung out to the depths of his being, and a stillness he'd never experienced before came over him. Huh. So this was peace. He'd found the one place in the world he wanted to live until the end of his days. It was right here, in Gunner's arms, completely, irrevocably possessed by Gunner Vance, body, heart, mind, and soul.

GUNNER LAY beside Chas, listening to his lover's breath settle into the light, even rhythm of sleep. He reached out and fumbled on the nightstand until he found the remote and turned off the TV. He sincerely hoped there was no one in the room next door, or they'd been treated to a rather noisy porn audio track. Neither he nor Chas had been able to stop themselves from shouting in pleasure. A lot.

The silence and darkness settled gently around him like the warmth of Chas's body against his side.

His mind drifted, caught somewhere between sleep and waking, and it dawned on him that he was happy.

It wasn't a state of being he could remember experiencing too many times in his life. It was nice. More than nice. It was… addictive. He could get used to this.

Going to work at a day job—minor security work for Spencer and Drago. Coming home at the end of the day to Chas. Taking him to bed, living out more of his fantasies, falling asleep with Chas in his arms….

Yeah, he could definitely get used to this.

His mind wandered more, and he pictured a neat little house. Nothing fancy. Poppy playing in the backyard. Maybe he would build her a swing. Or a jungle gym to climb on—

The image startled him to a more conscious state. He could actually see himself raising a family with Chas. Whoa. That was a hard left turn from where he'd ever thought of his life going before.

Small problem: he had no earthly idea how to get to that life.

Chapter Fourteen

CHAS WOKE up slowly, groggy, his eyelids refusing to open all the way. His limbs were heavy, his body half-paralyzed from how deeply asleep he'd been. Where was he, anyway? Motel room. Dark. A large shadow moved across the room, and he jolted fully awake, adrenaline screaming through his limbs.

He froze, staring, and the shadow turned and spoke. "Sorry. Didn't mean to wake you."

"G., what are you doing awake? It's the middle of the freaking night."

"Gearing up."

"Why?"

"Ounce of precaution, man."

"Are you planning to sleep in all that stuff?" As his eyes adjusted to the dark, he saw that Gunner was wearing a bulky vest, a utility belt, camo pants with pockets full of stuff, and combat boots, and was holding a helmet with elaborate electronic gear mounted to the top.

Gunner's smile flashed white in the dark. "I have slept in my tactical gear before. A lot. I was planning to get comfortable in the chair and snooze there so I wouldn't wake you up."

"You can come back to bed if you want."

Gunner snorted. "So you like the idea of cuddling with steel porcupines?"

"Not particularly. But I like snuggling with you."

Gunner's smile was more reluctant this time. "I like snuggling with you too. But duty calls."

"I thought you weren't expecting trouble tonight."

"I'm not."

"Let me guess. You're patrolling and standing guard anyway?" Chas murmured.

"Bingo."

"Should I be fully dressed and have my shoes ready to go too?"

"Wouldn't hurt."

Chas groaned and rolled out of bed. Sex with Gunner was rather more athletic than he was accustomed to, and he was a little creaky as he dressed. Gunner moved over to stand behind him as he put his shoes on the floor. Big, powerful hands kneaded his shoulder muscles with just enough force to make him groan with pleasure.

"I'll give you a full back rub tomorrow," Gunner murmured.

"You know how?"

"Standard SEAL training. We have to keep one another fully operational in the field."

"Ooh. SEALs giving each other full-body massages. Kinky," Chas mumbled.

Gunner made a sound of disgust that spun Chas around to face him.

"What?" Chas asked, startled.

"It's one of the many reasons I couldn't come out as gay. We did give each other rubdowns, in addition to sleeping, eating, and bathing together. Some of the guys would have been afraid that I might be attracted to them and that such contact would get sexual."

"But if it was your job and they were just your coworkers…." Chas frowned. "It's not as if being gay would make you attracted to every single male you worked with."

Gunner rolled his eyes. "I wasn't attracted to any of them. They're hairy, obnoxious macho jerks like me. No, thank you. Honestly, I have no idea what you see in me."

Chas laid his palms on Gunner's stubbled cheeks. "You and me, we have a very long history together. We've been friends, confidants, brothers, heck, even enemies. I can't imagine my life without you in it."

"You spent the past ten years without me in your life," Gunner muttered.

"And it sucked. No, thank you," he echoed.

Gunner swept him up against all that tactical gear and the hard, powerful man beneath, and it was almost too sexy to stand. Then Gunner leaned down, kissing him hard at first and then gentling the kiss to a long, deep, intimate thing that communicated how much Gunner cared for him.

"Not to be cliché," he murmured against Gunner's warm, resilient lips, "but is that your pistol poking me in the belly?"

Gunner let out a silent gust of laughter against Chas's mouth. "That's a breaching tool. I'll show you how it works sometime. My pistol's around the side of my hip a little bit more."

Chas stepped back, and in the faint glow from a streetlight outside, Gunner gave him a guided tour of a SEAL's operational gear. It was impressive how much crap Gunner carried around with him. Chas commented, "You're like a walking Boy Scout manual. You've got every eventuality covered."

"If only. No matter how prepared we are, we can always count on the bad guys to come up with something that we haven't anticipated. The name of the game in the field is being willing and able to improvise."

"That's why you'll be a good lover. We just need to tap into your natural ability to freestyle."

"If you say so," Gunner muttered, sounding a little shy.

Chas chucked him under the chin. "Never fear. I'm creative. Our sex life will never be dull."

"Can't say as I was actually worried about that."

Chas stared up at Gunner in the shadows, trying to make out the expression in his eyes. "Meaning you don't plan to have a lengthy love life with me, or that you believe we'll keep it fresh and hot for a long time?"

"The latter—" Gunner broke off, reaching for his ear with his right hand.

"What?"

"Hush."

Chas fell silent and heard the faintest of sound coming from Gunner's earpiece. Someone was speaking on the radio frequency Gunner was monitoring.

"Gotta go," Gunner bit out.

"What's happening?"

"Spence and Dray have company. They need me to help out."

"Where are they?"

"In the woods above the motel. They've got five tangoes moving around behind the building, and there are only two of them. Spence and Dray can't keep track of all of them alone."

"The bad guys are already here?" Chas asked in dismay. Without having to be told, he stomped into his running shoes and quickly laced them up.

"You can stay here. The tangoes appear to be running reconnaissance right now."

Chas squawked, "You want me to stay here by myself with bad guys closing in on me?"

"On you and Poppy," Gunner said dryly.

"It's a *doll*. I'll be all alone. I waited for you under that desk for two hours that first night in Misty Falls, and it was a goddamned nightmare. I can't do that again."

"The only other option is to come out in the woods with me, and you don't know anything about operating in stealth and darkness. I don't even have a pair of NODs for you. You'd be blind out there."

"I can hang on to your belt," he said desperately. "Please don't leave me in here. I'm a sitting duck."

Gunner huffed. "I can take you out into the woods and find you a hidey-hole. You'd have to hunker down there and would still have to sit and wait it out. But you wouldn't be in here."

"I'll take it," Chas declared.

Gunner rummaged in one of his two big duffel bags. "Put this on." He held out a black floppy hat with a wavy brim.

Chas jammed it on his head and then stood still while Gunner striped his face with a stick of camo grease that looked like a black version of children's glue sticks.

"Put on a coat. You'll get cold sitting still at night," Gunner ordered.

Chas shrugged into a thick zip-up hoodie and threw his jacket over it as Gunner pulled down a microphone boom in front of his mouth and murmured into it.

"Okay. Spencer and Drago know the plan. They advise that we should go out the back way."

"The back way?"

"The window. And bring the doll."

Right. They had to pretend they had Poppy with them if this ruse was going to work. Chas tucked Poppy 2.0 into his coat and nodded gamely at Gunner that he was ready to roll.

It was exciting to be included in a SEAL operation, but it was also scary as hell. Breathing too fast, he followed Gunner into the bathroom and waited for him to climb out the window. Honestly, Chas was impressed at how easily Gunner maneuvered his big body and all his gear out that narrow opening. It was almost as if he'd practiced doing that a time or ten.

Gunner's gloved hand came into view and waved for him to come out.

Chas climbed onto the toilet seat and then onto the nightstand. While he was pondering head first or feet first, Gunner whispered, "Head first. I'll catch you."

That solved that. Chas grabbed the edge of the windowsill and pushed his torso through the opening. Big, familiar hands grasped his shoulders from below, and Gunner whispered, "Kick your feet over your head. You'll do a flip and land on your feet facing outward."

Trusting Gunner to keep him from killing himself in the move, Chas threw his feet over his head. He landed in a crouch, startled at how easy it had been. The big shadow that was Gunner moved around in front of him and breathed into his ear on the way past, "Grab my belt. I'll go slow. Try not to make much noise."

They moved off into the bushes and brambles. How Gunner found his way through them, Chas had no idea. But for the most part, they moved unimpeded into the woods, always going steadily uphill. Gunner led them at an angle more fully behind the main structure of the motel. As Chas's eyes adjusted to the dark, he saw that the undergrowth thinned out as they moved higher up the slope. Gunner was absolutely silent. Chas never heard him take a step, never even heard him breathing.

As for himself, Chas winced every time he shuffled through a patch of dry leaves or exhaled hard. The noises sounded twice as loud as normal in the utter silence. And to think, at least seven other men were creeping around out here too. And some of them meant to kill him.

The more he thought about it, the scarier it got. The sense of this being a giant game wore off and the cold, hard danger of being hunted like prey settled in his gut like a lump of lead. He hated violence in all forms. He'd spent too much of his life being a target of it and watching people he cared about be affected by it.

He hated that Gunner was out here at risk, and he hated that Gunner had to be prepared to do violence to protect him and Poppy.

Eventually, Gunner stopped beside a big, jagged boulder. He pointed to Chas and then to the indentation at the base of the massive rock. That space didn't look very big, and the boulder looked in danger of tumbling forward and crushing anyone beneath it. Frowning, Chas crouched and crawled under the overhang.

"Get comfortable," Gunner breathed as he spread some sort of cloth over him. "You'll be here a while."

Chas reached up to drag the edge of the cloth aside, leaving him a slit to peer through. Otherwise he would get claustrophobic for sure. Gunner scooped up handfuls of twigs and leaves that he sprinkled over the cloth. He stood back, made a few adjustments, and flashed Chas a quick thumbs-up.

And then he was gone, as silent as the night that settled around Chas.

GUNNER HATED leaving Chas, but he had no choice. His teammates needed him. Apparently Spencer and Drago had spotted five tangoes but thought there might be a sixth one out here somewhere.

The hostiles had parked down the road a couple hundred yards in two SUVs and had fanned out from there. Drago had visual on two guys sitting across the road from the motel, one using some sort of sniper rig. Two more had circled around behind the motel and were more or less together. Spencer was tracking them. The fifth one had headed for the top of the ridge Gunner was currently about two-thirds of the way up. His job was to get eyes on number five and check out a possible sixth tango. Easy peasy.

Except the hillside in this area ended with a nearly vertical stone face about twenty feet tall, with the top of the ridgeline above that. He had to make a dicey free climb on loose, unstable rock without making any noise. He stowed his short-barreled urban assault weapon across his back and commenced the climb.

He was perhaps four feet from the flat summit when he heard movement above his head. He froze, clinging precariously to the cliff face by his fingertips and his left foot. His right knee was bent by his hip as he froze in the middle of reaching for another foothold.

Whoever was creeping around above him was doing so stealthily, moving with exaggerated care. But the guy wasn't rolling from heel to toe, which was resulting in leaves crunching and the occasional scuffing noise. Not Special Forces trained, then.

Gunner's left leg was trembling with fatigue before he felt safe enough to pull himself up the rest of the way onto the ridgeline, lying flat on his stomach. He gazed around cautiously. Off to his right, he saw faint movement. That would be the guy who'd walked past.

But then he heard a twig snap off to his left.

Crap. There was a sixth guy up here, and he'd come up between him and his apparent patrolling buddy. Freezing in place, he let only his gaze move. No decent cover within several yards in any direction. There was a shallow gully just by his right side, though. For lack of any better options, he eased inch by inch to the right until his body lay in the depression. Moving his hands slowly, he grabbed fistfuls of leaves and dirt and did his best to cover himself.

Footsteps scuffed to his left at a range of about thirty feet.

He went completely still, relying on the human eye's tendency to focus on movement rather than on unmoving shapes.

The bastard walked past his head, no more than ten feet from him. Gunner didn't even blink as the guy eased past, his boots at eye level. The hostile was lean in build, medium height. Dressed in black, but not heavily equipped. He was carrying a tricked-out Howa Type 89 Assault Rifle, however. It was the preferred weapon of the Japan Self-Defense Forces. The one this guy was carrying had a video sighting system that would allow a user to hold it away from the body and aim the weapon around corners. Not super useful out here, but hey, if it made the guy feel badass, more power to him.

Spencer and Drago wanted to capture one of these guys tonight. Question him and find out who he worked for and what the hell they wanted with a little kid. This one was a good hundred yards behind his buddy. If Gunner could take him down silently, Hostile Number Five might not realize he'd lost his partner for long enough that Gunner could drag this one away.

To that end, he let the guy move about twenty-five feet past him. Then Gunner pushed up, rising to his feet specter-like behind his unsuspecting target. He moved slowly at first, then picked up speed as he closed the last few yards.

He got an arm around the hostile's neck before the guy had any idea Gunner was even there. But dammit, the guy had excellent hand-to-hand combat training. He flipped Gunner over his shoulder, and only Gunner's own training allowed him to twist midair and land on his feet, still clinging to the guy's neck, which was now bent down in front of him. He made a fast move to one side to get behind the guy again, but the idiot jerked hard against the countermove. It was the kind of flashy move a movie martial artist would make but no sane fighter ever tried in actual combat. Not if he wanted to live. Sure enough, a sharp cracking sound split the night. It sounded like several stalks of celery being snapped in half all at once.

The hostile went limp in his arms, and Gunner swore silently. The guy had broken his own neck with that stupid move, for God's sake. He lowered the hostile to the ground as the man's paralyzed body gurgled its last few breaths. Life faded from the man's dark, staring eyes, and Gunner closed the guy's eyelids with his thumb and forefinger.

Dammit.

He turned, scanning the woods in the direction this guy's partner had gone. At least he knew that Hostile Number Five didn't have any backup now. Maybe he wouldn't be as stupid as this guy had been and kill himself with some ill-advised hero move.

Gunner moved off quickly, covering a lot of ground for about three minutes before slowing and scanning the forest with the heat-painting feature of his NODs. Spencer and Drago would be wearing clothing that minimized their heat signatures, but the hostiles didn't appear to be doing the same.

He crept forward, paralleling the cliff. He was close enough to look down on the motel and started when he spotted two men emerging from the woods across the road. Apparently the hostiles were beginning some sort of assault on his and Chas's room. Jeez. Good thing Chas and the doll version of Poppy weren't there.

In front of him, a figure rose silently out of a bush and surprised the living hell out of him. The hostile had almost no heat signature, just his hands and throat lit up on Gunner's gear. Bastard had been well hidden in a thick stand of brush, sitting perfectly still.

Gunner froze midstep as the hostile moved over to the edge of the cliff and trained his weapon toward the motel. This must be the overwatch guy providing sniper support. Either that, or his job was to pick off Gunner and Chas if they tried to flee.

Gunner eased slowly off to his left, counting on the shooter's concentration on the area below to keep the guy from noticing him. When he'd traveled a ninety-degree arc and was directly behind Number Five, Gunner started forward. This time he drew his Ka-Bar knife as he approached the target.

He jumped, wrapping his left arm around the shooter's throat and pressing the flat edge of the knife against the guy's chin in an obvious declaration of intent to kill if the guy gave him any hassles.

Fortunately, this guy went still, his body utterly relaxed. Not that Gunner took it for surrender. Not yet.

Flipping the knife blade to place the sharpened edge against the shooter's throat, he used his free hand to key his microphone. He muttered low, "Number Five in custody. Number Six is down."

Two sets of clicks in his ear were all the acknowledgment he got from Spencer and Drago. Which meant both of them were close behind their own targets. It also meant they were ready to move on to the second phase of this operation—chasing off the remaining targets so they'd have time to question his captive.

All of a sudden, gunfire exploded off to his left, where the ridge sloped down almost to the level of the motel, and from the trees across the street. The man in his arms jolted violently, and Gunner pressed the razor-sharp blade harder across the guy's throat.

There were shouts and returned weapons fire, interspersed with the distinctive double taps of Spencer and Drago's weapons. *Pop-pop. Pop-pop.* Their pace of fire was unhurried, undoubtedly precise, also undoubtedly herding the remaining hostiles toward their vehicles in a way meant to make them think they were vastly outnumbered and needed to retreat if they wanted to live.

Somebody cried out below. Spencer or Drago must have decided to nick one of them. That was a ballsy call, but maybe the hostiles needed a little more convincing to bug out.

It was incredibly difficult to hit a moving target at all, let alone control where on a body a bullet struck. Shooting for the leg or head were stunts that only worked in Hollywood. In the real world, snipers aimed at the center of mass and were happy with any shot that hit a vital area.

Without warning, the guy Gunner was holding let out a shout. It sounded like he said, "Run!"

He tightened his arm across the guy's throat until the dude was gasping and started clawing at Gunner's forearm. The man went limp, but Gunner held the choke hold a bit longer to make sure the guy was well and truly passed out.

Then he lowered the man to the ground and worked fast to secure his wrists behind his back with zip ties. He stuffed a bandana in the guy's mouth as he started to revive and stepped back, pointing his pistol at him. The hostile regained consciousness and glared up at him, testing the zip ties once and then subsiding.

Yippee. This one might live long enough to answer a few questions.

Gunner heard running footsteps and took a quick glance at the road below. Four figures in black were running at full speed in the direction of the SUVs, puffs of dirt kicking up behind them every few seconds. Drago was continuing to shoot at their heels, no doubt to convince them not to stop and circle back for their two missing teammates.

Engines roared to life, and the man at Gunner's feet struggled violently. Just figured out he'd been left behind, had he? Sucked to be him.

Two large black vehicles roared past, and Drago shot out the rear window of the last one for good measure. Gunner grinned and hoisted his guy to his feet, giving him a little shove along the ridge toward where it dipped down to street level.

"I'm coming up on your left, Gun," Spencer transmitted over the radio.

"Roger."

Spencer's dark shape materialized beside him, and the shoulders of the bound hostile drooped. He'd been planning an escape attempt, had he? Too bad, so sad.

"Take this one down to the room?" Gunner asked Spencer.

"Good a place as any for a conversation."

They marched the guy down the hill and met Drago coming across the road. Gunner unlocked the motel room door and ushered the prisoner inside. "You two have a chat with this guy. I have a little cleanup to do, and I need to retrieve Chas."

"Why don't you pack up the baby's gear, and when you've collected them, go ahead and hit the road," Spencer said quietly.

"Good idea. For the record, I put the sixth hostile in a throat lock, and he flipped me. I kept my grip and he tried to twist sideways out of it. Snapped his neck before I could let go. He died immediately. I swear I didn't kill him intentionally."

"I know you better than that, Gunner. You don't lose control in a fight. Hell, I wouldn't offer you a job unless you were a complete professional."

"Thanks," he replied gruffly.

Spencer nodded. "Photograph the corpse, police the area for any evidence that would lead back to you, and leave him. He's their problem to deal with… assuming they don't leave their own behind. Then you guys get out of here. We'll deal with this gentleman."

Drago had already hog-tied the prisoner with ropes he couldn't possibly wiggle in, let alone escape from.

Gunner nodded and quickly packed his and Chas's stuff and stowed it in the car. He came back for Poppy's stuff and efficiently tucked her gear into the baby bag and slung its cloth strap over his shoulder.

"That's a good look on you," Drago commented.

Gunner looked up, startled. The guy didn't sound like he was being sarcastic, and a genuine smile lit Drago's face.

"If they made these things in camo cloth, I'd like them better. The pink is a little loud for my taste," he replied wryly.

Spencer and Drago grinned as he ducked outside for the last time.

Gunner was just closing up the car when the motel manager came outside, looking suspicious. The guy demanded, "I heard noise out here. You boys causing trouble?"

"No, sir. I thought I heard some folks hunting in the woods, though. Gunshots woke me up. I couldn't get back to sleep, so I decided I'd go ahead and pack the car so we can get an early start in the morning."

"Don't forget to turn in the key when you check out," the guy grumbled.

"You bet. Good night, now."

The manager wandered back inside, and Gunner sighed in relief. He jogged around the end of the motel and headed up the hillside toward where he'd stashed Chas. Poor guy must be losing his mind after hearing all that gunfire.

It had been a hell of a night. First the emotional roller coaster of epic sex with Chas, and then a hunt in the woods and the unexpected shock of killing a guy. Even if it was the dead man's fault and a total accident, it was still stressful.

He could really use a hug from Chas right about now.

Which shocked the ever-loving hell out of him.

Chapter Fifteen

IT WAS official. He'd had a full nervous breakdown. Lying under this stupid boulder had not only chilled him to the bone but stretched his nerves until they'd totally snapped. Every noise made him jump, every rustle of breeze rattling through the branches sent him into a new panic.

His cell phone said he'd only been out here about a half hour, but it felt like several lifetimes. How in the heck did Gunner stand living with this kind of tension all the time? How was the guy not a complete wreck? A whole new level of respect for Gunner's training and guts came over him. He'd had no idea how rough a job this was.

As the clock continued to tick, he had way too much time to reflect on Gunner's chosen profession. The guy did this all the time. This was a normal workday for him. Hunting other human beings was his career.

Chas despised that with every fiber in his being.

It couldn't possibly be good for Gunner to live as a killer, to think as a killer, to *be* a killer. How did any human soul walk away unscathed from the knowledge that they'd taken the lives of others?

He had to find a way to talk Gunner out of doing work like this anymore—while Gunner still had a little soul left to save. Urgency to get him to quit the security field and find something, anything, less violent to do raged through him.

As soon as they made it off this hillside—if they made it off this hillside—he was going to have a talk with Gunner about it. While he waited to find out if they even got to have the conversation, he began to figure out his plan of attack.

Something was moving on the hillside below him. Oh God. It was big and dark. A person. He froze, feeling more trapped and exposed and vulnerable than he ever had in his life. It was awful. He was going to die and he was never going to get to tell Gunner he lov—

He spied the face of his killer.

Gunner.

Oh, thank God.

As Gunner's familiar form neared the big boulder and bent down to pull back the camo tarp, Chas burst out of the hidey-hole, rolled clear of the overhang, gained his feet, and practically leaped on Gunner.

"Sweet baby Jesus. I was sure you'd been killed when you didn't come back for me," Chas murmured against his neck.

"It just took a while to clear the area. I'm fine."

Gunner squeezed the stuffing out of Chas, and right now, he loved feeling those big, strong arms around him better than just about anything else on earth. "You sure you're okay?" Chas asked. "I heard gunfire. A lot of it. I thought you were dead—"

A warm mouth pressed firmly against his, stilling the stored-up babble of terror that had come spilling out. Distracted by the kiss, he fell silent, kissing Gunner back enthusiastically.

"Better?" Gunner murmured when the worst of his panic had subsided.

"Yeah," he sighed. Lord, he was a mess. "Are you okay?" He took a small step back and commenced running his hands up and down Gunner's arms, across his shoulders, down his ribs.

"Really, Chas, I'm fine. But I do need you to stay here a couple more minutes while I take care of one last piece of business. Then I'll be ready to head out."

And just like that, the panic roared back. "Oh no, you don't. You're not leaving me alone again!"

"I would really rather you stayed here."

"No. Effing. Way."

Gunner huffed. "I have to go photograph and search a body. You don't want to see that."

"A dead—" Chas broke off, too shocked to finish. Oh God. It was as bad as he'd feared. Gunner was standing there, talking as calmly about death as if they were discussing the weather. "What on earth happened out here?"

"It was an accident. The guy did something super stupid and broke his neck. I couldn't let go fast enough."

"You killed him?" Chas gasped.

"No. He broke his own neck in a dumbass attempt to slip the grip I had on him. Assuming he wasn't trying to actually kill himself. Which is also possible."

"And you're not completely freaked-out?" Chas demanded.

"Chasten. I'm United States Navy SEAL."

"I know. But… someone *died*. You're so calm. Too calm."

"Death comes with the job. We're trained to be calm about it. And honestly, this guy was colossally stupid or suicidal. Either way, I wouldn't have been able to stop him. He moved too abruptly for me to react and turn him loose." Gunner shrugged, and Chas stared at him in horror.

"How can you be so… casual… about this?"

"Death is never casual," Gunner snapped.

Chas's eyes widened. Okay. So Gunner wasn't completely soulless about having killed some guy. That was a hopeful sign. "You seem so relaxed out here. How is that possible? Bad guys were running around trying to kill you—kill us—and you're all Mr. Chill. You're so… in your element."

Gunner glanced around. "Welcome to my office."

Chas took a deep breath. Through the haze of his outrage and residual panic, he still sensed what an intimate thing it was for Gunner to share this side of himself with anyone who wasn't a SEAL. Not that he hated any of it one bit less.

He asked in resignation, "So, where's this body you have to photograph?"

"A hundred yards or so along the ridge above us. We'll have to go around the ridge in the opposite direction, which is a bit of a hike up the cliff to the top. It's a nasty free climb. Not long, but tricky. It's about a half mile to go around, so we'd better get going."

Chas volunteered reluctantly, "I used to rock climb. It probably won't be that big a challenge for me if you want to go straight up."

"You did?" Gunner blurted.

"I'm not a total couch potato."

"I took you for more the ballroom dancing type."

Chas grinned. "Oh, I've done that too."

Gunner rolled his eyes. "I hate dancing."

"That's because you've never done it with me."

They reached the ridge, and Gunner showed him where he'd climbed the cliff face. A quick scan with a red-lensed flashlight showed an easier section of rock off to the left a bit, and they chose to scale the wall there instead.

"You go first," Gunner said. "Be careful of loose rock. This shale cracks off super easily. But I'll be right behind you."

"So you can spot me from behind? Or ogle my epic glutes?"

The white flash of Gunner's teeth indicated that he'd smiled.

"But what if I'm the better climber? Then I should be spotting you," Chas asked seriously.

Gunner snorted. "You couldn't catch me if you tried. I weigh half again what you do."

"I know. I've had sex with you, remember?"

And just liked that, the air around them took on a charge that made it crackle and snap across his skin.

Chas mapped his route up the wall and started the climb. It was significantly easier than the walls inside climbing facilities and provided plentiful foot- and handholds. The only difference out here was that he had to carefully test each ledge to make sure no loose rock gave way before he put his weight on it.

In short order, they stood atop the ridge. Chas breathed a little hard, but Gunner was huffing too. Hah. He'd kept up with a SEAL for a couple of minutes.

"Lead on," Chas murmured.

Gunner pulled down the eyepiece thingy mounted on top of his helmet and took off confidently into the trees. Chas stayed close on his heels, amazed at how silently Gunner slid through the forest, ghostlike. He had to admit, it was sexy seeing him in his native environment like this. It was the difference between a racehorse standing in a stall and the same racehorse flying around a track at forty miles per hour—the former was pretty, but the latter was impressive.

Gunner stopped abruptly. "Stay here."

The reason they were up here slammed home. A man had *died* near here. Chas thought he smelled something. Whether it was blood or urine or both, he didn't know and couldn't tell. He was probably just being hypersensitive or imagining it altogether. But God, he hated this.

He waited while Gunner moved forward toward a hump on the ground. It appeared that he frisked the body, probably looking for identification. Several bright flashes indicated that he had photographed the dead man too.

In each brief flash of light, Chas caught a silhouette of a nose or the angle of a shoulder. That had been a human being. The dead man had a family. Friends. Hopes and dreams for his future. And he'd died at Gunner's hands.

Chas didn't understand the nuances of some guy breaking his own neck versus Gunner doing it for him, but he didn't much care about the distinction. Gunner had been fighting with the guy violently enough that the guy died, and Gunner had barely batted an eyelash when telling Chas about it.

He watched grimly as Gunner moved in expanding circles around the corpse, staring intently at the ground. Now and then Gunner stopped and dug at something or moved a few leaves around. Eventually he backed away from the corpse, dragging a stick with some dead leaves still attached to it like a broom.

"Okay. Let's go," Gunner said.

"Aren't we going to bury him?"

"His guys ought to come back for him. That way his family can bury him properly."

"But what if somebody else finds the body? Won't the police get involved? You could get in serious trouble."

"I made damned sure I left no evidence behind for law enforcement to find. I'm in the clear."

Chas's teeth ground together at how casually Gunner said that. *No big. I got away with murder. It's fine.*

Gunner was speaking. "...is a courtesy of war. You let the other side collect their dead and give them burial rites."

"There's an etiquette about these things?" Chas exclaimed, appalled.

"Keep your voice down. We don't want the guy in the motel room to know we're still out here."

"What guy in what motel room?"

"The dead guy's buddy. I captured him and handed him over to Spencer and Drago. They're undoubtedly stuffing him into the back of their SUV as we speak and taking him someplace else where they can have a little conversation."

And his panic was back.

He was surprised when Gunner led him along the ridge, hopped off it when it was no more than three feet above the level of the motel parking lot, and led him directly to their car. "What about all our stuff?"

"I already packed everything. We need to roll before the other hostiles work up enough courage to come back looking for their friends."

SHOCKINGLY, CHAS managed to fall asleep and only woke when the sun rose behind them, flooding the interior of the car with bright light. With morning came a little emotional distance from the night's events. He was less freaked-out today about a guy having died. He'd known Gunner practically his whole life. He would never kill anyone whom he didn't absolutely have to.

He also believed Gunner's version of events. The bad guy had done something boneheaded to break his own neck before Gunner could let go of him. Gunner had never been able to lie to him, and he hadn't been lying last night.

Chas might not like the fact that a man had died, but it was a far sight better than Poppy dying—or Gunner, or himself.

They were driving along a two-lane westbound road. Rolling farmland and forest surrounded them. Gunner looked beat. "Where are we?" Chas mumbled.

"Central Missouri."

"Can I take a turn at the wheel?" Chas offered.

"Nah."

"C'mon. Let me help. You don't have to be a superhero all the time. You haven't been getting nearly enough sleep the past several days."

"Well now, whose fault would that be?"

Chas grinned. "My point exactly. It's only right that I drive a bit while you catch a nap."

Gunner relented and pulled over for them to swap seats.

And so it went through the day, with them taking turns driving while the other napped.

At least a dozen times, Chas started to bring up the subject of Gunner calling a halt to the violence of his life, but every time, he chickened out. Gunner seemed to have fully hit his stride after last night and was in full-on badass mode. Now was probably not the moment to ask him to walk away from the job and never look back.

But soon. Soon he would have to tell Gunner that he couldn't live with knowing his lover was a professional killer.

They made good time and drove through the day and late into the night before Gunner finally called a stop. Chas's whole body felt beat-up from sitting in a moving vehicle for so long, sleeping in cramped positions, and from the forced inactivity. He hated to think how Gunner's back felt.

But they'd put nearly a thousand miles between themselves and that nightmare in Kentucky. The Rocky Mountains rose in front of them, hulking black shadows against the night sky, more an absence of stars in the dark than physical shapes.

Gunner murmured, "Let's wait until daylight to take on driving through the Rockies. Particularly since we won't be taking main roads."

Given that the idea of driving off a cliff scared the hell out of him, Chas agreed quickly. They were somewhere between Colorado Springs and Denver, just entering the Front Range, when Gunner pulled into a state park and followed the signs to a camping area. It was deserted at this time of year, and the ranger at the front gate told them to take whatever camping space they wanted.

"Camping?" Chas exclaimed. "What happened to hotels with running water and, oh, flush toilets?"

"We're roughing it tonight. Staying off the grid."

"You may like 'roughing it,' mister, but I am a huge fan of my creature comforts, thank you very much," Chas declared.

"We'll have all the comforts of home," Gunner argued. "Roughing it is when you're getting snowed on without any cover, sleeping directly on frozen ground, have to pee into a bottle, and don't take a shower for a month."

Chas stared at him in open horror. "No amount of money on earth could entice me to do something like that."

"How about a choice between life and death?" Gunner responded practically.

"Well, if I was going to die, I might do all that. But—" He broke off. "Are we in life-or-death danger?"

Gunner shrugged as he pulled out a flimsy-looking gray-green tent and started putting it up.

"Don't you shrug at me, Gunner Vance. I want to know. Exactly how much danger are we in?"

"I'll let you know when I talk with Spencer and Drago and find out what the guy I captured had to say."

"And when is that going to happen?"

"Oh, I'm sure he's talked by now. Obviously Spencer and Drago are still tracking down information or they would've already called us."

"How can you be so patient about all this stuff? Don't you want to know who's got it in for Poppy and why?"

Gunner pounded in the last stake with a rock and looked up grimly. "Yeah. I do," he answered flatly. "Grab that pole and lift it when I tell you to."

In a few seconds, the tent went from being a bunch of nylon on the ground to a fully erected shelter. It barely came up to Chas's waist, though. Appalled, he watched Gunner crawl in.

"Pass me the sleeping bags, will you?" Gunner called from inside. "They're the black cylinders about the length of my forearm."

"You mean these hard pillow things?"

"That's them."

Chas passed in the sleeping bags, which appeared to explode from their storage bags.

From inside the tent, Gunner said, "If you're nice to me, I'll tell you what all the noises you hear tonight are. Otherwise you get to spend the night wondering."

"What noises?"

"You'll see," Gunner answered cryptically.

They ate sandwiches they'd bought during a fuel stop a few hours back, and Gunner tossed Chas an apple that he commenced munching. With intense distaste, Chas relieved himself against a tree as if he was eight years old again, and then crawled into the tent—on his hands and knees, for crying out loud.

"I feel like a freaking dog."

"You'd make a cute puppy."

"There is no part of this that I like," he declared.

Gunner grinned as he unzipped his combat boots and set them just inside the flap. "Aww, c'mon. It's not that bad."

"I can see my breath," Chas complained. "And the ground is hard. I'm gonna have bruises in the morning just from sleeping."

"I put foam pads under the sleeping bags."

Chas lay down experimentally. "Could've fooled me."

"Oh, you'd know the difference. You'd have pebbles and sticks digging into your back if I hadn't."

"This is barbaric."

"It's nicer than the way mankind lived for millions of years."

"I, sir, am not a caveman," Chas announced indignantly.

Gunner's chuckle floated out of the darkness. "I put a bottle of water by the top of your sleeping bag for you. It's deceptively dry in this part of the country. Easy to get dehydrated, especially when it gets cold."

"Speaking of which, I'm shivering."

"You have to mummy up your sleeping bag."

"What the heck does that mean?" Chas demanded.

"At the top of your sleeping bag's zipper, there's a drawstring. Pull it until the top of the bag forms a hood around your head. If it gets really cold tonight, you can tighten it down until there's only a tiny hole left to get fresh air through."

"You do realize I'm claustrophobic," Chas grumbled.

"Think of it as sleeping in a coat."

Chas thrashed around, hating the confinement of the sleeping bag and unable to get comfortable on the hard *alleged* pad. He wasn't at all convinced there actually was a pad beneath him. He could totally see Gunner not giving him one as a joke. He opened his mouth to accuse Gunner of that very thing when a haunting noise, almost like a ghost moaning, made him freeze.

"What was that?" he asked in a whisper.

"An owl."

"Oh."

He listened for the sound again but instead heard what sounded like bones rattling nearby. "What's that?" he whispered a little more urgently.

"Wind rattling tree branches against each other."

"Oh." Chas tried to block out the night sounds, but damned if he didn't hear something moving outside. Close. "*What's that*?"

Gunner replied deadpan, "A bear. And it's going to rip through the tent and eat you if you don't be quiet."

Holy crap. Chas lay perfectly still in his sleeping bag for long enough to hear Gunner breathing deeply. He'd fallen asleep with a freaking bear outside? How dare he—?

And then it hit him. There had never been a bear at all. The jerk had just wanted him to stop asking questions. Furious at Gunner for tricking him and more furious at himself for falling for it, he turned over with a huff and closed his eyes, determined to get the best night's sleep ever, just to spite Gunner.

When he woke again, green-tinted light with an odd glowing quality to it met his confused gaze. His nose and cheeks were freezing, but the rest of him was toasty warm. And darned if he didn't feel well-rested. He rolled over and was startled to see Gunner's sleeping bag flat and empty.

Chas sat up fast and hit the ceiling of the tent with his head. A strange sliding noise startled him. What on earth?

He unzipped his sleeping bag and quickly rezipped it as frigid air poured into his warm little cocoon. The tent zipper moved and he lurched, looking around frantically for a weapon. He flung an arm out of his sleeping bag and grabbed his shoe, holding it up menacingly.

Gunner's head poked through the opening. "Morning, sunshine."

Chas scowled at Gunner but then stared over his shoulder in disbelief. "Is that *snow*?"

"Why yes. Yes, it is. I believe they have it in New Hampshire too. You know, white stuff. Falls from the sky. Accumulates in the driveway and is a pain in the ass to shovel?"

"Ha, ha. Very funny. How much fell overnight?"

"About six inches. It's why the tent is so warm this morning. Stuff's a great insulator. Eskimos knew what they were doing building igloos."

"This is cozy?" Chas squawked.

Gunner laughed. "God, you're fun to camp with."

"Fuck off," Chas bit out.

"Can I interest you in driving to town for a hot breakfast? Maybe a nice stack of pancakes slathered in maple syrup?"

Gunner remembered that was his favorite breakfast of all time? "I don't know whether to be charmed that you remember I love pancakes or livid that you're trying to sweet-talk me after making me sleep in a tent in a blizzard."

"I vote for charmed. I am a charming guy, after all."

Chas tried to stay mad, but when packing up the tent devolved into a snowball fight that he lost hopelessly, he ended up laughing as hard as Gunner. Rosy-cheeked, his hands wet and half-frozen by the time the tent was packed up and stowed in the trunk, he realized he was happy as Gunner drove away from the campsite.

Happy was not a state he often associated with himself. He managed cozy on a reasonably regular basis. Satisfied with a good day's work. Occasionally he even got to content. But happy? Joyous? Thrilled to be alive and with this man at this moment?

Impulsively, he leaned across the car and grabbed Gunner by the neck, planting a big, sloppy kiss on his mouth.

"What was that for?"

"I love you, dude."

Oh, holy God. The words were out of his mouth before he knew they were coming. He hadn't even had that thought consciously, but the words just spilled out.

Gunner's face froze into a mask of shock.

Should he retract the statement? Make a joke out of it? Pretend he'd never said it? His brain locked up, and by the time he decided to blow it off as a casual comment, Gunner had turned to face the road and was staring straight ahead with robotic concentration.

Shit, shit, shit.

Chapter Sixteen

GUNNER SQUEEZED the steering wheel like it was a cobra and he was choking it to death. Chas loved him. Love. Goddamn.

Love.

The big *L*. The real deal. Serious. Adulting. Commitment.

Shit, shit shit.

He was supposed to say it back, right? Wasn't that how it worked? But did he even know if he loved Chas? Sure, he'd loved him like a brother forever. Loved him as a friend. But that wasn't what Chas was talking about.

It felt as if the rules of the game had suddenly changed. Instead of playing the football he was familiar with, he found himself in a rugby game with only the faintest idea what the hell was going on, where he was supposed to go, what he was supposed to do. Hell, maybe this was a cricket match. He had *no* idea how that game worked.

Breakfast was a quiet affair. They ordered food at a local diner, gulped it down, paid the check, and hit the road. They barely spoke two words to each other the whole time. Gunner knew why he was freaked-out, but why was Chas freaked-out?

Although it was not as if he was about to ask Chas to clarify on his earlier declaration of love.

He stared at the road, not really seeing it, driving on autopilot. His mind raced in circles. Did he love Chas? How would he know if he did? Was there some test for it? Would he feel different? Act differently? Did it come to a person like a revelation—boom, all of a sudden it was there?

Wasn't he at least supposed to say thank you or something in response to Chas's declaration? God, he sucked at this relationship stuff. No doubt he had feelings for Chas. Big ones. Deep ones. Adding sex to their relationship had totally changed the equation and left him not knowing at all how things worked between them anymore. It had always been so easy being best friends. They could talk about anything, were always there for each other no matter what. Had he sacrificed all of that for the sex?

He turned down Chas's offer to drive, preferring to keep busy concentrating on the road winding ever deeper into the Rocky Mountains. Winter had come to the higher elevations, and snow lined the roadways and coated the slopes around them in black-and-white relief. Only the deep, faded green of the pine trees interrupted the stark, photo-like contrasts. As they neared the Continental Divide, even the pine trees gave way to just snow and rock—white on black, light on shadow.

He headed more north than west as the roads allowed, making his way toward Wyoming. He'd never been to Yellowstone National Park, and now was as good a time as any to see it. It lay at the junction of

Idaho, Montana, and Wyoming and took most of the day to get to, given the back roads they took when they could and the poor condition of the main roads when they were forced onto them.

Dusk was falling as they pulled into a magnificent lodge just outside the park, a huge log structure decorated with rustic furnishings and exceptional taste. Even Gunner could tell it was a classy place. Chas made a quiet "Ohhh" as they stepped into the lobby.

"I figure I owe you a night at a nice place after forcing you to camp last night," Gunner said gruffly.

"I'd hate for this place to get shot up, though," Chas muttered under his breath.

"Even if the bad guys figure out we're here, they won't be able to get here tonight. This isn't the easiest or fastest place in the world to get to."

"You said that last time."

"If nothing else, I'm betting they spent today dealing with the body of their guy. They either buried his remains or had to collect his body and get it shipped home."

"Any word from Spencer and Drago?"

"We've been in cell phone dead areas most of the day. I'll call them when we get to the room."

He was relieved Chas was talking again. The silence in the car had been almost total today, and it had been unnerving. Chas was usually the gregarious one who carried the majority of the conversation. But he'd barely spoken a word since that fateful declaration this morning.

Not that Gunner minded silence in general. Most of the guys he worked with were taciturn types, and SEALs ran most of their missions in complete silence.

They became adept at communicating through looks, facial expressions, and subtle hand gestures.

But Chas was an expressive person and used his words to convey pretty much everything he felt or thought. Gunner appreciated knowing in general what was going on with Chas without having to try to figure it out.

They checked into a deluxe suite using one of the credit cards Drago had provided. It was set up not only to be easily trackable but to report back to Charles Favian whenever somebody else tracked its use. When the tangoes chasing them figured out they were here, Favian ought to be able to warn them that the thugs were inbound. In theory.

Now that they'd caught one of the bad guys, the game would be to stay one step—or ideally several steps—ahead of the hostiles and not engage with them again until he and Spencer and Drago were prepared to take them out for good. From here on out, they would be leading the bad guys into traps and not the other way around.

They hauled in all the baby gear, and Chas carried in the doll. When a woman asked to see Poppy 2.0 in the elevator, Chas murmured that she was asleep and had had a long day. Gunner traded amused looks with Chas as the woman got off at her floor and they continued up to the concierge level.

Gunner opened the suite's door and held it for Chas.

"This is more like it," Chas declared, standing in the center of the spacious living room and turning in a full circle.

A fire burned cheerily in the fireplace, and tall picture windows looked out upon a valley straight out of a picture postcard. White snow blanketed the slopes and weighed down the boughs of the fluffy pine trees. The narrow black ribbon of a running stream cut through the valley floor, and a herd of elk drank from it. The last light was just fading, and as they watched, the valley slipped into peaceful night.

Gunner had to admit, it was darned near perfect.

Chas exclaimed from the bathroom, "Oh my God! You have to come see this! There's a giant hot tub in here."

Gunner stepped into the doorway and spied Chas already running water to fill the huge tub. The fireplace turned out to be two-sided, and the hot tub stood next to its far side. Chas looked up, his entire face lit with joy. "Order up a bottle of wine, will you?"

"I don't know anything about wine."

Chas straightened thoughtfully. "Ask for a port. It's a red dessert wine, but with some brandy added in. More kick than regular table wines. I think you'd like it."

"Will you like it?"

"I love the stuff. I'm a cheap drunk on it, though."

Gunner grinned. "I'll order two bottles."

Chas rolled his eyes, but at least he smiled a little. Profound relief flooded Gunner. He hated being at odds with Chas.

While they waited for the big tub to fill, he placed a call to Spencer. "Hey, it's Gun. Any information forthcoming from our guest?"

"Oh yeah. Took waterboarding him once, but then he sang like a canary."

"And what did he sing?"

Chas tugged on Gunner's sleeve, doing charades to indicate he wanted to hear too. "I'm putting you on speaker phone so Chas can hear too," he told Spencer.

"I'm doing the same. Drago's on with me."

"Great. We're all here, so tell us what you learned," Gunner said impatiently.

"Our prisoner works for the Oshiro gang." Spencer paused for a moment. "But he had an interesting tale to tell."

Drago picked up the narrative. "Apparently the Oshiro gang is dealing with some internal politics. The old Oshiro leadership wants to sit pat on its drug smuggling in the United States. But a group of younger Oshiro lieutenants wants to go international. They think there's more money to be made if they control both ends of the smuggling chain from Asia to North America."

Chas asked, "What does that have to do with Poppy?"

"According to our prisoner, the splinter group of pro-expansion Oshiro guys kidnapped Poppy. Our guy thinks it was some sort of show of force to intimidate the Tanaka gang."

"Do they want ransom for her?" Chas asked.

Spencer answered, "Our prisoner didn't know. He thinks the Oshiro guys who took Poppy want something else from Kamiko's grandfather, Yuzio Tanaka. He's the head of his clan. We think it's possible they're trying to get control of a port currently controlled by the Tanaka clan."

Drago took over. "Charles Favian has been digging around. He talked with the folks over at the CIA's Asia desk, and they say Yuzio Tanaka and his son, Kenji, have had a serious falling out and aren't on speaking terms."

Gunner frowned. "Meaning what? The Oshiros aren't going to get what they want from kidnapping Poppy because Grandpa is pissed off at Poppy's daddy?"

"Potentially," Drago answered grimly.

Chas frowned at Gunner. "What does that mean?"

Gunner answered, "It means they'll need to dispose of Poppy, assuming they can get ahold of her again. They can't just give her back when they can't strongarm Grandpa into doing what they want."

Spencer said, "I think we have to proceed on the working theory that once these guys figure out the old man isn't going to bend, they will ultimately kill Poppy."

"She's a baby!" Chas exclaimed in a combination of horror and dismay.

Drago replied, "She's a Tanaka. Which means she's smack-dab in the middle of this feud, whether she deserves it or not."

"Who doesn't love their own grandkid?" Chas demanded indignantly.

Gunner heard the shrug in Drago's voice. "Ol' Yuzio may not believe in giving in to extortion, even if Poppy is his own blood. It may not be about love. It may be purely about the principle of the thing."

Spencer added, "J. Paul Getty refused to pay ransom for his grandson's return after a kidnapping. He said he had a bunch of other grandkids, and if he gave in on one of them, they all would be in terrible danger."

"Didn't Getty end up coughing up a couple million bucks for the kid?"

Spencer snorted. "Only after the grandson's ear was sent to a newspaper."

"That's cold, man," Gunner commented.

"There's a wrinkle to all of this," Spencer said grimly.

"Which is?" Gunner asked when Spencer didn't continue right away.

"Kenji Tanaka told me he got a ransom demand five days ago, and his people thought it came from the Oshiro gang. But other Oshiros had already contacted Kenji's father with different demands. Sounds to me like the two branches of the Oshiro gang are working at cross purposes with each other. And possibly, they each have different plans for Poppy."

Gunner frowned. "Either way, that doesn't bode well for her. Clearly we need to smack down whatever Oshiro gang members try to come after her until we can hand her off to her daddy."

"Exactly," Spencer replied.

Chas gasped beside him. Yeah. Gunner felt the kick in the gut too. Their kiddo was caught up in the middle of a nasty and dangerous mess. Any time money and power were involved, bad people would be prepared to do terrible things.

Spencer continued, "A friend of Drago's at the agency collected a DNA swab from Kenji yesterday and is personally flying it to the US to be compared to the swab we took from Poppy. We should have results on that in a couple of days."

Chas looked ready to puke, which Gunner totally related to. The idea of losing Poppy, of having to hand her over to a stranger, made him feel faintly ill as well.

"I don't want to do anything too dramatic until we have the results of the DNA test," Spencer said. "Once we know she's the right kid, I'd like to draw together both factions of the Oshiro gang and eliminate them both or least give them a good spanking, before we hand her back to Kenji Tanaka. I'd hate to return her only to have something bad happen to her because his family's enemies are embarrassed."

"Where's the Oshiro prisoner now?" Chas asked curiously.

Spencer chuckled. "He's comfortably ensconced in Chez Barn at the back of our property. He's not going anywhere."

"What are you going to do to him?" Chas blurted.

"Nothing for now. We'll be putting him on a hook and dangling him for the rest of the Oshiro boys to come and get shortly. We still have a few things to arrange before we let them know where their guy is."

Chas frowned. "I don't mean to tell you guys how to do your job, but should we be luring the bad guys there when Poppy's just across the street?"

Spencer grinned. "If you were the bad guys, would you look for her there? It's the last place anyone will think we stashed her. Plus, we're very close if we need to get to her to protect her."

Chas frowned doubtfully.

"Will the Oshiros come for their guy?" Gunner asked.

"Don't know," Drago answered. "It'll depend on who he knows and how much they value whatever criminal activities he's engaging in here in the States. If he's a low-level thug, maybe not. If he's a little higher up the chain of command, I expect they will want him back."

"If nothing else, it's lousy for morale not to recover your guy. I think the odds are better than not that they'll come after him. Particularly if we dangle Poppy in front of them too," Spencer added.

"You wouldn't!" Chas exclaimed.

"Not the real Poppy, of course," Spencer said quickly.

Gunner noted how protective Chas had sounded. He'd gotten pretty attached to the munchkin. Unfortunately, he knew the feeling. The little cutie was irresistible. Made a guy think about rug rats of his own someday.

"What do you want us to do in the meantime?" he asked.

"Stick to the plan," Spencer replied. "Keep playing hide-and-seek with whatever Oshiro guys are following you while we try to figure out which faction is chasing you and how to draw out both factions at the same time."

Gunner concurred. Aloud he asked, "How's Poppy?"

"She's great. Cute as a button," Spencer replied.

"Is she making noise? Baby babbling or crying?" Chas asked anxiously. "When she's afraid she goes completely silent. Is she safe? You're sure these Oshiro guys can't get to her?"

Drago answered more gently than Gunner would have guessed the guy was capable of. "She's babbling up a storm. The gal from the agency who's watching her speaks some Japanese, and Poppy seems to be responding very well to that. As for her safety, we've got that place protected like Fort Knox. Spencer and I have called in a few favors, and some of our friends are supplementing the already formidable security team at the estate."

"Why don't you guys start swinging back around toward this side of the country over the next few days," Spencer suggested. "If this comes to a fight, I'd rather do it on my home turf."

"But we'll be leading reinforcements back to possibly even more Oshiros!" Chas protested.

"I swear to you, Chas. We've got this under control," Spencer responded. "With the team we've got in place around Poppy, she's safer than any baby on the planet. I stand by our plan of taking out as many of these Oshiro dudes as we can before we hand her over to her father."

Gunner ended the call after that and watched pensively as Chas wandered into the bathroom, trailing his fingers in the hot tub's bubbling water. The bottles of port arrived. Gunner signed for them and carried them into the bathroom, where Chas now sat in the tub, staring out the window.

Gunner stripped silently and slid into the tub beside him. "You really love kids, don't you?" he asked quietly.

"Yeah. I do."

"You're going to be a great parent."

Chas sighed. "I don't know if it'll ever work out."

"I learned in SEAL training that if you want something bad enough, you should refuse to give up on it until you get it."

"I'm no SEAL, Gunner. I'm just a slightly neurotic kindergarten teacher from a small town without much of a dating pool."

Gunner turned to stare at Chas. "Are you kidding me? You're a great catch. And God knows you're the most loyal friend I've ever had. Why you stuck with me for all these years, I'll never know."

Chas glanced up at him. "You were a bit of an ass-hole there for a while."

"Still am, last time I checked. But I'm working on being better."

"When you're not going all SEAL on me, you're fine just the way you are," Chas declared.

If only. "I'm sorry about this morning," he murmured.

"What do you have to be sorry about? I'm the one who blurted out something stupid and awkward."

Gunner frowned. "I'm no great expert on relation-ship shit, but I hear that expressing your feelings is sup-posed to be a good thing."

Chas laughed. "Wow. Spoken like the most clue-less man ever. You realize you just verified all the ste-reotypes about strong, silent males being emotionally unavailable, right?"

"Like I said, I'm no expert at relationships."

"Or feelings, apparently."

"Or deep conversations."

"Or basic manners," Chas added.

"Hey, now. I know how to say *please* and *thank you*. And I call women *ma'am*." He poured a glass of the deep burgundy port and held it out to Chas. "Here. Drink."

"A toast," Chas murmured, waiting for Gunner to pour himself a glass.

"What shall we toast?"

"To Poppy being safe."

"Well, duh. Anything else you'd like to toast?" Gunner asked.

"To old friends, new lovers, and hot sex."

Gunner grinned. "Hear, hear. And all the better when they come in a single package."

Chas sipped his port appreciatively. "Thanks for coming to Misty Falls to rescue me when I called. I was pretty sure Poppy and I were going to die."

"I'm glad you called me. It was lucky I was able to come right away to help you." Gunner leaned back, savoring the jet of hot water pounding his muscles.

"What will you do when you go back to work?" Chas asked.

"Regarding what?"

"Are you going to take up Spencer and Drago on the job offer?"

"Undecided."

"Can I throw in a vote for going the history professor route?"

"It's a little late for that."

"It's never too late to follow your dreams. And I'd rather see you in a job where you won't be risking your life on a regular basis. You're my guy, and I want to keep you safe."

"What? You're going to protect me from any bad guys who show up?" Gunner asked humorously.

"Anyone who wants to hurt you is gonna have to go through me."

Gunner froze. Repeated the words in his head. Absorbed them through every pore of his skin like the rare and precious blessing they were. Very few civilians in his life had ever had his back unconditionally. He'd been so busy protecting Chas and Poppy, he hadn't really stopped to register the depth of grief and loss he felt at losing his SEAL family.

He reached out and looped his arm over Chas's shoulder, pulling him close against his side. Chas turned a little and laid his head on his shoulder.

"I think I may love you too," Gunner murmured.

"I beg your pardon?" Chas squawked, jerking upright.

"Jesus. You don't have to act like I just told you I was going to kill the president."

"Say it again," Chas demanded.

"Aww, now you're making it weird."

"Say it."

Gunner huffed. "I think I love you." He waited expectantly for a moment and then grumbled, "Aren't you supposed to say it back?"

"You mean the way you did this morning?"

"You're such a jerk sometimes," Gunner muttered.

Chas's beautiful eyes narrowed. "You let me know when you're sure about your feelings, and then we'll see if I say it again... double jerk."

"You do realize I'm a SEAL. And I'm in water, my native environment. Are you sure you want to challenge me here and now?" he teased.

Chas snorted. "As if you'd ever hurt me. You don't have it in you."

The humor drained from Gunner's chest. "No. I don't. You mean too much to me."

"A bit of advice from the guy in this relationship who's good at emotions? Be careful of making promises you can't keep."

"I promise, Chas. I'll never hurt you."

"That's a broad statement. If you mean you'll never lay a hand on me, that I can believe. You're not the type to speak with your fists. Never have been. But emotional hurt is inevitable in all relationships. It's the partners' capacity to forgive that defines the relationships that will last."

"That's some wise shit."

Chas rolled his eyes. "Drink your port. Clearly I need to get you a little drunk before we discuss your feelings any more."

"They warn SEALs about getting drunk and hopping into bed with frog hogs, you know."

Chas frowned up at him. "What in the world is a frog hog?"

"Groupies in bars who hang out around SEAL bases looking to sleep with a SEAL."

"You know I'm not interested in you just because you're a SEAL, right?"

Gunner snorted. "Yeah. I got that memo a long time before I joined the teams."

"And you know I wasn't trying to seduce you when I asked you to come rescue me, right?"

Gunner's arm tightened across Chas's shoulders. "The thought never crossed my mind."

Chas tilted his head up and kissed Gunner's jaw.

He turned his head, tilted his chin down, and met Chas's mouth with his own. Port on the tongue of his lover tasted amazing—spicy and pungent, with subtle notes of hot hillsides and bright sunshine.

Chas turned, threw his leg across Gunner's hips, and straddled his lap, which brought them eye to eye. "I'm right here, G. What *are* you going to do about me?"

Gunner's junk stirred as Chas's crotch floated lightly against his, the bubbles swirled around his penis, and the combination of heat and strong wine went to his head a hell of a lot faster than he expected them to.

"I do believe, Mr. Reed, that I'm going to make love to you in a hot tub, regardless of how cliché that might be. Then I'm taking you to bed, making love to you again, and spending the rest of the night holding you in my arms."

Chas smiled, his eyes and entire face brilliant with the joy and love for life that Gunner had never been able to get enough of. Chas had always been the light to his darkness, the laughter to his taciturn nature, the reminder to reach beyond his darkest depression.

Their lovemaking was slow and intimate to-night. They stared into each other's eyes as Chas's body slipped down onto Gunner's erection like a cus-tom-made glove. The bubbles tickled Gunner's balls, and the heat relaxed his entire body until all he could do was hold on to Chas's waist and thrust up languidly for what seemed like forever.

Eventually, however, Chas's body became taut in his arms, his own back arched up and into his lover, and they finished together, sharing mutual groans of satis-faction against each other's necks.

Chas went limp, resting on Gunner's shoulder, floating lightly in the water. They stayed like that until Gunner became aware of the pads of his fingers turning into prunes. He climbed out of the hot tub and lent Chas a hand to do the same. Then he led Chas over to the fireplace, where heat poured out, warming the whole room. He and Chas dried each other off using thick ter-ry cloth towels.

He finished with a quick towel-dry of his hair. Chas grabbed the half-consumed bottle of port and headed for the king-sized bed facing the picture win-dows. They propped up the pillows and passed the bottle back and forth, drinking it as they stared out at the night.

"What's that?" Chas asked, pointing.

Gunner looked at the faint green shimmer in the sky. "That's the northern lights."

"We don't see them often in Misty Falls. There's too much ambient light from the houses and streetlights."

"They're incredible when you get up into the Arctic Circle. Remind me to take you on vacation up there sometime and show you."

Chas snuggled against his side without comment, but he seemed to like Gunner's talk of a long-term relationship.

Maybe it was the port talking, but he could envision spending a very long time with Chas. They... fit.

Never in a million years had he seen this reunion coming, nor the direction it had taken. Things were moving fast, really fast, between them.

Too fast, perhaps?

Was it supposed to happen like this? A thunderbolt out of the past that knocked him completely on his ass? Was he being a fool for love? Was this no more than a hot sexual infatuation with his first real lover? How in the hell was he supposed to know?

One thing he did know. He hated the unanswered questions rattling around in his head. And as sure as he was lying here, he had no idea what to do next with Chas. Hell, he barely had any idea what came next in his own life. How was he supposed to know what kind of life he could offer Chas... if any?

Chas hated danger. Hated the unknown. No way would he want to sit at home waiting for Gunner to come home from dangerous assignments. Especially not now that he'd had a taste of what Gunner's life in the field was like.

Dammit. The very mission that had brought them together would be the thing that would push them apart. It figured. He never could catch a break when it came to his personal life. Never had. Never would.

Chapter Seventeen

FOR CHAS, the next few days passed in a blur of being sick of sitting in a car, staring at thousands of miles of pavement, and overall general exhaustion. After their romantic interlude at Yellowstone, Gunner had inexplicably shut down. He wasn't laughing, wasn't joking around and shooting the breeze. Hell, he was barely speaking to him.

What had gone wrong? Chas had plenty of time to replay the evening while they drove across the country back toward the East Coast. For the life of him, he couldn't figure out what he'd said or done to make Gunner withdraw so completely into his own personal emotional cave.

One thing he did know: now was not the moment to spring his demand on Gunner that he find a safer job if they were going to have a long-term relationship with each other. That left him feeling grumpy and frustrated too, not in any mood to break through Gunner's sullen silence.

By the time they hit Virginia, he finally resolved that whatever was going on in Gunner's head was the guy's problem to solve—not his. He washed his hands of trying to show Gunner Vance how to be a normal human being and have a normal human relationship. The SEAL in him had won, apparently. Which sucked rocks.

If a faction of the Oshiro gang was following them back across America, they saw no sign of the black SUVs nor of any armed men. Chas wasn't sure if that was a good sign or a bad one. Gunner was tense, always watching everything and everyone around them. But Chas didn't know if that was real concern or just habit. Either way, Gunner's tension was contagious, and Chas was a nervous wreck by the time they finally pulled into the driveway of the old farmhouse late that night and were greeted by Spencer and Drago.

Chas and Gunner fell into bed without talking much to their hosts. They'd been driving nearly around the clock, taking turns napping and only stopping for fuel, food, or pit stops.

God, it felt good to stretch out on a comfortable bed that wasn't vibrating or rumbling, without cranking his neck and back into unnatural angles not meant for human beings.

Gunner groaned under his breath beside him. Chas felt Gunner move, pressing a hand against his right rib cage. He'd been doing that a lot recently.

Chas murmured, "Any chance you cracked a rib in your parachuting accident?"

"I'm thinking I cracked about four of them."

"Four?" Chas exclaimed, sitting up. "Why on earth didn't you stop and get those checked out?"

"Nothing to do for cracked ribs but let them heal."

"Can't you bandage them or something?"

"Elastic strapping helps make the pain bearable, but I still have to breathe, and every breath flexes them."

"Simple breathing hurts you? How long has that been going on?"

"The docs gave me some sort of epidural painkillers in the hospital and said it would last a couple of weeks. It has been starting to wearing off for the past few days."

"And you never said anything before now?" Chas exclaimed, indignant.

"It's just a little pain. No big deal."

"Four broken ribs is *no big deal*?"

"They're only cracked. Actually my spine is the worst of it. I messed up some disks, apparently."

Chas flopped back down to the mattress, aghast. "And all that sex we had. Did that hurt you?"

"Some. Although I was a little bit distracted from my pain."

Chas swore heartily. Enough to make Gunner chuckle, in fact, and to make him swear some more.

"Language, Mr. Reed. Language."

He turned his back on Gunner in a huff.

"Sleep while you can, Chas. Things could get exciting around here for the next few days."

"I have no desire to find out what constitutes 'exciting' in your world. Not after spending the past week with you."

"Aww, c'mon. The road trip was fun."

"Except for the part where we were chased, a guy died, and you took a freaking prisoner."

"You ain't seen nuthin' yet, kid."

"That's what I'm afraid of."

"How about tomorrow we go visit Poppy? Would that make you feel better?"

"You're bribing me. And it's totally working, you giant jerk."

"Sweet dreams, Chasten."

Chas huffed. "Same to you." God, he hated it when Gunner managed him like this. But the guy had always known how to handle him like nobody else. In bed and out of it.

GUNNER WOKE up a whole lot sorer than he was willing to admit. As for Chas, he was asleep on his stomach, his face mashed against the mattress, his jaw slack. The guy looked wiped out. The past week had been hard on both of them, but Chas wasn't used to the fast pace and high stress of working in hostile environments.

Moving stealthily, Gunner rolled out of the bed and padded barefoot across the room. He slipped out into the hall and eased the door shut so Chas could sleep a little more.

Spencer and Drago were either still asleep or not in the house. Maybe they were taking care of their prisoner. Gunner fiddled around with the coffeepot on the kitchen counter until he got it to start brewing, and then he went into the living room to work his way through a yoga stretching routine. The athletic trainers who worked with the SEAL teams swore by flexibility for injury prevention and longevity as an operator.

He took it slow, gradually working out the kinks and creaks. By the time he heard Spencer and Dray moving around in the kitchen, he felt like a normal human being again and not a stiff stick-figure imitation.

He strolled to the back of the house, following the smell of bacon frying, and found Spencer, who obviously noticed how gingerly he was moving. "How are you feeling, Gun?"

He poured himself a cup of coffee and sat down at the table. "Creaky. I'm forced to admit—reluctantly—that the admiral may have been right to sign my termination papers."

Spencer swore under his breath. "You really should come to work for us. The vast majority of what we do isn't strenuous. It takes more brains than brawn to be a good security consultant."

"I'm seriously considering it."

Drago clapped him on the shoulder as he plunked down a plate heaped with scrambled eggs, bacon, and toast. "Glad to hear it. Look forward to having you on the team."

Something warm spread through his gut. Apparently he needed to feel like part of something larger than himself, some sort of brotherhood of like-minded souls, more than he'd realized.

"How soon do you think someone will be coming for your prisoner?" he asked.

Drago slid into a chair across the table. "Soon. And based on past incidents with the Oshiro gang, they like to come in with overwhelming numbers. We anticipate at least six, and possibly many more guys than that, to come after him."

Gunner stared at both men. "You're not seriously thinking about going into a firefight against a bunch of hostiles with just the two of you, are you?"

"We'll have you too," Drago said jauntily.

"Still. Three against a couple of dozen isn't ideal."

Spencer shrugged. "We should have plenty of reinforcements, assuming we can get the Oshiro boys to come to us."

"And who would these reinforcements be?" Gunner asked.

Drago grinned. "I might have made a call to an old friend over at the FBI. Turns out the feds are plenty eager to get ahold of whoever shot up a peaceful little New England town. When I told him I might be calling in the next few days with information as to the location of the shooters, he and his people were all over it."

Gunner swallowed a bite of the hearty breakfast. "And how, exactly, are we bringing the Oshiros to us?"

"Easy. We're going to make sure our prisoner sees Poppy, and then we're turning him loose."

"Are you actually going to release him, or are you going to make him think he escaped?"

"He gets to escape. We'll control the direction of his egress from the property to make sure he catches a glimpse of Poppy on the way out."

"When does this little maneuver go down?"

"This afternoon."

"So we'll need to be prepped for a full onslaught by Oshiro muscle by tonight?" Gunner asked.

Spencer nodded. "Yep. Gonna be a busy day. We need to recon the woods around here and figure out where we want the fight to go down."

Gunner looked up quickly. Chas stood in the doorway, looking stressed, but not completely freaked-out. Which was good, given what was coming, but bad if it meant Chas was getting used to the violence and death of Gunner's world. A fierce desire to keep one part of his life pure and clean and simple swept over him. And that part of his life was Chas.

"Hungry? I'm cooking eggs and bacon," Spencer asked from over by the stove.

"Both sound great. I like my eggs sunny-side up if you're taking orders."

"Coming right up."

Chas, of course, was no dummy and asked, "What will you guys do if both parts of the Oshiro gang show up here? Can you take them all on by yourselves? Couldn't that be a lot of people?"

"Possibly," Gunner answered evenly. He waved a half-eaten piece of bacon at Chas. "You have to understand. SEALs practice force multiplication tactics. One SEAL is the equivalent of ten fully trained soldiers from most other armies in the world in a firefight."

"A firefight?" Chas echoed in alarm. "You're planning on having a shootout with an entire crime gang? Are you guys *nuts*?"

Chapter Eighteen

CHAS SAT on a blanket in the front yard of Spencer and Drago's house, playing with Poppy. She'd squealed in delight when she'd seen him and Gunner, and had run to them and grabbed their legs when they'd gone across the street to fetch her for this little outing.

It had choked him up, and if he wasn't mistaken, it had choked up Gunner a little too.

Of course, with the prisoner about to be released and herded past him, this was no simple little playdate. A half-dozen commandos were hidden in the trees around the house and yard, and Gunner had assured him one of the best snipers in the business was out there somewhere, ready and waiting to assassinate anyone who tried to mess with Poppy while she played innocently in the grass.

This was no life for a little kid. She should be able to grow up in peace and safety without having to worry that bad guys were going to jump out and grab her at any time. That was, of course, the only reason he was going along with any of this madness.

If he was ever going to have a family of his own, he couldn't do it around men like this, who lived lives like this, who drew danger to themselves at every turn.

Chas's stomach dropped to his feet. No matter how much he cared for Gunner, he wasn't sure he could give up on his own dream of one day being a parent. If Gunner refused to give up being some sort of private mercenary one step removed from being a SEAL, Chas couldn't—wouldn't—do that to his hypothetical children.

The plan today was for Spencer and Drago to strategically let their prisoner escape. The two of them were going to "chase him," but in fact they were guiding him past the house and out to the main road. The idea was for the guy to see Poppy playing with Chas and report back to his people where the kid was, and that only three guys were protecting her.

Chas listened intently for noises to indicate that the prisoner had made his escape as he rolled a ball across the blanket to Poppy. She rolled it back to him, laughing. That game lasted for about a minute, and then she was up and running, chasing after a leaf dancing on the wind.

Chas jumped up and raced after her, scooped her off her feet, and spun her around until she howled with laughter. His instructions were explicit. Keep himself and Poppy on that blanket in the front yard at all costs. Apparently it had something to do with sight lines and fields of fire—none of which gave him warm fuzzies to contemplate.

Gunner had assured him that all of the shooters out here kept having to shove down an impulse to grab the toddler and race into the house to hide her. Funny how he didn't worry about his own safety much. Ever since Leah Ledbetter had died on his porch, he had been mainly focused on keeping Poppy safe. Gunner seemed to feel the same way.

It was as if a parenthood switch had flipped on in their heads. Suddenly, the child was by far the most important thing—her safety, her happiness, her well-being. Some of his students' more obsessive parents began to make a little bit more sense, now that he thought about it.

"Chichi?" Poppy said, screwing up her face into an adorable frown.

"I'm told that's a nickname for daddies, Squirt. And as much as I'd like to be your *chichi*, I'm Uncle Chas. Can you say Chas? Chas?"

"Cha?"

"Good! Chas! Uncle Chas!" He poked himself in the chest. Lord, she was growing and changing and learning new things even in the short time they'd known her.

"Unca?"

"Yes! Uncle Chas!"

"Unca Cha!" She flung herself at him, and he caught her in a bear hug, laughing with her.

"Such a smart girl. I hear your name is Kamiko."

She leaned back and studied him very intently with somber black eyes.

"Kamiko?"

"Ka."

"That's you." He touched the end of her nose. She smiled, and then he tickled her until she was laughing and squirming wildly.

He almost missed the faint sounds of shouting from the woods behind the house and looked up sharply. Belatedly, he remembered Drago's instruction to pretend to see or hear nothing. The less competent the Oshiros thought the people holding Poppy were, the less force they would likely bring to bear in trying to get her back. At least that was the hope.

Chas rolled onto his back and held Poppy up in the air, her chubby limbs flailing and her laughter clear and carrying. But he couldn't bring himself to leave her so exposed, even knowing that the escaped prisoner would have no access to weapons of any kind.

He rolled over onto his hands and knees with Poppy lying on her back beside him. He used his body as a living shield while he surreptitiously looked around the yard for movement.

He saw a flash in the trees but had no idea if it was the escaping prisoner, a sniper watching him, or Spencer and Drago herding the prisoner toward the road as they "chased" him south off the property. Poppy pulled her thumb out of her mouth and reached out to grab his chin with her wet fingers.

"Ee-yew," he said in exaggerated disgust, making a horrified face. Poppy giggled on cue and grabbed his nose. "You're quite the tease, missy. Gonna lead your daddy on a merry chase, aren't you?"

A pang of grief at not being there to see her grow up almost made him cry out in pain at how sharply it hurt. He sincerely hoped she was not Kenji Tanaka's daughter and that he and Gunner could keep her as their own for a little longer. If he was being honest with himself, he desperately hoped they could keep her forever.

He knew it for the fantasy it was. Not only the part about keeping Poppy, but also about settling down and having a family with Gunner.

At this point, he didn't even know if Gunner wanted a long-term relationship with him, let alone a permanent one that included kids. The guy's declaration of love had been less than stellar and certainly didn't inspire any confidence that Gunner planned to stick around any longer than it took to return Poppy safely to her family.

He sighed.

Poppy yanked at his ear and he yelped, his attention snapping back to her. "So that's the way you want to play it, do you, kiddo? The tickle war shall now commence! Prepare to giggle!"

GUNNER SAT in the woods under his ghillie net—a sniper's camouflage gear—peering at Chas and Poppy wrestling and laughing on the grass. Right there was everything, everyone, he wanted in the whole wide world. If he could have Chas and Poppy for the rest of his life, laughing and loving and happy, he would die a happy man.

But damned if he had any idea how to get it. Chas was miffed at him for the way he'd told Chas he loved him, and Poppy's father would take her back as soon as the DNA evidence proved she was Kamiko Tanaka. Which Gunner's gut told him she surely was. The perfect Norman Rockwell moment playing out in front of him was an illusion. Guys like him didn't get happy-ever-afters.

If he was lucky, he might get to retire with the aches and pains left over from using his body far harder than it had ever been built for. He would get to relive past glories now and then when he got together with the old gang, assuming he made it to retirement alive.

At least Chas could go back home, resume his normal life in his little house, teaching kids and finding happiness with some lucky guy someday.

But him? He didn't fit into normal. Had no idea how to do it. Hell, he probably didn't even deserve it. His entire life until the past week or so had been a lie. Maybe this was karma coming back to bite him in the ass. The universe was dangling the perfect guy, the family, the happiness he could've had in front of him, taunting him.

God, this sucked.

He heard movement off to his left and swung his weapon in that direction, scanning the woods intently.

There. A glimpse of black clothing. That would be the prisoner. The guy was running, stumbling, looking back over his shoulder. Gunner heard Spencer and Drago behind the guy a bit, making a lot of noise, shouting back and forth and making sure the idiot kept running in the correct direction to go right past the house, see Poppy, and then hit the road.

The prisoner passed between him and the house, about fifty feet in front of Gunner. As the guy realized a clearing was off to his left, he slowed and moved away from it, toward Gunner. Dammit, they needed the guy to see Poppy.

Gunner picked up a rock and heaved it at a tree between himself and the prisoner. It hit with a *thunk* and the prisoner lurched away from the sound in panic. He practically bolted right out into the front yard before he contained his panic enough to stop.

Gunner watched in satisfaction as the prisoner crouched low now, moving along behind a line of brush and brambles just inside the tree line. In the yard beyond, Poppy let out a squeal, and Chas's warm laughter rose to meet the piercing giggles.

Poppy, who'd been lying down, pushed up to her feet and took off running across the grass, straight at the prisoner and Gunner's positions. Chas, racing after her, scooped her up and carried her back to the blanket, blowing raspberries on her tummy as he went.

Perfect. The Oshiro guy could not have failed to see Poppy clearly enough to positively identify her. Now, to chase him off the property and into town to call in reinforcements.

A swift-moving shadow off to Gunner's left startled him. Damn, Drago was good. He moved with every bit as much stealth as a SEAL would have, and every bit as quickly.

Drago deliberately scuffed his feet through a small hollow that had collected a deep layer of dried leaves, and the noise was impressively loud. Gunner's last glimpse of the prisoner was of the man sprinting full-out toward the main road, paralleling the long front lawn about fifty feet inside the trees.

The bait had been taken. Now all they could do was wait and hope the Oshiro gang took it and came after Poppy.

In the meantime, he was going to spend a few minutes playing with her before they had to return her to the safety of the Brentwoods' estate across the street. He missed her laughter like crazy, as it turned out. And oddly enough, he missed squeezing her chubby little legs and tickling her feet until she laughed. It was official. He'd lost his mind.

Or maybe you've lost your heart. To a little girl with an infectious laugh.

CHAS WAS subdued at supper, but he took comfort in noting that Gunner was equally subdued. The two of them missed Poppy terribly, and neither of them had liked having to hand her back over to the nanny, even if it was for safekeeping.

Spencer was asking Drago, "The call with your buddy at the FBI went well?"

"Oh yeah," Drago answered, grinning. "He was all over wanting to know where the shooters from Misty Falls might be. I told him I know they're in the Washington DC area and that he should put a tactical team on standby."

"Did he believe you?" Gunner asked.

"I gave him plenty of details that never made the news about the Misty Falls shooting. He and his team will come running if we need backup."

"What's to keep your buddy from tracing the phone call and figuring out who you are and where you are?" Chas asked curiously.

"I used a burner phone and routed the call through encrypted internet servers all over the world. He won't be able to trace it."

"May I just say, as a civilian, it's scary as hell realizing how easily you guys can avoid law enforcement when you want to?"

Spencer leaned back, laying down his napkin. "That's why we're so particular about who we train to do what we do. People who go into our line of work are investigated exhaustively and then put through the emotional wringer. Our training is designed to strip away all layers of artifice and deception and lay bare the core of a person. Many a SEAL wannabe has washed out not because they couldn't hack the training but because the instructors simply didn't trust him."

Chas frowned. "I get that young recruits start out as white-hatted hero types. But over time, as you all do… awful things… doesn't that take a toll on a guy? Don't people—what do you call it when a SEAL goes bad?"

"A big problem," Gunner supplied dryly. "That's what we call it."

Spencer nodded. "Now and then somebody cracks. People thought I'd gone bad when I disobeyed my orders to arrest Drago and bring him home. There was a rather concerted effort to bring me in, get me off the street, and make sure I didn't go on some kind of rampage."

"Did you crack?" Chas asked curiously.

Spencer smiled over at Drago. "It was a close thing. But Dray got me through it in one piece."

Drago reached out to squeeze Spencer's hand affectionately. "We saved each other. I think I was in worse shape than he was when we found each other."

Chas looked on with envy at the two warriors who'd found true love with each other. God, he would love to have that with Gunner. But the guy was so emotionally closed off, he didn't think he'd ever get there. Sadness washed over him. Such a waste of a human heart.

Gunner stood up, gathering plates. "I'll clear the table if you guys will lay out the topographical map. I want to go over the plan one more time. Now that I've walked the property and have visuals on it, I want to see it on paper."

Spencer stood as well. "After we go over it here, how about we walk through it outside in night conditions?"

Gunner nodded. "Perfect."

Chas winced. Not perfect. He hated running around in the dark, particularly when there were bad guys in the darkness out to kill him, or worse, out to kill Gunner. "How fast do you think your prisoner dude will get in touch with his friends and lead them here to attack us?"

"Two, maybe three days."

"So, tonight?" Chas asked sarcastically.

Drago harrumphed. "Fuckers have been moving faster than we anticipated almost every step of the way."

Spencer shrugged. "We'll be ready for them tonight, regardless. They do seem desperate to impress the bosses back in Japan."

Gunner added, "Either that, or the bosses in Japan are breathing fire at them to get the kid back so they don't look like incompetent fuckups to the Yakuza brass."

Chas fretted through the map session. His job was literally to stay in the house and stay out of the way. Period. He hated every second of the talk about the guys moving around in the woods trying to flush out targets, what search patterns they would use, and where they would go to hide if they got overwhelmed by too many bad guys at once.

Faced with three violent special operators, it wasn't as if he could stand up and make an argument for finding a way to do this nonviolently. Maybe contact the Oshiro clan. Explain that they weren't getting the kid back and should call off their war dogs. Maybe negotiate some sort of truce between Grandpa Tanaka and whoever was in charge of the Oshiro gang.

He was privately appalled when Drago brought out huge bags of gear and weapons that the three men methodically commenced inspecting, cleaning, oiling, and loading with ammunition. Every lens got polished, and even the knives got sharpened before they declared their gear ready to go. Nope. This thing was going down violently if Gunner and his friends had anything to say about it.

Chas allowed that they probably wouldn't start the shooting, but he had no doubt they would retaliate aggressively when the shooting started.

And then it was time for the midnight walk-through. He followed Gunner to the back door, murmuring, "I don't like this. Be careful out there."

"Relax. There's nobody out there, Chas. This'll be a stroll through the woods. Wanna come along?"

"No!"

Gunner grinned. "Why don't you go on up to bed and try to get some sleep? This'll take a couple of hours."

"Sleep?" he squawked. "Are you mad?"

"What else would you do late at night, given that I won't be there to have epic sex with?"

Chas punched Gunner's upper arm. "Can I call you if I freak out?"

"Like on my cell phone?" Gunner blurted.

"Yeah."

"Not ideal. Even a silenced cell phone makes some noise."

"Yeah, but if nobody's out there—"

Gunner cut him off. "I have an idea. How about we give you a headset? You can listen in on us as we run through the plan and patrol the property. And if you freak out, you can ping me on the radio. I'll set up a secondary frequency for you that'll be private just between you and me."

"You can do that?"

"Of course. The SEALs use only the best equipment. I can monitor two frequencies at once."

That would work. He'd meant to ask why, if nobody was out in the woods tonight, Gunner was concerned about running silent, but the headset suggestion derailed him. And besides, he knew the answer already. They were being cautious, operating as if the worst-case scenario was going to happen and the bad guys would show up this evening.

Gunner spent the next few minutes showing him how to operate the headset, change frequencies, and transmit. It didn't distract him from the coming violence one bit, however, nor from how relaxed Gunner was about going into a bloodbath and possible death.

Gunner startled him by transmitting loudly in his ear over the radio, "How do you hear me, Chas?"

"Umm, super loud."

Gunner grinned. "In military parlance, we rate loudness and clarity each on a scale from one to five. So I've got you five by five, which means you're very loud and very clear."

"Fine," Chas said off the radio. "You're five by five by five."

"What's the third five for?"

"Fuck-off factor."

Gunner grabbed him by the back of the neck and pulled him close for a hard, hot kiss. "Go to bed."

"Wake me up when you come in?"

"Count on it."

"Okay, then. Five by five by zero."

Gunner kissed him again and then turned and disappeared into the night as Chas stood at the back door, watching him jog into the trees, hating every single second of this. One second Gunner was moving away confidently, and the next he was just… gone.

He probably ought to have more faith in Gunner's ability to keep himself alive. But if it came to him or Poppy getting hurt or Gunner doing something stupid and heroic, stupid and heroic would win out every time.

Chas didn't know what time it was when he felt Gunner's heat slip under the covers behind him. Strong arms went around him, and he leaned back against Gunner's muscular body, loving how it felt like home.

"Have fun playing GI Joe?" Chas murmured sleepily.

"Had a blast."

"Please tell me you didn't kill anyone."

"I didn't kill anyone. Go back to sleep."

"Mmm. Sweet dreams."

"If they're of you, they will be."

"Love you," he mumbled, already slipping back into unconsciousness.

He thought he heard Gunner whisper, "Love you too," but he wasn't sure if that was real or part of the dream he was already drifting into.

Chapter Nineteen

GUNNER SAT out in the woods in the dark again, ghillie net draped over him, NODs in place over his eyes. God, he'd love to have drone coverage of the farm right now. Something with look-down infrared capability that could tell them if, when, and where any incoming hostiles approached. As it was, they were having to do this old-school, using boots on the ground and eyes on the forest.

Spencer and Drago were out here too. Drago was covering the barn where they'd held the captive, and Spencer had the rear approaches to the house.

From his position on the west side of the long north-south yard, Gunner saw in the front windows Chas playing with the Poppy-sized mannequin. Now and then, he tossed her up in the air and pretended to laugh with her. At the moment, Chas was sitting on the couch, no doubt suffering through a children's movie, with Poppy 2.0 tucked in the crook of his arm beside him.

The costumer at the CIA, whom Drago had called on to create the fake Poppy doll, had done a fantastic job of creating a copy of the child. The only giveaway that the doll wasn't real was how still it was. Real

Poppy was always in motion, wiggling and exploring. She never sat still or watched an entire movie.

Spencer radioed, "Your turn to run a patrol, Gun."

"Roger." He stood up slowly and moved off into the trees toward the road. He would go to the end of the grassy lawn and cut across in the woods between the yard and the road, and then patrol up the east side of the yard. He would set up shop over there until it was time to make another circuit of the front of the property.

It would be bold of the bad guys to come right in the front way. Drago thought they would sneak in from the back. Gunner worried that if the hostiles had enough guys, they might feel confident enough in their superiority to just come straight in, guns blazing.

He'd made it almost to the turn to cross in front of the house when a rustle of movement caught his attention. He froze, carefully scanning the trees. He spotted a blip of heat down low. It could be a small animal, maybe a rabbit, or it could be a human lying on the ground. His own ghillie net was woven through with material that diffused and disguised his heat signature. It was possible that the bad guys had the same technology, hence he didn't automatically assume that little slash of heat was a sleeping bunny.

He moved off to his right, swinging wide of the position of the possible hostile to take a better look. It was slow going moving in complete silence, but in about ten minutes, he paused to scan again.

Sonofabitch.

"I've got three clustered heat signatures," he breathed. "They're lying low, not moving. Correct positioning for a team to be surveilling the house."

"Hold your position," Spencer murmured. "I'll join you. Dray, move in to cover the front of the house."

Gunner waited impatiently until Spencer slid up silently beside him and touched him on the shoulder. A tap from Spencer's hand signaled him to move out. Proceeding at roughly the speed of a glacier, Gunner eased forward. Dammit, the signatures were gone.

He moved forward more quickly, and in about two minutes, he stared in disgust at what had clearly been an observation hide. Bastards hadn't bothered to put back the sticks they'd stuck vertically in the ground to hold up their camo netting. A fallen log had provided cover from the front and explained the tiny slit of heat he'd seen. The log had hidden the rest of their heat signatures.

"Do they have heat-seeking gear?" Gunner asked. "Is that how they saw me coming and bugged out?"

"I think we have to assume that," Spencer replied grimly.

"Which means if they were watching the house, they saw only the one heat signature of Chas inside. They know Poppy's not in there."

"Where did they go, then?" Spencer asked. He sounded as frustrated as Gunner felt. He should've shot the guys as soon as he spotted them. He probably wouldn't have gotten them all, but the fuckers wouldn't have disappeared without taking a hit.

"Looks like they left," Drago announced.

"Now what?" he asked Spencer.

The other SEAL considered for a moment. "Lemme make a quick call to Poppy's security team across the street."

Gunner counted the seconds impatiently until Spencer reported, "All quiet over there. But I've told them to be on high alert."

"And us?" Gunner asked.

"We hold our positions and wait."

Gunner huffed. He hated the idea of sitting and waiting until the Oshiros decided to make a move. It was the right call, but he was itching to take these hostiles out and get on with his life. His life with Chas, dammit.

He knew patience was one of the SEALs' greatest virtues, and Spencer was right to call on it now. But God, it was hard. He sank to his haunches and scanned in a three-sixty around the position. It was a good spot for a hide, on a slight rise with clear sight lines in every direction.

He probably ought to bring his SEAL-instilled patience to bear on Chas as well. The guy'd said he loved him again last night but had been more asleep than awake when he did it. This morning Chas had made no reference to it and didn't seem to remember doing it. But Gunner could wait the guy out. He would say it again. And next time Gunner would make sure Chas was wide-awake to hear him say it back.

The stars wheeled slowly overhead and the night grew colder. Through his binoculars, Gunner watched Chas go through the motions of putting Poppy 2.0 to bed and moving around the house, turning out lights and generally shutting down for the night. He took pleasure in watching Chas's slim, athletic silhouette through the windows, and a warm feeling filled his gut at the mere sight of him. Lord, he had it bad for Chas.

The last light, his and Chas's bedroom light, winked out in the front corner of the house, and darkness fell inside the structure. Chas wouldn't be asleep, if he had to bet. The poor guy would be lying in bed, jumping at every creak the old house made and at every puff of wind blowing outside.

A half hour passed with nothing happening. If the Oshiro soldiers were out here, Gunner had to give them credit: they were patient compared to most civilians.

Spencer murmured, "Dray, report."

"All clear in the back. They haven't come around here to jump the house from this side."

"Gun, report."

"All quiet in front."

"I don't like this," Spencer replied. "We know they were here. Why aren't they hitting the target?"

"They had to have IR gear. They must've figured out Poppy's not in there."

"So they just left? We killed one of their guys and held another one captive. Why wouldn't they at least try to kill one of us? Vengeance is serious business for guys like these."

Gunner had no answer. Spencer wasn't wrong.

Spencer sighed. "Let's run a carousel."

He was referring to a maneuver where they would move clockwise around the house, circling it while remaining equidistant from one another. It was an effective way for a few people to patrol a large area.

"Gun, swing out close to the road and see if there are any vehicles parked down there."

"Wilco." Which was short for *will comply.*

He headed into the woods and was nearly to the front property line when he spotted a single heat signature. The guy appeared to be lounging against something, and there was a big, faint blob of heat just beside him. Vehicle engine block that was still warm. The guy was leaning against a car. Two more blobs indicated a total of three vehicles parked a dozen feet or so off the road.

Gunner reported low, "I've got one tango guarding three vehicles which appear to be hidden just off the road."

Dray said tersely, "Three vehicles? That means we're looking at a dozen or more tangoes."

"Sounds about right," Spencer replied.

"Then where are they?" Gunner demanded.

"I know where they're not," Drago replied. "And that's here. This place is as quiet as a tomb. We've got no action at all on our property."

Gunner didn't get it. Spencer was absolutely right—the hostiles should be out for blood. If nothing else, they would need to show the big bosses they were being effective, at least in part, after having lost custody of Poppy in the first place. Why hadn't Chas or the three of them been attacked?

Had something spooked them? Had they changed plans? What the hell were he, Spencer, and Drago missing?

He wouldn't normally be alarmed that things weren't going to plan. That was pretty much ops normal for a SEAL mission. But Chas was involved in this one. He didn't like using Chas as bait if they had no idea what the tangoes were doing. They needed more warm bodies, more resources out here if they were going to press ahead with tonight's confrontation.

"We should call in the FBI," he murmured. "Get a tactical team out here to scour the area. Their cars are here… the tangoes have to be close."

"We don't have any idea how many guys there are or who they are, at this point. They're not acting at all like the bulldogs who followed you and Chas. Those guys tracked and attacked you relentlessly. We can't afford to call in a tip to the FBI and have it be wrong. If it is, the next time we call, the FBI will ignore us."

This was why Spencer had been the team leader. He consistently made the right call, even if it was the hard call. Gunner sighed and moved closer to the road. He muttered, "I'm half tempted to grab the car guard and demand to know where his guys are."

"Last resort maneuver," Spencer replied. He sounded tense. He obviously didn't like the fact that the bad guys had disappeared either.

Drago murmured, "I'm heading for the road."

Gunner's gut twisted. This was a clusterfuck... he felt it in his bones. Every operator's instinct he had was shouting at him. Something bad was about to go down, and they weren't where they needed to be. And Chas was a sitting duck in that big house all alone—

Tat-tat. Tat-tat-tat.

"Gunfire," Gunner bit out, running toward the sound. "Direction of the road. My tango just jumped into vehicle number three."

Spencer's voice came over his earpiece, breathing hard. Dude must be in a full sprint toward him. "Those shots are coming from the Brentwoods' place."

Full-blown, holy-shit panic exploded in Gunner's gut. The bad guys had figured out where Poppy was? How in the hell—?

He cut off the thought. Didn't matter right now.

"I'm right behind you," Drago grunted, also obviously running full-out.

"Don't cross the road, Gun," Spencer bit out. "Wait for us."

More gunfire exploded. A lot of it. Gunner guesstimated that at least a dozen weapons were involved in an exchange of fire. Crap, crap, crap.

Reluctantly, Gunner screeched to a halt just inside the tree line about fifty feet behind the last vehicle. Spencer knew him too well—the guy knew he would charge in headfirst if Poppy was in danger. *C'mon, Spencer. Get here already.*

"Hurry," Gunner ground out over his microphone.

It was probably no more than sixty seconds until Spencer tapped his shoulder twice, indicating he should hold his position. *Dammit.* Drago arrived in perhaps sixty more seconds, but it was the longest two minutes of Gunner's life.

Spencer took point, leading them away from the vehicles around a bend in the road. Frustratingly, it was also farther away from the Brentwood property. Gunner schooled himself to patience as sporadic weapons fire continued.

Spencer indicated with hand signals that they would cross the road in stealth mode, one at a time. Gunner felt ready to explode with impatience. His urge to barge in, guns blazing, was almost uncontrollable. Were it not for Spencer and Drago grimly flanking him, he'd have done just that.

In the farthest recesses of his mind where he was still vaguely rational, he was thankful for their steadying presence. They moved into the woods on the far side of the road and quickly encountered the tall iron fence that surrounded the Brentwood estate.

Spencer reached out with one knuckle to touch the fence, and no spark jumped. Dammit. This fence was supposed to be electrified!

It made their ingress easier, though. The three of them scaled the fence quickly, pulled themselves up to the top, and rolled over the spiked tips of the fence using their bullet-resistant vests to cushion the points.

Gunner dropped to his feet and took off after Spencer, who was already running away from him. It was gratifying to finally move fast like this, and the sprint burned off some of the excess adrenaline that had been clouding his brain function.

He'd never been on this property, but fortunately Spencer and Drago had been running exercises on it for months while they trained the Brentwoods' security staff. Spencer angled off to the left as the trees thinned and a massive mansion came into view. It was a brick-and-stone castle that looked as if it had been lifted straight off some grand British estate.

Muzzle flashes came from several of the downstairs windows. Which meant the hostiles hadn't made it into the house. That was good. Bad news: there were multiple tangoes shooting back at the house from the edge of the lawn.

"That place got a panic room?" Gunner bit out.

"Oh, yeah. I'm sure the Brentwoods and Poppy are all locked up bank-vault style."

Drago growled, "They had better be locked up or heads are gonna roll on the security team we trained."

"So we're hunting?" Gunner asked.

Spencer's wolflike smile was all the answer he needed. Excellent. These fuckers were trying to hurt his baby girl. He had no compunction about killing every last one of them.

The three of them fanned out, moving more slowly now. They eased through the trees, steering clear of the rolling expanse of manicured lawn. Drago muttered that they'd taught the security team not to bother trying to shoot at anyone beyond the grass.

That made sense to Gunner. The security staff's odds of hitting targets in the woods would be too low without sniper training and weapons, and the goal was to keep intruders out of the house, which meant said intruders would have to cross the lawn to get to the main structure.

It didn't take them long to see muzzle flashes ahead of them. Four of the Oshiro gang members were lying at the west edge of the lawn behind a low brick wall. Unless they were sitting there shooting at the house for the hell of it, Gunner figured they were supposed to give someone cover as that someone tried to reach the house. Which meant the incursion would probably come from the north or south, at right angles to these yahoos.

He and Spencer and Drago had discussed their rules of engagement at the kitchen table yesterday, and they'd agreed that if the Oshiro boys were using lethal force, they would match it. Which meant the men in front of them were dead and just didn't know it yet.

Spencer indicated that he would take the shooter on the far end, Drago would take the nearest guy, and Gunner should take the two in the middle. They crouched no more than twenty feet behind the targets, weapons at the ready. After a few quick clicks on their primary radio frequency to verify they were ready to roll, Spencer gave the go signal.

Gunner exhaled and double-tapped two shots into the back of his first target's head, then shifted quickly to his second target. The guy had rolled onto his side to look behind himself, and Gunner sent two rounds into his neck above where body armor would end.

It was quick and brutal. But then, that was a nature of the job. He raced forward to check his kills while Spencer and Dray did the same. And then they were off, sliding toward the south end of the estate in search of the next team trying to capture or kill Poppy.

They'd been moving forward quickly for perhaps three minutes when Gunner's earpiece came to life, startling him. Once they'd engaged the enemy, SEALs rarely spoke at all. They relied on hand signals and their superb training to know what to do next and what their teammates would be doing.

Except it wasn't Spencer talking in his ear. It was Chas, talking on the secondary frequency in the headset Gunner had given him.

Chas asked low, "Gunner, did you guys just come back to the house?"

He clicked the radio twice. He'd taught Chas yesterday: one click for affirmative, two clicks for negative.

Chas whispered urgently, "Oh God. Then there's someone in the house."

Gunner's entire being exploded with tension. He reached up and touched his throat, transmitting back a single word. "Hide."

Spencer whipped his head around to glare at him as he broke operational silence.

There was no help for it. Gunner murmured, "Chas says there's someone in the house with him."

Spencer hesitated for no more than a millisecond. "Go."

Gunner nodded and spun, taking off running at full speed, silence be damned. Chas was in mortal danger.

Chapter Twenty

CHAS LOOKED frantically around the bedroom. Where to go? They'd talked about it last night. Think. What had Spencer told him about where to hide? His panic was so bad, he couldn't remember anything past the overwhelming urge to run and keep on running.

Laundry chute. There was an old laundry chute in the house that Spencer thought was big enough for him to climb inside, but Drago had been against him using it. He'd said it trapped Chas and gave him nowhere to run. Something about shooting fish in a barrel.

Think.

It sounded like the person or people had come in the kitchen door. He'd heard the distinctive squeak of the old hinges perhaps thirty seconds ago. Since then he'd heard nothing. They could already be upstairs. He raced over to the door on bare feet and locked it. Not that the old-fashioned lock would slow the bad guys down for more than a second or two.

He turned to face the room. Closet? Too obvious. Under the bed? Same. Behind the curtains?

He'd be visible. Could he squeeze under the dresser? Probably not.

Out of options, he ran over to the window and heaved the old wooden sash open as he looked outside. It was a solid twenty-foot drop to the ground. Knowing him, he'd break his leg if he tried to jump down there, and then the bad guys would find him and kill him anyway. He glanced left and right and spied a rain gutter overhead. He probably shouldn't try to hang from that. They weren't usually attached that firmly and were made of flimsy aluminum. But it gave him an idea.

He punched out the screen and winced as it hit the ground with a faint metallic clang. Quickly, he climbed up onto the windowsill, sitting first and then reaching up to grip the top of the window frame. It was precarious as hell, but he managed to gain his feet standing on the open sill and reaching up to grip the rain gutter for balance. Carefully, he slipped his fingers behind the rain gutter, which was in fact quite loose, to grip the edge of the roof itself.

Using his right foot, he reached up and caught the edge of the open window with his toes and stepped down on it. Fortunately, the window was in good repair and slid shut until it rested on top of his left foot. That was as closed as he was going to get the thing. Hopefully, it would disguise his mode of exit from the house from a fast search by a bad guy.

From inside the house, he heard movement. A stair tread squeaked.

Oh God. No time to go slow.

He eased to his right until his left foot stood on the very last bit of the exterior sill, his fingers gripped the edge of the roof, and his right foot braced against a downspout at the corner of the house.

If he could just extend his right foot around the corner, he should catch the edge of the front porch roof....

It was right at the limit of his ability to stretch his body, and adrenaline probably gave him the last few centimeters he needed, but the toes of his right foot touched solid horizontal wood.

Okay. He was spread out against the wall, his body forming an awkward X. He might or might not have the foot strength to hold his body weight in this position long enough to move his hands farther to the right along the roofline.

A tremendous crash on the other side of the wall decided for him. The bad guys had just kicked in the door to his bedroom. Any second they would come over to the window and look out. He had to be off this wall by then!

Straining with every muscle fiber in in his body, he pushed his feet against the edge of the porch and the edge of the windowsill. Then, moving carefully, frantically, he edged his fingers to the right, one hand at a time. Right, left. Right, left.

His toes could no longer maintain contact with the windowsill, and his left leg swung down alarmingly, nearly pulling his left hand off the roof.

His left hand cramped with the effort of hanging on. His fingers slipped a few millimeters, and it felt as if all the skin was being scraped off his fingertips by the rough asphalt roofing. Grimly ignoring the burning pain, he pulled with all his strength on his left hand and inched his right hand to the right.

Reversing the process urgently, he pulled with all his strength on his right hand and lurched his left hand to the right. Oh God. It felt like his left hand was on fire. He thought he felt blood begin to drip down his left wrist.

He repeated the procedure one more time, and the entire ball of his right foot was abruptly able to plant on the sloping porch roof. He pushed hard on the foot, taking weight off his arms and giving them a much-needed rest.

He only allowed himself a few seconds, though. He had to get around the corner before the bad guys got done searching the bedroom.

He heard a shout from inside the house and a grunted reply in a language he didn't understand. Spurred on by the bad guys feeling bold enough to yell back and forth, he inched his hands the last few feet along the roof until he was able to crouch on the front porch roof, breathing so hard his chest hurt. He lay down flat on the surface and commenced low-crawling across it.

A big old crepe myrtle's branches overhung the other corner of the porch, providing decent cover from anyone who might glance up here.

The wood beneath him gave a loud creak and he winced, speeding up his frantic crawl toward a hiding spot.

At last. He huddled in the fine branches of the crepe myrtle, praying they hid him. Enough leaves blessedly clung to the branches to provide reasonably thick shadows beneath the overhanging boughs.

He looked down over the edge of the roof. He could jump down from here, but there was precious little cover in the yard. He would have to run for the trees and make it to the woods unseen, and then he would have to play commando with whoever was inside the house. He was barefoot and had no coat. Not to mention, he had no weapon and no fancy heat-seeking night vision gear.

Nope. He had no interest in playing hide-and-kill with the bad guys. He was safer up here.

"I'm coming," Gunner grunted into his ear. "Where are you?"

"Outside," he dared to whisper, praying the microphone was sensitive enough to pick up the bare thread of sound.

"Outside?" Gunner echoed. "Where?"

"Porch roof, near the tree."

"Brilliant. Stay put. I'm going to go in and clear the house."

He clicked the microphone twice. Emphatically. In fact, he repeated the double negative click for good measure.

"Don't worry," Gunner muttered. "They're dead men walking."

Chas flinched. The cold violence in Gunner's voice was unlike anything he'd ever heard from him.

It was cold out here, and Chas began to shiver. He hugged his knees to his chest and lay on his side on the rough roof shingles. The angle of the roof was uncomfortable as hell, and when the wind blew, he shivered harder and crepe myrtle twigs poked him painfully. But he was alive. So far.

He tried to distract himself by attempting to spot Gunner coming. But he never saw even a hint of movement. He wasn't sure whether to be impressed at how good Gunner was or depressed at how bad he was at doing the whole Special Forces thing.

He listened intently, expecting to hear gunfire inside the house at any second. But as the minutes ticked by, silence reigned. Did he dare ask Gunner what was up? Or would transmitting give away Gunner's position?

He opted to remain silent and just wait, but it was hell. Was Gunner lying only a few feet away from him, hurt or maybe even dying? Should he be brave enough to check on Gunner? The thought of just cowering here while something happened to him—

It was unbearable. He reached for the button on the headset to transmit. Maybe just one click to see if Gunner reacted.

Click.

A long, long pause.

Click.

Oh, thank God. Gunner had clicked back. Reassured, he hugged his knees more tightly to preserve his meager body heat. His toes were never going to feel warm again.

Without warning, gunfire exploded nearby and he lurched violently.

Sweet baby Jesus. Was Gunner hurt?

GUNNER DIVED under the dining room table just in time to avoid being shot. It had taken him longer than he'd wanted to creep across the lawn to the house, but he dared not rush in like some unthinking idiot and get himself wasted without knowing how many hostiles there were and if they'd posted a lookout outside the house.

He'd finally low-crawled all the way to the back door, which had conveniently been left open. He didn't even have to oil the damned thing to get past the squeak. He'd just slipped inside low and scanned the kitchen quickly. Clear.

He considered the door to the basement, but he doubted the hostiles had started there. They'd be double-checking to make sure Poppy wasn't really hidden somewhere upstairs and likely be planning to kill anyone who got in their way.

He'd cleared the half bath and butler's pantry beside the kitchen and was just turning into the dining room when a hostile rounded the corner from the living room. It was a close thing to double tap the guy and then dive for cover.

His target went down but squeezed the trigger of his weapon as he toppled over, spraying lead all over the damned room.

So much for the element of surprise. Dammit.

A male voice called out from somewhere upstairs.

Fuck, fuck, fuck.

Gunner grunted, "I'm okay."

The voice called back, "Keep searching."

He moved quickly to the downed hostile and checked for a pulse. The guy was dead. He crouched beside the corpse for thirty seconds or so, and nobody came rushing downstairs on the attack.

Okay. He'd gotten away with his ruse. Better, he knew at least one more hostile was upstairs.

He spun low and fast into the darkened living room. He avoided the soft spot that creaked in the floor by the front window, and quickly cleared the room. After a quick check of the big office, it was time to head upstairs.

He took each step with care, easing his weight onto the tread slowly enough to prevent the casual squeak.

He skipped the first step above the landing that always squeaked, and crouched lower and lower as he approached the second floor. The landing in front of him was empty.

He stopped a few steps from the top, almost lying on his belly to peer through the railings down the central hall. He saw a shadow move into the right rear bedroom—Spencer and Drago's master bedroom.

He pushed upright and ran lightly down the hall before pausing beside the doorway. All at once he spun inside. The man across the room, currently peering in a closet, turned in surprise. Assuming that the bad guys had control of the house was the man's last mistake. Gunner double-tapped his weapon into the guy's torso.

On the assumption that the guy was wearing body armor, Gunner charged forward immediately after he shot, while his target was still flying backward and slamming into the wall. Drawing his Ka-Bar knife from his ankle sheath as he leaped, he jumped on the hostile's chest and drew the blade under the guy's ear and across his throat fast and deep.

He leaped back as the hostile went limp beneath him, shoved the blade in its sheath, and spun out into the hall, kneeling on one knee, waiting for a response to the gunfire.

The house was eerily silent.

He began a methodical search to clear the house. He cleared the bedroom across the hall and worked his way back toward the stairs. He'd almost finished with the second floor and was getting ready to head downstairs when he heard a click in his ear.

It took him a second to figure out what it was. Chas. On their private frequency. He had no doubt heard the gunfire and was scared shitless. Gunner clicked back. He hoped that held Chas for a few more minutes. He wasn't willing to break silence until he'd cleared the entire house.

He headed downstairs and, in an abundance of caution, cleared the ground floor again. Then he headed down to the basement, which was dark, damp, and blessedly empty.

Now to make a circuit outside.

But first, a quick call to Chas. The guy was probably losing his mind if he had to guess.

"Hey, babe, it's me. The house is clear, but now I have to check around a bit in the woods. Are you gonna be okay holding your position on the roof, or do you want me to come get you first?"

Chas sounded scared but in control of himself, whispering, "As long as you're safe, I'll be okay up here. Do your job."

"Love you, Chas."

"Love you too."

Sonofabitch. They'd finally managed to tell each other they loved each other at the same time like normal people did. Of course, they'd had to wait until the middle of a shootout to pull it off.

Nope. Nothing normal about the two of them.

CHAS WATCHED the yard and surrounding woods intently while he waited for Gunner to come get him. It was quiet for several minutes, but then he thought he saw someone moving toward the house in the woods along the driveway.

Horrified, he reached for his throat microphone button. "Incoming," he breathed. "Paralleling the driveway." He thought quickly about the compass directions and added, "East side. In the trees."

A single click was the only response.

Satisfied that he'd been helpful to Gunner, he lay still in his odd little hiding spot, praying harder than he'd ever prayed before. He prayed for Gunner to be safe and for himself to live through the night. He prayed for Poppy and Spencer and Drago, and for Mr. and Mrs. Brentwood, who'd been kind enough to take in Poppy and protect her.

He had no idea how long he'd been up on the roof—a while—when he heard what sounded like the entire Maryland police force coming down the road, sirens screaming. From his vantage point on the roof, he saw the glow of what had to be dozens of light bars illuminating the main road.

Welp. The cavalry had arrived. Only hitch: it had headed for the Brentwood estate and not here.

Should he continue to stay put? Or maybe get down and make a run for the road and all those lovely armed police?

As soon as the thought crossed his mind, he dismissed it. He trusted Gunner with his life, and if Gunner said to stay here, he would do that. He might hate Gunner's profession, but he knew without a shadow of a doubt that the man was extremely good at his job.

Maybe time passed faster knowing the police were nearby, or maybe it was just knowing an end to this nightmare night was in sight. But before long, Gunner murmured in his ear, "It's all clear out here. Either that or the bastards are better than me."

Chas sincerely doubted the Oshiro gang members were better than a SEAL. "I'm willing to bet my life on your being better," he murmured back. "Can I get down, go inside, and get warm now?"

"Yes."

Praise the Lord and pass the potatoes. He uncurled and was shocked at how stiff he was. He whole body felt like a board. He dangled his feet over the edge as he pushed back on his belly, shoving himself backward until his hips hung off the edge of the porch. Letting go, he controlled his fall and rolled all the way back to his feet.

And then Gunner was there, wrapping him up in a crushing hug.

"Jeez. You're an ice cube. Let's go inside," Gunner murmured.

He followed Gunner up the front steps and into the living room. Chas reached for the lights, but Gunner grabbed his wrist. "Leave the lights off."

"Any reason why?"

"Well… yeah."

"Care to tell me why?"

"Umm, there's a dead guy in the dining room. Thought I'd spare you that sight."

"There's a *what*?"

"There were two hostiles in the house. I neutralized them both. Surely you heard the shooting."

"I was in denial. Shouldn't we tell the police?"

"We will. Once the situation across the street is contained. I'd rather not siphon off FBI resources until all the tangoes over there are dead or in custody. When Spencer reports that he's in the clear, I'll let him know we've got a couple bodies over here."

"Right. But gross."

Gunner guided him across the living room to the sofa. "I'll go get us some blankets."

Chas nodded, watching Gunner move swiftly upstairs. That was when the smell of blood abruptly overpowered his nose. His stomach threatened to revolt, but then Gunner was back, handing him shoes and wrapping him a thick blanket.

Gunner sat down and pulled him against his side. "When you called to say there was someone in the house, I swear it took twenty years off my life."

"Really?" Chas replied. "I figured that would be normal everyday stuff to you."

"Not when it's you in danger."

"Aww. Feeling a little warmer now."

Gunner murmured, "They say sex is a great way to warm up."

Chas laughed under his breath. "We don't know everyone's safe over at the Brentwood place yet. Speaking of which, should you head over there?"

"The FBI will have brought a small army with them. I would just be in the way."

"I'm glad you're here, Gunner."

"Me too. You did good. How in the hell did you make it onto the porch roof?"

"I went out the bedroom window. It was a stretch, but my rock-climbing skills gave me an edge."

"Nice piece of climbing. That took serious strength."

"I figured if the bad guys found me, they might kill me. Turns out that's a pretty good motivator to try hard."

Gunner said sharply, "They would have killed you for sure—and me—if I hadn't killed them first."

They sat in silence for a moment. Then Chas said, "It seems disrespectful to sit here like this with two dead men in the house."

"My sympathy for them is limited."

"They were still human beings," Chas responded mildly.

"Human beings who made very bad choices."

Chas shrugged beneath his cocoon of blankets. "I'll never approve of killing."

"Can you accept that it's necessary sometimes?" Gunner asked in obvious alarm.

Chas frowned. "In theory. But in practice, I have to ask myself if there was another way to handle all of this. I mean, you guys set them up. You laid an ambush and then killed them when they walked into it. Why couldn't we have tried something else first?"

"Because that's not how people like this operate."

"You don't know that for sure. You didn't even try anything else."

"I cannot believe we're having this conversation," Gunner muttered. "I just killed two men to save *your* life. And Spencer and Drago are picking off hostiles in the woods across the street to save Poppy's."

"I don't like it," Chas replied stubbornly.

"So you'd have preferred to die rather than have me take out the guys who came in here to kill you?" Gunner asked in disbelief.

"I could've tried to run away. If you hadn't come, that's what I would have done. In that scenario, you wouldn't have had to kill those guys. Which I suppose means their deaths are on my hands too." He fell silent as the reality of that sunk in and appalled him.

"Stop, Chas," Gunner said sharply. "They broke into this house intent on killing you. Their team had already figured out Poppy wasn't here. They had no reason whatsoever to come in here except to kill you. It was revenge, straight up. Don't start feeling sorry for a couple of violent killers who were bent on murdering you. They would have chased you down, and believe me, they'd have caught you. They were wearing the same kind of tactical gear I was."

"I hear you. But—"

"No buts. Some people are simply in need of killing."

"I can't agree with that," he declared. "I hate all of this."

"Hell, I hate killing. But in my world, it often comes down to kill or be killed. If you can accept that, then we're okay. But if you can't, then we've got a problem."

Chas clamped his mouth shut so he wouldn't say something he could never retract. But God, it was hard. He was not the bad guy here for being unable to accept outright killing as a viable option for dealing with problems. Sure, he'd had to defend himself a few times over the years. But punching a guy a few times was a far cry from putting a bullet in his head.

Where did it stop? This wasn't a sanctioned SEAL mission, but Gunner thought it was okay to kill in this situation. What if a more casual friend's life was threatened? Was it okay then? Or what if the threat was slightly more vague? Was a lethal response still okay? What if an asshole in a bar assaulted Chas? How much violence was okay then? Or what if Chas really, really pissed him off? Would Gunner resort to violence in that situation?

No matter how many ways he turned it over in his head, examining the morality of it from every angle, he couldn't find a way to accept murder as a necessary evil.

"I'm sorry, Gunner. I just can't."

Gunner's arm tightened around his shoulders briefly, convulsively, and then fell away from him.

Gunner stood up swiftly, silently, every inch a predator, and disappeared into the night, leaving Chas to sit alone on the sofa with his regrets and a dead man in the next room.

GUNNER EXHALED hard in frustration for at least the hundredth time. How could Chas do this to them? How could he ask him to choose between the only kind of career he knew and their love?

He and Chas had spent most of the night separately writing out statements for the police and being interrogated by the FBI after the agents had secured the Brentwood estate. A few dead Oshiro gang members' bodies had been collected and the rest of the gangsters arrested. It had taken hours to clear the entire grounds of the estate, but eventually Mr. and Mrs. Brentwood, Poppy, and the nanny/bodyguard friend of Drago's had been let out of the panic room. They were all spending the night at the Brentwood mansion under heavy FBI guard.

Gunner's interrogators had made him start at the beginning, when he'd gotten that frantic phone call from a childhood friend begging for help, and had him walk them all the way through to clearing the house and killing the intruders.

The good news was initial forensics indicated that the weapons the Oshiro gang was using were the same types that had shot up all those people in Misty Falls. The FBI was inclined to be lenient with several ex-Spec Ops types who'd taken down the perpetrators of the Misty Falls massacre, and he, Spencer, and Drago had all been released around dawn.

The house was taped off as a crime scene, so they'd picked up Chas, piled in a truck, and driven to a local diner, where they'd ordered a mountain of food and dug into it.

Spencer and Drago put their heads together across the booth to discuss something in private, which left him and Chas sitting side by side in awkward silence.

Gunner muttered the one thought that had been on his mind ever since their disastrous talk last night. "How can you ask me to choose between you and my job? You know how much it means to me. It's not just some nine-to-five gig for the paycheck, and you know that too."

"It's not that simple," Chas ground out under his breath.

"Then explain it to me. For God's sake, help me understand."

"Tell me something, Gunner. If you had to choose between what you believe in most and me, could you do it?"

Dammit. "Depends on what you mean by 'what you believe in most,' I suppose."

"The thing you believe in above all else. Your deepest, most closely held belief. For example, my deepest belief is that love is the answer to most of what's wrong in the world today."

"I have no idea what my deepest belief is," he argued, frustrated. God, he hated having to dig around in his feelings as if they were some dead animal he was dissecting.

"Well, I know you believe in your teammates. They're family to you, and you'd do anything for them, right?"

"Yeah."

"Could you choose between letting your teammates die or letting me die?"

"That's not fair. I'd try to save all of you."

"Can you choose between a life with your SEAL family or with me?"

"I think I already have."

"Could you give up being a soldier, being a warrior, for me?"

"It's not that simple. It's not as if I can unlearn all the things I know how to do. I'll always be a warrior, whether you like it or not."

"Could you quit killing?"

"I'd give that up forever in a heartbeat if my work allowed for it."

"Does that mean you're willing to go back to college, get that history degree, and settle down to teaching with me?" Chas pressed. "And never pick up a weapon again? Never harm anyone again?"

Gunner squeezed his eyes shut tightly and asked grimly, "Are you making that a condition of our continued relationship?"

"What if I were?"

"I asked first."

It was Chas's turn to sigh. "That's what my heart wants. In my head, I don't think it would be fair. I got into this relationship knowing who and what you are."

Gunner exhaled hard. Again. Why couldn't Chas understand what his career meant to him? He tried to explain. "Look. I love working with men like Spencer and Drago. It's who I am. More to the point, it's who I want to be. I like this version of myself. I'm strong, self-sufficient, and I can protect the people I care about."

"I do understand the allure of all that. Believe me, I got picked on a lot more than you did as a kid. But I also grew up. I learned how to use my words to deflect most idiots and my fists to deflect the rest. I don't *need* your protection. But I don't condone killing people. That's my line in the sand."

"I hear you, Chas. I even believe you. But I still want to be able to look out for you."

"At some point, you're going to have to acknowledge that I'm an adult and can take care of myself."

"It's not about you. It's who I am. SEALs are in the business of protecting lives. Of using violence when necessary to stop bad things from happening to innocent people. Violence is a tool, not an end in and of itself."

"You're splitting hairs," Chas accused.

"They're important damned hairs. They make the difference between me being the murderer you accuse me of being and an honorable warrior protecting his country and its people."

"I'm not questioning your patriotism. Just your chosen methods for defending it."

"Aren't you splitting hairs by saying it's okay to use some force, but it's not okay to use lethal force?" Gunner accused.

Chas didn't answer. He merely turned away, staring out the window of the diner in stony silence.

So that was it? They were over? Because Chas couldn't wrap his head around what SEALs did and why? He refused to believe that they couldn't find a way through this. The alternative panicked the living hell out of him. Gunner knew deep down in his gut that he would never love another man the way he loved Chas. And furthermore, he was pretty damned sure he would never find another man who loved him the way Chas did.

"You were happy enough to have my SEAL skills at your beck and call when you and Poppy were in trouble. Isn't it a wee bit hypocritical to wring your hands and claim I'm being too violent now?"

"Pulling me out of a dangerous situation and killing people are two entirely different things!"

"No, Chas. They're not," he ground out. "I was prepared to kill anyone who tried to hurt you the night I came to Misty Falls. I was equally prepared not to kill anyone tonight if they didn't escalate the situation enough to make it necessary." He took a breath and continued more calmly, "Sometimes there are going to be jobs where the rules of engagement are to kill or be killed. But I promise you I never kill when it's not absolutely necessary."

Chas was silent.

What the hell was going on inside Chas's head? His stony expression wasn't giving away a thing. Gunner asked reluctantly, "Is that enough for you?"

"I honestly don't know," Chas said quietly.

Gunner squeezed his eyes shut hard, shocked to feel an excess of moisture in them.

From across the table, Spencer said, "Drago and I agree on what should happen next. We want to run it by you two."

Gunner looked up bleakly. It was hard to care about a damned thing when his heart was cracking like a sheet of ice that had just had a wrecking ball dropped on it.

Chapter Twenty-One

CHAS COLLECTED Poppy out of her car seat, which had been strapped into one of the plush leather seats on the private jet Kenji Tanaka had sent for them. Poor kid was cranky and out of sorts after spending almost twelve hours inside the jet. They'd stopped in California to refuel and had gotten out and stretched their legs, but the toddler was pretty much done with being confined.

She wriggled furiously, starting into what he expected was about to be a total meltdown. "Your turn to chase her," he murmured to Gunner. "Ready?"

Gunner rolled his eyes and slipped his backpack off, then set it down beside him.

Chas set Poppy down and she took off like a shot with Gunner right behind her, heading for the elaborate planters filled with tropical foliage and flowers that lined the arrival walkway at Honolulu International Airport.

Chas watched listlessly as Gunner scooped up Poppy and blew raspberries on her tummy until she squealed with laughter. God, they were good together. He would have loved to raise a family with Gunner. The two of them were just different enough that between them, they would have made an excellent set of parents.

Chas turned to Drago. "And you're sure the DNA match was positive? Kenji Tanaka is definitely her father?"

"One hundred percent positive." Drago added low, "Sorry, dude. I know how close you and Gun have gotten to her."

"I'm sure Tanaka will let you visit her from time to time, if you'd like to," Spencer said from Drago's other side. "After all, he owes her life to you, Chas. You saved her from the Oshiros that night in Misty Falls."

If he was a hero, he didn't feel much like one. He felt as if the past few weeks had ripped his guts out, thrown them on the ground, and stomped around on them until they were bloody mush.

They climbed into the big SUV Spencer had rented, and Chas put a deeply—and loudly—annoyed Poppy into her car seat one more time while the guys loaded bag after bag of military gear into the back of the vehicle. He crawled in beside the screaming toddler and pulled out her blue stuffed elephant to waggle it in front of her.

"Mr. Elephant is sad when Poppy screams like a baby. She's a big girl now. Can she tell me how old she is?"

Gradually, he calmed the tantrum with his one-man puppet show. They drove for a while, heading inland on narrow winding roads through lush tropical jungle. They pulled into a gated drive, and Drago, who was driving, punched in a code on the security pad. Then they wound a long way back through more jungle.

Eventually a clearing came into sight, with a wooden chalet-style house surrounded by huge covered porches in the middle of it.

"Home sweet home," Spencer announced.

"How'd you know about this place?" Gunner asked from Poppy's other side.

"Borrowed it from a friend a few years back for R and R after a long deployment," Spencer answered. "I called and asked him if he'd mind if we shacked up here for a few days while the handoff gets made."

"How's this handoff going to work?" Chas asked without any enthusiasm.

"Tanaka's flying to Hawaii, and his security team is going to make sure the Oshiros haven't followed him. When he knows he's in the clear, he's going to come here, collect Poppy, and then go home to Japan. Pretty straightforward, actually."

Chas closed his eyes for a moment. He was not going to indulge in some huge drama fit in front of these hard, controlled men who wouldn't know a real emotion if it bit them in the ass.

They unloaded the car and left him to explore the house with Poppy, and predictably, they disappeared into the woods to reconnoiter and do their whole SEAL paranoia thing. The house was authentically decorated with lots of rustic wood furniture, high ceilings, rattan ceiling fans, and glass doors everywhere that opened up to let the warm breezes flow through. It would have been insanely relaxing were it not for the fact that in the next few days, he would lose Poppy forever.

He knew she'd never been his, but dang, he'd come to love the little squirt. Even now, when she was exhausted and fussy, her natural cheer and good nature shone through.

He plopped her into the bathtub for a nice warm bath and then stretched out on a bed with her for a nap. Predictably, she crashed immediately. He, however, was not so lucky.

This whole bizarre adventure was almost over. In a few days he would fly back to Misty Falls, resume teaching, start repairing his shot-up house, and pretend to put his life back together. Thing was, he was never going to get it back together, not really. Not after Gunner.

GUNNER FOLLOWED Drago into the house. Spencer had volunteered to take the first watch outside. He went hunting and found Chas and Poppy curled up together on a bed, so cozy it hurt to look at them. He made a memory of this moment to hold in his heart for all time, but it tasted bitter knowing that memories were all he would ever have.

How had it gone so bad, so damned fast?

Drago poked his head in the door. "Get some sleep, dude. You've got the late shift tonight, and with jet lag, it's gonna be a bitch."

At least traveling west meant his body clock thought it was five hours earlier than local time. But he knew from long experience that any major time shift took a toll. Gunner backed out of the room, leaving Chas and Poppy to sleep undisturbed, and went into another room down the hall to nap alone. It sucked, pure and simple.

Welcome to your future, man. Sleeping alone with buckets full of regrets.

His dreams were of Chas.

He woke up feeling worse than before he'd gone to sleep.

At midnight, he geared up and headed outside to relieve Drago. "How's it looking?" he asked the former CIA man.

"All quiet. I went exploring outside the fence, and just over that ridge"—he pointed at the big one south of the lawn—"there's a dirt road. Could pose a bit of a security problem."

"How thick is the jungle up that way?" Gunner asked quickly.

"Not thick enough to stop a bunch of tangoes from hiking down and setting up shop along the edge of the trees."

Gunner studied the tree line intently. "They'd have the high ground. It would put us at a serious disadvantage in a firefight."

"Maybe you could recon a few fallback positions if we had to bug out of the house?"

"Will do."

Drago nodded and went inside, leaving him alone with the night. The insect noises here were unique, and as he explored the north side of the property, he familiarized himself with the various clicks, chirps, and buzzing noises.

He found a gardener's shed just inside the north tree line, but it was too flimsy to make for decent shelter in a gun battle. He pushed deeper into the jungle in search of defensible positions. The best he found was a small rise, an outcropping really, on the north face of the valley, about halfway up. It appeared to be made of volcanic rock and had a line of boulders across the south edge of the little plateau that would provide decent protection. The jungle on each side of the position was thick as hell and would cause no end of problems for anybody trying to sneak up on them. The hillside above was steep and rocky, alternating scree fields that would be hell on ankles with thick stands of trees and vines.

He made a note of how to get to it again and actually cut a narrow path to it. He spent the next hour or so positioning piles of dead logs beside the new trail and pulling back curtains of vines and tying them back just enough that a well-placed machete blow would send them cascading down into the path.

Well satisfied with his work, he headed back toward the house and spent the remainder of the night roaming around the edge of the grounds.

The next day was tense. Tanaka's people called first thing in the morning. They were on the island and finalizing their security before coming to get Poppy.

Gunner and Chas spent the morning playing with her, and every minute was a dagger to his heart. Chas didn't look like he was holding up any better.

Lunchtime came and went without a call from Tanaka, and then suppertime came and went.

"What do you suppose the hang-up is?" Chas asked nobody in particular as darkness fell outside.

"They must've spotted some of the Oshiro gang," Drago guessed. "They're probably doing exactly what we did—setting up a trap and luring the bastards in."

"Let's just hope they get them all," Gunner said fervently. "I'd hate to end up in another firefight." He glanced sidelong at Chas for any reaction to that remark, but Chas's jaw was tight as he stared out one of the big window walls.

"Well, it's about time to start night patrol," Spencer said. "You guys get some rest, eh?"

Drago headed upstairs to grab a nap, and Gunner stood reluctantly to follow. He hated to leave Poppy when he had so little time left with her.

"Rest," Chas said softly. "You need your strength to kill whoever wanders onto the property."

"Snark is beneath you," Gunner replied evenly.

Chas looked up sharply. "You're right. I'm sorry. I just hate all of this."

"Me too."

Their gazes met for a moment of shared under-standing. They were both hurting bad over having to give up Poppy.

Gunner dozed upstairs for a few hours but grew restless at around midnight and couldn't get back to sleep. He got up, geared up, and eased the door to Poppy and Chas's bedroom open to look in on them. They were both sleeping peacefully.

Then he backed out and quietly headed down-stairs. Spencer and Drago were both outside, probably doing their shift change now. He poked his throat mike to murmur, "I'm awake and in the kitchen grabbing a snack. Nobody shoot me, eh?"

"Can't sleep?" Spencer asked, obviously on the move. Heading for the house, no doubt.

"Nah. Gut's jumpy."

"Mine too," Drago reported.

"Mine three," Spencer added dryly. "Stay sharp, Dray."

"Always am."

Gunner listened idly to their banter as Drago head-ed out and Spencer headed in. While he was making himself a sandwich, he made one for Spencer too. When his friend came in the back door, Gunner handed him a plate.

"Nice hide you built, Gun," Spencer commented, taking a bite of the ham sandwich.

"Here's hoping we don't need it—"

"Problem," Drago muttered in both of their ears. "I've got movement on the south ridge."

"Stay here," Spencer ordered tersely. His plate rattled to the counter and he was out the door without another word. "Head count?" Gunner heard Spencer ask.

"Six. Maybe a few more."

Aww, fuck. Not good.

"Get Chas and Poppy up. Be ready to move out with them," Spencer ordered.

"Wilco," Gunner bit out, racing for the stairs.

He woke Chas first. "Get up. Get dressed. Grab a couple of blankets and the emergency bag for Poppy. I'll get her. If you still have that headset I gave you, put it on. Meet me downstairs in one minute."

Chas's eyes were huge with fear in the dark, but he nodded and rolled out of bed, fumbling into shoes as Gunner leaned over the crib and scooped up Poppy, blankets and all.

"Get her pacifier and some bottles," Gunner ordered over his shoulder. "We may have to keep her quiet."

He moved swiftly downstairs, trying not to jostle the toddler and wake her up any more than she already was. She was mostly asleep now, and he needed to keep her that way. He turned off the kitchen lights and the single lamp burning in the living room, plunging the house into darkness.

Chas came downstairs, breathing hard. "Now what?"

"Get the bottles and join me in the living room."

Chas joined him in a minute and sank down on the sofa beside him and Poppy. "What now?" he breathed.

"Now we wait for instructions. Spencer and Drago are checking out the movement Dray saw on the south ridge."

"How long will it take?"

"Not long," he replied grimly.

"Do we know which part of the Oshiro gang is here?" Chas asked.

"Does it matter?" he countered.

They sat in the dark, listening to the night sounds while Gunner reviewed the route to the fallback position.

And then the thing he feared happened. The animals outside started to go silent. Not good. Not good at all. Spencer and Drago knew how to move quietly enough not to disturb the night creatures. But incoming hostiles? Probably not so much.

Gunner stood up, moved over to the living room doors, and pushed one of the big glass sliders open. The quiet was even more noticeable now. "Get ready to move out. Fast. We'll run full-out across the lawn. Do your best to keep up with me."

"What's wrong?"

"Insects have gone silent. There are definitely people moving around out there."

"If we're going to have to run, do you want me to rig up a sling for you to carry Poppy on your back?"

"You know how to do that?" Gunner asked in surprise.

"Of course. My kids' moms do it all the time with their babies." Gunner watched in surprise as Chas pulled out the carrying sling he sometimes let Poppy sleep in on his lap. They slipped her into that, and Gunner threw the cloth strap over his shoulder and across his chest. Then Chas folded one of the blankets like a bandana and crossed it the other direction diagonally across Gunner's back and under Poppy, making a second envelope. Chas moved in front of him and tied the ends securely across his chest.

Gunner shifted around a few times, bouncing on his toes.

"Feel secure?" Chas asked.

"Yeah. That's good. Thanks." He stared down at Chas, who stared back up at him. It was all there between them. The friendship, the love, the happy ever after they couldn't have.

"Are we going to be okay?" Chas asked, low.

"I'll die defending the two of you, whether you like it or not," he answered grimly.

Chas opened his mouth to say something, but Spencer's voice cut across whatever he'd been about to say: "Run."

Chapter Twenty-Two

CHAS CONSIDERED himself to be in damned good shape, but he'd never run so hard in his life. Gunner bolted out the door, took the lanai steps three at a time, and was off across the lawn like a high-speed train. Chas sprinted after him, watching the baby bag bounce against his back, his lungs gulping in great gasps of air, his thigh muscles burning like fire.

His shoulder blades itched with anticipation of a bullet slamming into his back, dropping him on his face and ending it all.

They reached the trees on the far side of several acres of lawn dotted with fruit trees, and Gunner finally slowed. He moved swiftly to the right for a few yards and then plunged into the jungle, disappearing from sight.

Chas lurched forward, frantic not to lose Gunner. He suspected the guy would keep on going and not look back to realize he'd left Chas in the dust. As he reached the spot where Gunner had disappeared, he was startled to spot a narrow strip of bare dirt. A trail?

He lunged forward frantically. He'd gone per- haps a dozen yards when a hand reached out of the undergrowth from the side of the trail and grabbed his upper arm.

A yelp escaped him before he bit back any more sound. "Don't scare me like that," he whispered angrily as Gunner yanked him off the path.

"Hush," Gunner murmured.

"Now what?"

"Now we wait and watch."

In the next few minutes, Chas heard a series of clicks over the radio. He assumed that was Spencer and Drago communicating with each other in some secret SEAL code.

Then, without warning, Spencer said in a bare whisper, "Gun, call Tanaka. Tell him to bring everyone."

Gunner swore under his breath as he pulled out a cell phone and quickly dialed a number.

Chas listened as Gunner said low, "We're under attack from a large force. Bring everyone you've got. The package is on the north ridge."

The person at the other end said something extremely brief, and then Gunner disconnected.

"What did he say?" Chas whispered.

"On their way."

"What's the package?"

Gunner glanced over at him wryly. "You and Poppy."

"Oh." He thought for a second, then asked, "How long until Tanaka's people can get here?"

Gunner shrugged. "Hopefully soon enough. Watch the south ridge. It should start to light up with muzzle flashes any time now."

"How many bad guys are there?"

"A lot. Spencer and Dray have counted at least a dozen. Perhaps as many as a dozen more could be out there."

"But Spencer and Drago are out there alone!"

"They'll be okay."

Chas frowned. "You don't sound too sure about that."

"SEALs always believe they'll win. We die believing we're going to win the fight."

"That's morbid," Chas muttered.

He shrugged. It was the truth. He started to untie the blanket harness holding Poppy. "Stay here and take her. I'm going to move off to the side and take up an overwatch position."

"What does that mean?"

"It means I'm going to set up long-range sniper support for Spencer and Drago. If they get pinned down out there, I may get a shot at the bad guys to give them a little extra cover."

"Won't the bad guys see you shooting?"

"This sniper rig has flash suppression and noise deflection. It'll sound like I'm shooting from somewhere else."

Gunner wasn't entirely surprised to discover that Poppy was wide-awake inside the sling as he transferred her to Chas's arms. The tyke had an uncanny instinct for danger that no toddler should rightfully have. But right now, he was grateful as hell for it. She was sucking furiously on her pacifier, the only outward sign of her stress.

Gunner said grimly, "At all costs, keep her quiet. Even if you have to put your hand over her mouth and plug her nose until she passes out. This is life-and-death."

Chas nodded, his eyes wide.

"I won't be far away. If you see men coming across the lawn and I stop shooting at them, head on up this path. At the top of it, there's a rocky outcrop with some big boulders. There's a little pit dug behind them. Get in that, cover up with blankets as best you can, and stay there. One of us will come for you."

He had no more time to give Chas hints or advice on how to survive the unfolding shitshow. Spencer and Drago were horribly outgunned and having to retreat fast down the south ridge. They would hit the house any second, and they would need covering fire.

Gunner shoved into the thick underbrush, using his machete to cut his feet loose when they tangled hopelessly, brute forcing his way some fifty feet west of Chas and Poppy. He began looking for an opening to see the valley as he made his way uphill.

He found a spot and flopped down behind a fallen log, working at top speed to unfold his tripod, uncover his sight, and take up a shooting position. And not a second too soon.

The infrared designator on Drago's chest lit up as he exited the trees on the other side of the valley not thirty seconds after Gunner began scanning through his weapon sight. Spencer wore a similar designator that would allow Gunner to differentiate them from the hostiles.

"I've got you in sight, Dray," he announced calmly, watching Drago run, crouching, in a zigzag to the crawl space beneath the house. Gunner did the math fast on distance and windage and made his corrections, dialing them into his weapon carefully.

A heat signature popped out of the trees almost exactly where Drago had emerged a few seconds before, and Gunner lined the hostile up. A smooth pull through his trigger and the heat signature flew backward.

This was a long-range rig, which meant he was firing large-caliber rounds. At only a few hundred yards' range like this, they would hit with enough velocity to tear a body in half. *Chas would purely love knowing that.*

He swung his sight down the tree line and picked out another heat signature. It was at the wrong angle to show him a designator, and he held his shot until he got visual on Spencer.

There, to the left of the house, was the second infrared friend-or-foe designator. Spencer was crouching just inside the tree line. Which meant that the other heat signature was a valid target. Gunner lined the guy up and took the shot. *Splash two.*

Apparently the hostiles had thought better of simply charging the house based on the resistance Spencer and Drago had already put up. Knowing those two, they'd been moving all over the hillside, convincing the incoming thugs that there were a dozen or more good guys defending this valley.

The next half hour or so settled into a strange stalemate. Nobody fired a weapon, and Spencer and Drago patiently held their positions, not giving themselves away.

As for him, Gunner identified the positions of at least ten men and mentally marked them for later shooting. But he, too, silently held his ground. What the bad guys didn't know was that reinforcements were coming. The longer they waited to attack, the better for the home team.

The stalemate began to draw out long enough that Gunner began to question why the bad guys hadn't moved. They'd clearly organized themselves up in the jungle on that ridge, and in fact, there were now three clusters of heat signatures visible from his position not far inside the tree line. Why weren't they attacking?

Was it possible they were waiting for reinforcements of their own?

He keyed his mike and murmured, "Any chance these guys have called in their own backup, Spencer?"

Spencer answered with a single click. *Yes.*

Dammit. Sometimes he hated being right.

Whether the bad guys' reinforcements arrived or not, all of a sudden the pause was over. Without warning, all three groups of hostiles charged down the hillside toward the house.

Gunner lined up targets and fired at them as fast as he could. As best as he could tell, he'd hit about a dozen by the time they broke out into the open and rushed the house.

He saw Spencer easing back toward the front gate, and he made out Drago backed up to the northern edge of the crawl space. Gunner waited until the groups reached the house and took up positions to shoot the hell out of it, and then radioed, "Go."

Spencer and Drago took off running across the lawn while the bad guys opened fire on the house. The pair darted from tree to tree, using shadows for as much cover as possible. The moon had already set and it was pretty damned dark out here, which also worked to Spencer and Drago's advantage.

But neither man had made it to the north ridge by the time the fusillade of shooting stopped and one of the groups of hostiles swarmed into the house like so many infuriated fire ants.

"Hurry," Gunner muttered.

Spencer and Drago sprinted the last few yards and dove for cover.

"Clear," Spencer reported.

"Clear," Drago bit out.

"Chas and Poppy are on the trail. I'll meet you there."

"Take them up to the hide. We'll hold the line here as long as we can," Spencer ordered.

"Roger," Gunner replied.

He slogged back through the thick undergrowth to Chas and Poppy's position. They were gone. Good man. Chas had done as ordered and headed up to the fallback position. Gunner raced up the trail, leaving the various traps unsprung. Spencer and Drago would use them to cover their retreats when they came through.

He turned and ran up the steep slope. About halfway up, he heard the sound of a helicopter. Please, God, let that be Tanaka's men. He reached a clear spot in the path and turned to peer back at the valley through his infrared gun sight. A large helicopter settled squarely in the center of the valley in the only reasonably open area on the property.

He watched through his night optical gear in horror as a dozen men, mostly Caucasian, streamed out of the bird—dammit, this could be more Oshiro gang members.

But his chagrin turned to shock as the newcomers were cut down before their feet touched the ground. The pilot tried to bug out, but the copter came under withering fire and smoke started pouring out of the engine section. It slammed back down to the ground, and the pilot emerged with his hands over his head. The bastards in the trees shot him where he stood.

"What the hell was that?" Spencer whispered.

"I think the Oshiro factions just resolved their differences," Gunner replied dryly. "One side just slaughtered the other side. Although I couldn't tell you which bunch was which. But they sure as hell made our job easier."

Drago breathed, "I'm still counting at least two dozen hostiles out here. We're a long way from out of the woods."

Fuck, fuck, fuck, fuck. Gunner realized he was chanting the word with each step he took as he turned and sprinted up the trail. What were the odds they could go full defensive and egress out of this area with Chas and a baby in tow, and not get caught and mowed down like that pilot?

The terrain at the top of the ridge was rocky and open and provided precious little cover. There was no way to pass through this jungle without leaving a trail either. Not with an amateur and a baby.

They were well and truly screwed.

If this were a normal SEAL mission, he would call in all the air support that could be mustered, as well as whatever standoff support troops had been deployed along with the primary operating team.

He heard Spencer and Drago beginning to fire below him. Dammit. The hostiles were headed this way. They were running out of time to pull a miracle out of their asses.

God, he missed having all the resources of a SEAL team right now. Hell, they could call in a

search-and-rescue bird to come pluck them off this
mountain and fly them out—

It was a long shot, but what the hell. They were going to die up here. They were so ridiculously outnumbered and outgunned, it was laughable. If nothing else,
the hostiles could simply wait for the three of them to
run out of ammo and then hunt them all down and kill
them at their leisure.

Horror at the idea of Chas and Poppy being executed in cold blood made him stumble, and he jerked his
attention back to the path beneath his feet.

He spied the boulders ahead and put on one last
maximum burst of speed. He leaped for cover and landed hard beside Chas and Poppy, both of whom lurched
in surprise as he dropped down beside them. He frantically pulled out his cell phone and waited impatiently
as the call went through. It was a Hail Mary pass, but it
was all he could think of.

"Charles Favian. How may I help you?"

"Charles, it's Gunner. Use my satellite phone to get
my position. We're on Oahu. We're under attack and
we can't hold off this force for much longer. Do you
have any resources at all you can call in to help us?
We're desperate."

"Oahu, you say?"

"Yeah."

"I can't call in active-duty forces since you're not
on a government op, but there are a crap ton of retired
SEALs in Hawaii, and I know a few of them. Lemme
see what I can do."

Charles Favian was fucking brilliant. He was going to call in retired SEALs and appeal to them to help
two brothers in trouble. Now, if only some of those
SEALs lived damned close by.

Charles had kept him on the line, and Gunner heard him talking urgently on another phone. "Yes. Call everyone. These are the coordinates. There's a baby out there in the middle of it. Yes. And two SEALs. Spencer Newman and Gunner Vance. Team Ten."

He glanced over at Chas, who stared back fearfully.

"Are we going to die?" Chas asked grimly.

He smiled bravely and lied, "Nah. SEALs always find a way."

Spencer radioed urgently, "Fall back. I'll cover your retreat and trap the trail."

Gunner hung up on Charles, for they'd just run out of time. They were on their own now.

He set up his rig between two of the boulders to cover where the trail emerged and waited grimly for the final retreat. Drago came bursting out of the jungle first. He leaped behind the rocks and landed with the kind of grunt that gave away that he'd been hit.

"Chas, check him for wounds and do what you can," Gunner bit out, never taking his eyes off the trail.

In under a minute, Spencer also burst out of the jungle, but he was ducking as someone shot at him. Aiming over his head, Gunner sent a round down the mountain to give Spencer the cover he needed to make it behind the boulders.

That was it. They were done retreating. Now they would shoot it out until they ran out of ammo or died, whichever came first.

Spencer set up shop at the left end of the outcropping. Drago waited impatiently while Chas insisted on tying a bandage around his left thigh, and then he rolled to the right side of the wall of rock.

"Ammo check?" Spencer murmured.

"I've got a couple hundred rounds," Gunner reported.

"Same," Drago replied.

"I'm at about one-twenty," Spencer supplied.

Spencer didn't have to tell them to conserve rounds. They all knew they were massively outgunned.

Over the next few minutes, the bad guys figured out where they were and fanned out across the slope below. The good news was the thick undergrowth was giving them hell and slowing them down a lot. Which, at the end of the day, only prolonged the inevitable.

Grim determination to go down fighting settled in Gunner's gut. He'd been in some bad situations before, but none as hopeless as this one. If he had to die, this wasn't a bad way to go. He was with friends and the only two people in world he loved. It sucked that Poppy wasn't going to get to grow up and have a full life. She should've gotten a chance to be a kid, fall in love, have kids of her own—

He broke off the train of thought. He had no time for despair. Not yet.

But as the next hour passed and the bad guys methodically forced them to use their precious ammo fighting off wave after wave of attacks, the despair set in, whether he wanted it to or not.

Chas rendered basic first aid, tying strips of cloth over their various minor wounds as they got nicked by flying shards of stone. He also passed them water bottles and the precious clips of spare ammo. For her part, Poppy cowered in the lee of the rocks with her thumb or her pacifier jammed in her mouth. She whimpered from time to time, but silence didn't matter anymore.

The bad guys knew exactly where they were and were patiently wearing them down.

"Ammo check?" Spencer asked a shade wearily.

"Thirty-two," Gunner reported.

"Sixteen," Drago reported.

"I'm at twelve. Time to let them draw in close. Let's make the shots count."

Gunner knew what Spencer was saying without stating it aloud. They were going to die soon. It was a last-ditch SEAL maneuver to let their position get overrun and burn the last few rounds of ammo on point-blank shots that would take out as many of the enemy as possible before they were gunned down themselves. As a SEAL, if you had to die, you took as many of the bastards with you as you could.

"It's been an honor, sir," Gunner said formally to Spencer.

"Likewise," Spencer replied.

Drago just swore under his breath, off radio but loud enough for Gunner to hear. Then Drago transmitted. "I love you, Spencer Newman."

"Love you too."

"Jesus," Chas whispered off-mike beside him. "You guys sound like you're getting ready to charge over the rocks and go out in a blaze of glory."

Gunner risked turning away from his weapon sight long enough to smile ruefully at Chas. "Guess you were right. We should have found another way to handle this besides shooting it out."

Chas leaned over and grabbed the front of his shirt. "Don't you give up on me, Gunner Vance. Poppy and I are depending on you. Be the warrior you were trained to be, dammit."

He stared, stunned. "You mean it?"

"I'm not ready to die, and she sure as hell isn't. You fight for us."

"But I'm killing people. Loads of them."

Grim desperation vibrated in Chas's voice. "Poppy deserves to grow up. You and I deserve a shot at happiness. You do whatever it takes to give us all a future. You hear me?"

"Yeah."

"You were right. You kill whoever you have to. And stay alive, dammit."

He nodded and turned back to his sight. Huh. Chas finally got it. Funny how staring down death at close range could change a person's opinions about the whole kill-or-be-killed thing.

If he, Spencer, and Drago rotated shooting so that they never shot at the same target, they could still take out a fair number of hostiles.

He transmitted, "Let's rotate shots. Call your targets. Single shots only at close range."

"You sure?" Spencer asked.

"I'm not ready to go just yet."

"You heard the man," Spencer murmured.

Gunner settled in, readying himself to shoot like he'd never shot before. He reviewed the basics as he always did. He felt the calm washing over him. There it was. The kill zone.

A heat signature moved up the path toward them. "Mine," he said coldly. He pulled the trigger and the hostile's head evaporated. *Thirty-one rounds left.*

When the bad guys were coming in slowly enough, he took two shots to every one of Spencer's and Drago's to even out the ammo count. He was at fourteen, which meant Spencer and Drago were down to around six each, when he heard something from below.

A muffled bang.

Another one.

Several heat signatures lit up on the trail… but heading away from their position.

"What the hell is that noise?" Drago asked.

"Sounds like weapon fire," Spencer said wonderingly. "Muffled by the jungle. Hold your positions."

Gunner stayed at his weapon, poised to shoot anyone who came up the trail at them, but over the next ten minutes or so, not a single person charged their position. Sounds of weapon fire came from both ends of the valley and seemed to be converging toward the middle of it.

"Come look at this," Spencer said over his radio.

Shocked, Gunner left his weapon and moved over behind his boss, who was peering around the left end of the rocky outcrop. The entire hillside below them was lit up with muzzle flashes—two large groups of them, one coming in from their left and another group from the right. And between them, the Oshiro gang was slowly being crushed, rather like a nut in the jaws of a lethal nutcracker. For all the world, it looked like a military force executing a clearing maneuver on a battlefield.

"What the hell?" Drago muttered.

Even Chas poked his head around the rock to stare. "What is that?" he asked.

Gunner's phone vibrated in his pocket, and he pulled it out. "Go ahead," he murmured at Charles Favian.

"Do you see them yet?" Charles asked, sounding positively gleeful.

"You mean the massive line of shooters advancing up the hill toward us?" Gunner asked.

"They're SEALs. Well, retired SEALs. I've got them on a satellite video feed here. They say there's another group of shooters taking out the same guys they're trying to take out, but they don't know who the new shooters are."

"Could be Tanaka's guys," Gunner replied.

"You might want to get on the phone with Tanaka's men and tell them they've got SEALs on the field helping them and not to kill our guys."

"Will do. Just a sec." Gunner took the phone away from his mouth and relayed the message to Spencer, who immediately got on his cell phone to call Kenji Tanaka.

Charles commented, "Satellite view shows the new arrivals have pretty much cleared out your bad guys. They should reach your position in a few minutes. Don't kill the good guys, eh?"

Gunner snorted. "We have just about enough ammo left to make a smiley face in a pumpkin."

"Good timing, then," Charles said. "The SEALs are operating on channel four if you want to say hello."

"Thanks," Gunner muttered.

Drago was already dialing up channel four on his radio. "Roger. Four adult males and one toddler. On the rocky outcropping about a hundred yards above your line. We're using IR designators if any of you gentlemen have the capability."

Gunner got his own radio switched over in time to hear someone respond in a gravelly voice, "We've got a few IR capable kits. We'll send those boys up your way first."

"We'll be watching for them," Spencer replied. "And I repeat, there are friendlies coming in from the other end of the valley."

"Roger. We see them."

Chas frowned. "What's happening?"

Gunner couldn't help grinning as he answered, "Tanaka's guys got here, and they appear to have come in from one side of the valley, and Charles Favian called a bunch of retired SEALs who live in the area. They came in hot from the other end of the valley. Between the two, they appear to have wiped out the Oshiro boys."

Sonofabitch. Tanaka coming for his own kid was not a surprise. But the SEAL brotherhood coming to the rescue like that for him and Spencer? That was a surprise of the best kind. This was why he loved his brothers-in-arms so damned much. When the chips were down, a bunch of crusty old ex-SEALs had answered the call. He and Spencer were still part of that brotherhood. They would be until they died. Leaving his active-duty SEAL team didn't make him any less of a SEAL. He would always belong to this very special family.

Something proud unfurled in his chest, and it felt as if he'd drawn his first real, deep breath in weeks.

It took a bit to sort out who all was who on the hillside. A few hostiles were found hiding and taken prisoner if they surrendered or eliminated if they tried to fight. But eventually a great bearded bear of a man emerged at the top of the trail, his assault rifle pointed at the sky.

"Ooh-rah," he said by way of greeting.

"Is the hill clear?" Spencer asked cautiously.

"Clean as a virgin's—" He broke off. "Sorry. Forgot about the kid. Yeah. Hill's clean. Y'all can come down now."

Gunner stepped out from behind the rock. "Man, am I glad to see you." He couldn't resist thumping the big ex-SEAL on the back.

"C'mon. I imagine the boys are gonna want to meet y'all. It's not often we get an excuse to come out and run a little target practice." He added, "Oh, and there's a bunch of Japanese fellas down in the valley who are all kinds of worked up to see the kid y'all have up here."

Gunner snorted. He would bet.

The hike down to the valley floor didn't take long. The SEALs had obviously cleared out the logs, vines, and other traps on their way up. They stepped out of the jungle, and several dozen men milled around, armed to the teeth, chatting and laughing as if they were holding a team reunion. A group of similarly armed Japanese men stood apart, speaking quietly among themselves.

A big cheer went up when they stepped out of the woods.

Poppy must have sensed she was safe at last, for on cue, she popped her thumb out of her mouth and let out a wail fit to raise the dead. That made everybody laugh, and Chas hugged and joggled her until she calmed down.

The next few hours passed in a blur. The contingent of Tanaka's men made a discreet departure before law enforcement arrived, and not long after, police showed up to take control of the scene. The retired SEALs pitched in, fetching bodies and laying them out for identification. All in all, some forty Oshiro gang members died in the valley.

As far as Gunner, Spencer, and Drago could tell, both factions of the Oshiro gang had taken heavy losses out here tonight. If nothing else, the entire Oshiro gang had been taught a painful lesson on how seriously the Tanaka family—and the SEALs—took her safety. Gunner doubted they would ever try to mess with her again.

A few SEALs had taken incoming fire and had had minor injuries, but nothing life-threatening.

At about dawn, Spencer took a phone call and then strolled over to have a conversation with the ex-SEALs who'd stuck around. As one, they all piled expectantly into their vehicles.

"C'mon," Spencer said to Gunner. "Get Chas and Poppy and load them up."

Gunner frowned. Spencer wasn't usually the cryptic type. It was part of why he'd been a good team leader. He shared all he knew with his guys.

Spencer drove, and Drago rode shotgun in the front seat. Gunner and Chas flanked Poppy in the back seat.

"Where are we going, Spence?" Gunner asked when they reached the outskirts of Honolulu.

"Kenji Tanaka texted me an address. He said to bring reinforcements."

"Does he know that means a whole platoon of SEALs?"

Spencer shrugged. "I'm just doing what the man said."

Gunner got the distinct feeling Spencer knew something he wasn't sharing. They pulled into a massive estate that sprawled beside the ocean, with several acres of manicured lawn stretching around a magnificent Asian-inspired home.

A half-dozen silent Asian men in dark suits watched while all the SEALs piled out of their vehicles and surrounded Gunner, Chas, and Poppy in a tight phalanx. They made their way into the house, and Gunner was aware that for so many men, they moved exceptionally quietly into a huge living room.

Six gray-haired Japanese men sat around a table in what looked like some sort of formal meeting. One man stood stiffly at the foot of the table, with no chair for him.

A younger Japanese man, perhaps in his thirties, rushed forward when they came in, and Poppy caught sight of him and squealed.

"I'm Kenji Tanaka. And that's my daughter."

Poppy waxed more cautious when Kenji approached, eyeing him carefully. It took him a couple of minutes of speaking to her in Japanese for her to be absolutely sure he was her father. But she eventually held out her arms to him, and Gunner's heart shattered as she threw herself into her father's arms.

Tears ran down the man's face as he held his daughter tight. If he'd needed any more proof that this was Poppy's father, the tears did it. Only a parent could react that way to the return of their missing child.

Chas made a tiny sound beside him, a barely audible keen of grief and loss. Gunner looped an arm over Chas's shoulders, pulling him close to his side. Only the two of them would understand the agony the other one was feeling in this moment of what should be a joyful reunion of father and daughter.

One of the gray-haired men, the one sitting at the head of the table, spoke formally in English to the man standing at the foot of the table. "Sora Oshiro. Your grandson's American gang of thugs stands accused of kidnapping my granddaughter. While I do not blame you for the sins of your descendent, you would do well to pass along this message to him and his people. Any further attempts to strongarm my business operations will not be tolerated. And any action that in any way endangers any member of my family will be met with swift and deadly force."

The man at the foot of the table bowed his head in a pose of humility.

The speaker swept a hand toward the tight cluster SEALs still hovering close to Poppy and her father.

"Not only has your grandson angered my family, but he has also angered this family. I assure you, So-ra-san, the family of Navy SEALs is perhaps the only one more formidable than my own. And your grandson and his gang are now their enemy."

Gunner noted the SEALs around him going out of their way to scowl at the man being berated at the foot of the table. And if he knew them, the retired SEALs were memorizing the man's face carefully.

"My granddaughter not only has the full protection of the Tanaka Clan, but she also has the full protection of the United States Navy SEALs. The next time the Oshiro gang would target me or mine, tell your grandson to remember that and weigh how many more of his people he wishes to lose."

The man at the foot of the table bowed deeply and left the room without ever speaking a word. In a few moments, the sound of a motorboat speeding away broke the silence.

Without warning, the stern man at the head of the table broke into a big smile and stood up. "Welcome to

my home, gentlemen. I am in your debt for your protection of my Kamiko."

Well, then. Despite any differences with his son,
Grandpa wasn't immune to his adorable granddaughter,
apparently. Gunner glanced down at Chas, who raised
his eyebrows in response.

"Which of you is the teacher who rescued my
daughter?" Kenji asked.

"Umm, that would be me," Chas said, stepping
forward. "I'm Chasten Reed."

"It is a great honor to meet you, Mr. Reed. And the
soldier who helped you?"

Gunner hated the attention but cleared his throat.
"Master Chief Gunner Vance, Mr. Tanaka."

"Kenji, please. It would be my honor if the two
of you would consider yourselves part of my family
henceforth."

Gunner didn't know a lot about Asian culture, but
he suspected this was a rather big deal. "I'd be honored," he replied.

"Me too," Chas responded. "Especially if that
means I get to be Poppy's—sorry, Kamiko's—Uncle
Chas."

"It does indeed," Kenji said, smiling. "And you?
Do you wish to be Uncle Gunner to her?"

"I do," Gunner answered without hesitation.

Cheers went up around them.

Into the general joviality, Kenji said, "Breakfast
will be served shortly. Please stay and dine with us."

There was more laughter, and the Japanese men
at the table mostly excused themselves from the room.
Gunner suspected that if they were the local Yakuza
bosses, they would rather not hang out with a bunch of

SEALs, some of whom were likely cozy with local law enforcement agencies.

It took a while, but the local SEALs cleared out, leaving only Gunner, Chas, Spencer, and Drago sitting on the lanai with Kenji. Kamiko was fast asleep in his arms, but Gunner didn't blame the guy one bit for not wanting to let go of his daughter after just getting her back.

Kenji asked Spencer, "So what are your plans now that you've rescued my daughter and restored my reason to live?"

"Drago and I are starting a small private security business. Gunner here is considering coming to work for us. We hope to grow the business over time with more people of his skill."

"How can I help you?" Kenji asked. "You've already turned down a reward. May I at least help you launch your business?"

Spencer and Drago looked startled. Spencer murmured, "What do you have in mind?"

"I'm an architect. I would be honored to design and build you an office. Perhaps a training facility? Maybe some living quarters? You'll need cash for equipment, of course. And a few high-profile clients to get you started. I have extensive business contacts to whom I will recommend your firm in the highest possible terms."

Gunner grinned as Spencer and Drago gaped. Spencer finally managed, "That's more than generous. Really. It's not necessary—"

Kenji waved a hand. "I'll hear no protests from either of you. I insist."

Drago said, "How can we ever thank you?"

Kenji grinned. "Name the business after me if you must."

"Tanaka Security?" Spencer murmured.

Kenji laughed heartily. "My father would never stand for his name being attached to such an honorable endeavor. How about my nickname within my family? I'm known as the Black Dragon. The bad seed within my clan, as it were, because I refused to join the family business."

Spencer and Drago exchanged nods. Drago replied, "Black Dragons Incorporated it is."

"And as for you two," Kenji said, turning his attention on Chas and Gunner. "What can I do for you?"

Gunner was shocked when Chas reached for his hand and grasped it. He clasped Chas's hand right back. "We're alive, and that's all I could hope for. When we were up on that mountain last night and it looked like we were all going to die, I knew that all I wanted in life was a little house with Gunner and a family of our own someday."

Kenji smiled down gently at his daughter. "I can't give you children, but I can give you that house, and it will be my pleasure to do so. Also, I believe teachers do not make much money in your country. I would like to provide a retirement fund for you, Chasten. You should never have to worry about your future again."

Chas protested, "No, we couldn't accept—"

Kenji cut off Chas politely. "You two gave me my life, my future, back." He glanced down at Kamiko. "I insist on doing the same for you."

Chas looked over at Gunner helplessly.

Gunner responded, "You heard the man. I guess we're stuck sharing a house together and raising a family. Are you okay with that? I'm still going to be working with the guys and doing violent stuff now and then."

"If it means I get to have you, I'll find a way to tolerate it. Last night was… an epiphany for me."

Gunner asked cautiously, "How so?"

"You guys used your skills last night to save lives. Specifically, mine and Poppy's. I saw how intent the Oshiro men were on killing us. They had no care whatsoever for our lives, which begs the question of why we should show concern for theirs." He frowned, searching for words, and Gunner waited him out.

Finally, Chas said, "I guess I had to experience a situation where it was a choice between you guys killing or Poppy and me dying for it to really register why you do what you do."

Never in a million years did he think he would ever hear those words come out of Chas's mouth. But then, he'd never in a million years thought he and Chas would find their way back to each other again either. "You sure about that? You're not going to change your mind in a few months when I have to go on a dangerous job?"

"I have so much to live for now," Chas replied, squeezing Gunner's hand. "In the end, I didn't want to die. I want to see Poppy grow up, I want to live a long, happy life with you"—he smiled at Gunner—"and I want to have a family of my own. With you."

Gunner stared back, his heart so full he wasn't sure he could speak past the lump it made in his throat. He choked out, "I want all of that too."

Kenji laughed. "There you have it. I'm building you two a house. Your happily ever after home. Oh, this is going to be fun. I can't wait to get started."

Gunner smiled at Chas, so happy his heart hurt with joy. They leaned in simultaneously on the sofa to kiss each other. He murmured against Chas's lips, "I can't wait to get started either."

Chas mumbled back, smiling and still kissing him, "Count me in, big guy. Count me in."

New York Times and *USA Today* bestselling author CINDY DEES started flying airplanes while sitting in her dad's lap at the age of three and got a pilot's license before she got a driver's license. At age fifteen, she dropped out of high school and left the horse farm in Michigan where she grew up to attend the University of Michigan.

After earning a degree in Russian and East European Studies, she joined the US Air Force and became the youngest female pilot in its history. She flew supersonic jets, VIP airlift, and the C-5 Galaxy, one of the world's largest cargo airplanes.

She also worked part-time gathering intelligence. During her military career, she traveled to forty-two countries on five continents, was detained by the KGB and East German secret police, got shot at, flew in the first Gulf War, met her husband, and amassed a lifetime's worth of war stories. Cindy has turned many of her experiences into novels of military romance and suspense.

Cindy's hobbies include professional Middle Eastern dancing, Japanese gardening, and medieval reenacting. She can also be found often on various social media, hanging out with her friends and fellow readers.

Winner of a Golden Heart and Holt Medallion for writing, Cindy is a five-time finalist and two-time winner of the prestigious RITA Award for Romance Fiction, two-time winner of RT Book Review's Best Harlequin Romantic Suspense Novel of the Year, and is a Romantic Times Lifetime Career Achievement nominee.

She has published over sixty novels, including thrillers, adventure novels, epic fantasies, and many stories of military romantic suspense.

CINDY DEES

OUT OF
CONTROL

A Black Dragons Inc. Novel

Hot SEAL. Hot spy. Hot reunion. Can they work together to find a notorious terrorist without killing each other first?

When SEAL Spencer Newman accepts a dangerous mission to bring in CIA agent Drago Thorpe—the only man he's ever loved—he expects things to get FUBAR. He *doesn't* expect Drago to convince him to go rogue too.

Drago regrets ending their torrid affair by pressuring Spencer to acknowledge their relationship publicly, and he wants a second chance. It's always been a challenge to get the uptight SEAL to break the rules, but to eliminate a supposedly dead terrorist, they'll need to operate outside the law. Tension heats up as they track their target, but can they find him before their attraction explodes out of control?

www.dreamspinnerpress.com

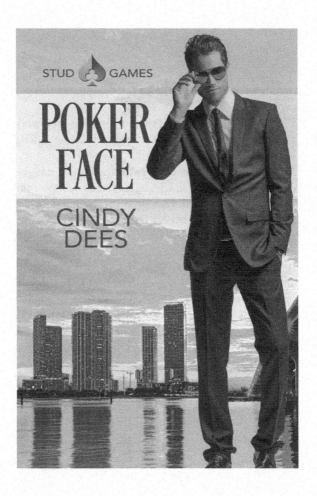

STUD GAMES

POKER
FACE

CINDY
DEES

A Stud Games Novel

Surveillance, seduction, and extra-dirty politics.

Christian Chatsworth-Brandeis has a problem. A huge one. The US senator he works for has run away with his latest mistress on the eve of a make-or-break fundraising event, and it's up to him to cover his irresponsible boss's tracks.

Stone Jackson, Senator Lacey's new bodyguard, looks enough like him that, with some extensive grooming, he might pass for the senator. Christian and Stone hatch a plan to substitute Stone for the senator, but Miami madness and the incendiary heat between them are throwing obstacles in their way. It's a race to find the senator and pull off the con of the century before the attraction between them spins completely out of control.

www.dreamspinnerpress.com

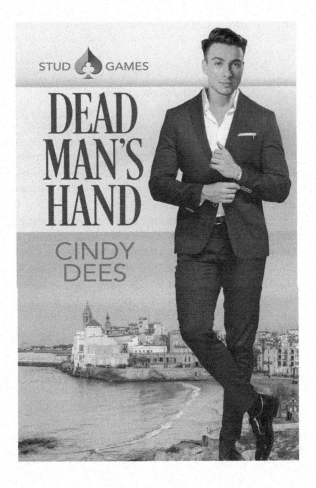

STUD ♠ GAMES

DEAD MAN'S HAND

CINDY DEES

A Stud Games Novel

Temptation, peril, and dirty poker.
Love is a high-stakes game.
When Collin Callahan, British secret agent, goes
up against math genius turned surfer bum Oliver El-
liot, the battle is epic—and so is the attraction. They're
pitted against each other in an exclusive, ultra-secret—
and ultra-illegal—poker match in Gibraltar, but when
players start dying and they could be next, they find a
common goal: catch the killer before it's too late.
Evenly matched at poker and romance, they each
wrestle personal demons that threaten to consume them
as the stakes climb. It's an all-or-nothing gamble with
both life and love on the line as they fight to be the last
seven-card studs standing.

www.dreamspinnerpress.com

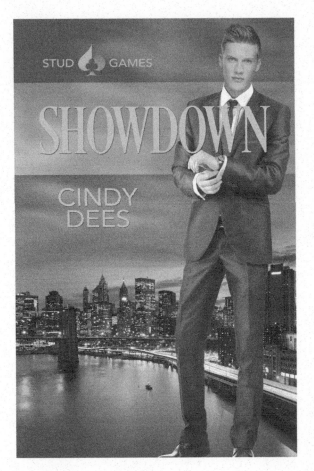

A Stud Games Novel

In crime, like in love, there can be no half measures….

Fashion model Zane Stryker needs money—badly. At almost thirty, his glory days are behind him, and he needs capital to start over. When his luggage is switched with a bag containing contraband he's forced to deliver, it's either the worst thing that's ever happened to him… or the best.

Enter Sebastian Gigoni, formerly of the British Special Forces, who has to decide just where Zane's loyalty lies and why. Sizzling attraction erupts between them, but that doesn't mean they can trust each other. They double down in a race for their lives—and their love—but are their purposes at odds? As they struggle to reconcile their goals, their consciences, and the needs of their hearts, one thing is clear—they must go all in or give up altogether.

www.dreamspinnerpress.com